DEADLAND

RISING

Part Three of the Deadland Saga

The search for hope

in a shambling world

RACHEL AUKES

DEADLAND RISING
Book 3 of the DEADLAND SAGA

Copyright © 2015 Rachel Aukes

Surprisingly Adequate Publishing
Edited by Stephanie Riva – RivaReading.com
Soldiers © Darren Whittingham – Fotolia.com
Warpaint font © Chepi Devosi – ChepiDev.com

ISBN-10: 1508583064
ISBN-13: 978-1508583066

For Lori, Glenda, and Eric

CONTENTS

UNCERTAINTY

CHAPTER I

The fresh blanket of snow created a pleasant illusion. With Des Moines covered in silent white, I could almost imagine that concealed underneath the disguise was not the charred, desolate remains of a city littered with hundreds of thousands of corpses.

Another round of shivers racked my body. I hugged myself to fight off the morning chill and slid off the hood of the Humvee. Pants, boots, a long-sleeve T-shirt, and a mid-weight jacket weren't nearly enough to ward off the looming Midwest winter. The cold wasn't the only reason why I was shivering, though. I shivered because I felt utterly empty and afraid.

We had nothing. No food, no supplies, and less than a day's worth of gas left.

A lot had changed in two days. I think we were all numb, still operating on autopilot. Ten of us were all that remained of Camp Fox. To call our ragtag group "survivors" was being generous.

Clutch leaned next to me against the Humvee. He watched me with those warm brown eyes. They were often his only betrayal of emotion. He tried so hard to remain stoic, always in control, but his eyes belied his hard-fought façade. He was exhausted...and worried. "How are you holding up, Cash?"

I forced a smile. "Hanging in there. You?"

He rubbed his neck. "Hanging in there." He handed me a bag of homemade granola he'd found while searching vehicles after the bandit attack alongside the Mississippi River.

As I chewed on a handful of crunchy seeds, nuts, and oats, I stared at the large store on the other side of the interstate in the far distance. Sitting on the outskirts of the city, the building had somehow survived the bombing of Des Moines. After the outbreak, the military had tried to stop the spread by bombing all large cities, but their attempts were too late to do much good. I pointed to the store. "That's a Bass Pro Shop. It could be worth checking out. If it hasn't been looted already, it would have winter coats."

Clutch let out a long, quiet whistle. "Awfully risky. I'd prefer not to get any closer to Des Moines than we are now."

"That's the same reason why most looters would have avoided it, too," I replied. "It's worth the risk. Now that most of the zeds have migrated south for the winter, this could be our best chance before these places turn into a free-for-all."

He pushed off the vehicle, opened the driver's side door, and pulled out a pair of binoculars. He scrutinized the area for long minutes before handing the binoculars to me. "It looks in good shape. There's going to be zeds still locked inside."

I adjusted the binoculars to see through the store's shattered windows but could make out nothing in the interior darkness. "We won't know until we check it out."

"Farmhouses would be safer."

"And looted already." I lowered the binoculars. "I don't want to go into a place that big and that close to the city, but we're going to freeze out here otherwise."

After a pause, he sighed. "I sure would like to get my hands on some decent fishing gear."

I chewed on my lip. "What do you say? It could be like Christmas for all of us. Just a couple months early."

Slowly, his lips curled upward. "Christmas, eh? Jase has been talking about wanting a new backpack. We still need to figure out a plan," he said.

"Plan for what?" Jase chimed in as he walked toward us, hefting a black garbage bag filled with river water ready to be filtered and boiled.

"We're going to check out that Bass Pro Shop over there." I pointed.

He cocked his head in that direction. "Cool. Count me in. After breakfast, though. I'm starving."

"You're always starving," Clutch retorted.

The insatiable teenager shrugged and headed straight for our small campfire, where Vicki was busy making some kind of wild herbal tea to go with a bucketful of walnuts and two small trout Frost had caught.

As we all gathered around the fire, Clutch and I shared our ideas regarding the store. While no one was excited about entering a sporting goods store so soon after the run-in with the bandits in a store far too similar to this one, everyone agreed that we would freeze to death without warmer clothes.

If only we had food and supplies, I would've preferred to skip the store and head straight for Fox National Park. Several of us knew the area blindfolded. Alas, we had neither food nor supplies, and there was snow on the ground. Overnight, we had changed from the survivors handing out the food to begging for food.

Marco, the only person in our group not from Camp Fox, was the only man left alive of a squad sent to search for survivors. Marco's home base was New Eden, a large sanctuary in Nebraska. He'd said New Eden had enough supplies to feed hundreds well into next year. Even better, the town had been built around a missile silo. They'd survived the herds by going underground, and could do it again. Marco was anxious to get back to New Eden, and his hope was contagious. The decision had been unanimous.

We'd accompany Marco to New Eden.

Little Benji finished breakfast first to hustle back to

playing fetch with Diesel, a massive Great Dane that stood taller than the boy and would protect his short master with his life. Benji had Down syndrome, yet he'd managed to survive the outbreak on his own and ride a bicycle for miles through a zed-infested landscape to search for his grandfather.

I chuckled while I watched the two chase each other. Benji, oblivious to the ruined world around him, proved more resilient than the rest of us. He didn't seem to carry the emotional or physical scars we'd collected since the outbreak. Sometimes, I wondered if we needed Benji more than he needed us. Frost smiled at me before turning back to watch his grandson play. The older man rubbed his knuckles, a sure sign his arthritis was acting up again.

A cold wind blew through. *"Brr,"* Hali said as she snuggled closer to Jase. The teenagers tried to look casual about their friendship, but everyone knew the pair carried a flame for each other. Even the apocalypse couldn't stop young love.

"Here you go, dear. This will warm you up." Deb poured steaming tea into Hali's water bottle. Deb was moving slowly due to her daily bouts of morning sickness. She wasn't showing yet, but Vicki had said the first few months of pregnancy were always the hardest. That Tack, Deb's lover, had died only a couple weeks ago, didn't help. The woman was struggling to hang on—physically and emotionally—and there wasn't a goddamn thing any of us could do.

"I say we take a full day in the store, pull together what we can, and then spend the night inside," Griz said before quickly adding, "Assuming it's safe."

"I was thinking the same thing," Clutch said. "But, I don't like how many assumptions we're operating on right now." Clutch and Griz could've been twins with how they thought alike, despite their different personalities. I suspected much of that came about because both men were Army Rangers and every day was another mission.

"Then we'd better get packed up and check out the place," Jase said. "Maybe I'll find a new backpack. Did I mention that I'd like a new backpack?"

"Every day," Clutch groaned, giving Jase a small smile before his features tightened. "All right, everyone. We head out in fifteen. Cash, Jase, and Griz, you're with me to recon the store."

"Got it," I said, echoed by affirmations from Jase and Griz.

Clutch continued. "Marco, you'll lead the second Humvee with everyone else crammed in. I know it won't be comfortable. You'll park at the far edge of the parking lot to watch for zeds. At the first sign of trouble, you'll radio us, and we'll rendezvous back here. Otherwise, we'll bring you inside once we have a defensible position for the night. Any questions?"

Griz spit out a piece of walnut shell. "Dibs on the candy aisle."

"Each man for himself," Jase said with a sly grin.

"Okay, the two words of the day are 'quiet' and 'careful,' everyone," Clutch said as he climbed to his feet. "This place could be a goldmine, or we could be walking into a buffet line for zeds. Let's pack up and roll out."

"Or a trap set by bandits," Vicki said bitterly.

I clenched my jaw. No one needed reminded. I jumped abruptly to my feet and focused on brushing walnut shells off my pants rather than on the truth in Vicki's words.

Twelve minutes later, we were driving toward the store. Adrenaline made my knees knock. I rubbed my cold hands together. For the size of their engines, Humvees had shit for heaters, though I'd be rubbing my hands together even if it was the middle of summer.

We all had weapons. Clutch still had his Blaser rifle that he'd owned for far longer than he'd known me. I checked my pistol: a Glock on which I'd spent an hour cleaning off its previous owner's blood. I holstered it and then checked both my knife and machete.

I hoped that none of us would have to waste what precious little ammunition we had left. I had to get up close and personal to use my machete, but I figured — hoped — that the cold temperature would have slowed down any remaining zeds.

Since the zed migration a couple weeks ago, I assumed that most of the zed population would've joined the herds as they headed south. With how few zeds we'd seen since the herds passed through, my theory seemed proven. Otherwise, going this near to a city was suicide. Of course, I also knew that if the zeds couldn't have gotten out of the building to join the herds, they would still be inside, safe from the elements and starving for food.

At the edge of the parking lot stood a lone, charred zed. Snow dusted its head and shoulders. Its eyes, nose, and ears were all burnt or rotted off, which explained why it wouldn't have known to follow the herds. It wore fatigues, and I wondered how it ended up here. We drove close enough to the frozen zed that I could read the bloodied and blackened badge it wore: Pvt Jonathan Hart.

What happened to you, Private Jonathan Hart?

As soon as the thought crossed my mind, I scowled and looked away. I'd never forget his name now. I hated humanizing zeds, even though they weren't anywhere near human anymore. That much was clear. It was as though they'd transformed, or *transhumanized,* into something entirely different. Except, when they wore something that revealed the person they'd once been, it added one more vision to an already overflowing cornucopia of nightmares.

Fortunately for us, the only other zeds in the parking lot except for Private Jonathan Hart were collapsed lumps on the concrete. Even covered by snow, I knew those lumps belonged to someone's family at one time. Hell, they could've been *my* family, who I'd abandoned in Des Moines when I'd selfishly fled the city during the outbreak.

I tried not to think about the greatest regret of my life, instead focusing on the massive store before us. *Be here, now,* I ordered myself.

Other than the completely demolished glass doors, likely from the bomb blast, the building from the front was in one piece and looked to be in pretty good shape. Unfortunately, through those shattered doors, I could see sunlight. A large section of the roof must've caved in, which meant the store wasn't going to be winning any prizes for being structurally sound. Not only would we have to be careful to not set off any more seismic events within the store, we'd have to deal with concrete, roof, and rebar while searching for supplies. The bright side was any zeds that had been trapped inside *should've* been able to get out and leave with the herds.

Griz whistled. "She looked prettier from a distance," he said from the backseat, pointing at the building.

"It's what's on the inside that counts," I replied optimistically.

"Depends," he said. "Are we talking about girls or stores?"

Jase snorted.

I rotated in my seat to find Griz smirking and Jase grinning from ear to ear. "You guys are hopeless."

It was then I noticed a green sprig weaved around Griz's helmet, another one of his personal air fresheners. Without deodorant, we'd all found new ways to deal with not having baths anymore. Today, his sprig reminded me of a laurel wreath, as though he were the mighty Apollo ready for battle. "What. No wreath for me?" I asked.

"If I make one for you, I'll have to make one for everyone," Griz replied.

"You made one for Benji," I said.

"The little trickster conned me into making him one."

"Diesel even has one on his collar," Jase added.

Griz shrugged. "He conned me, too."

I dramatically acted put out. "You made one for the dog before making one for me?"

"Yup," he replied simply.

"Time for game faces," Clutch said. "We're coming up on kick-off."

I smiled and shook my head at Griz before turning my attention back to the store.

Clutch drove around the perimeter of the building, where we found part of the western wall had collapsed from a fire. That explained the sunlight we'd seen, but the blackened debris worried me. "I hope the fire didn't burn through the store," I said.

"If it did, it'll be a quick trip," Clutch said as he brought the Humvee to a stop twenty feet from the main doors. We stepped outside. Gripping my machete, I searched the area for any signs of life. The only thing I saw was my breath in the cold air. After we spent many long seconds walking alongside the front and sides of the building, we stood outside the doors.

Inside the store, snow covered a portion of the

merchandise, making a playground of shapes that could be anything. We shared *the* look. The one where we both wanted to get the hell out of there, but knew we had to go in. It was the look of dread.

"It doesn't look looted," Jase said. "That's a good sign."

Clutch glanced upward, shading his eyes against the sun with his hand. "Well, we can't wait around. When the sun warms things up, the zeds will start moving around again. We need to either go in now or write it off."

"At least the snow will make it easier to spot footprints," Griz said, coming to a stop next to me.

I closed my eyes and turned my face toward the sun, feeling its warmth on my cold skin. After taking a deep breath, I turned back toward the team. "We're already here."

Clutch pulled out his handheld radio and clicked the mike. "This is Team Charlie. We'll check back in twenty minutes. Radio silence otherwise. Be ready to roll out if this run turns to shit. Do not come after us. Confirm."

"*Got it*," Marco's voice came through the radio in response. "*Be careful in there.*"

Jase took the first step forward. "Let's do this."

The four of us moved toward the hollowed-out front doors. As one, we stepped through the frames, our boots crunching on broken glass.

A single zed lay in our path in the entryway. Its skin was ripped from its body, flayed by glass shards, several of which were still embedded in organs.

"The thing must've been pushed up against the glass doors when the bombs fell," Griz said quietly as he gripped his machete.

Sprawled under a ceiling where the elements couldn't get to it, I could see the zed's organs, even its lungs and heart, beneath its shattered ribs. Its mouth moved only slightly, as though it was trying to tell us something. I'd seen horrific things before, but this zed caused us all to pause. It didn't attack, though with how ravaged its body was, it probably couldn't. Instead, it did nothing but lay there and watch us. Its gaze seemed more curious than sinister.

I couldn't take my eyes off the zed. Not until Griz put it out of its misery with a single thrust of his blade. I took a deep breath and swallowed. The aggressive zeds were so much easier to deal with. They'd come at me with evil in their eyes, and I instinctively fought back. Then, there was the tiniest minority of ones like this one that stuck with me. I called them Zen zeds, the ones that simply stared and never attacked. They haunted my nightmares worse than the violent ones, because these seemed like they retained a shred of their humanity. The act of killing them felt more like euthanasia than self-defense. I assumed they preferred death. At least, that's what I told myself.

Clutch began to move forward again, and the rest of us fell in behind him. We stepped cautiously until we were out of the narrow entryway and stood at the edge of the huge store. Clutch took point, and we followed him as he headed to the right, toward the boat section. Earlier, he'd said that he wanted to clear this section first. With its open spaces and the collapsed outer wall, it would be our Plan B in case we had to leave in a hurry and couldn't get out through the store entrance.

Rows of fishing boats sat in mish mashed rows on the floor, tossed and blackened by a surge of heat that must've hit the entire west side of the building. The bomb blast had been enough to break out all the glass. The sprinkler system must've still been working at the time of the bombing, as only the edge of the store had burned.

Fingers crossed, the good stuff was still safe.

Interspersed around the boats stood unmoving snow-covered statues.

Zeds.

I held my machete in a defensive position, ready to swing out at any moment. Griz came to a stop in front of the nearest zed. We encircled it, and my grip tightened on my machete. The duct tape I'd wrapped around the handle to give it a better grip creaked under my grasp.

Like Private Jonathan Hart, this zed's skin was crisped, and it had no eyes, ears, or nose. Slowly, Griz waved his blade in front of its face. It made no movement.

"Do you think they're dead?" Jase asked quietly.

"Maybe they're just frozen," I whispered back.

"I figured more would've migrated," Griz said. "But,

these must be in too rough of shape to drag themselves out of the store."

Clutch looked across the area. "We'll take them down one at a time. Don't get too close if you can help it."

Jase waved his arm in front of a zed. It didn't flinch or show any recognition. "Kinda hard, with them standing around like bowling pins all over the place."

"They must be deaf and blind," I said. "None of them seem to have sensed us."

"Let's keep it that way," Clutch said.

Griz swung and lodged his machete in the first zed's temple. He pulled out the blade and the zed collapsed. We all stood and watched as he wiped the blade on the zed's shirt.

Clutch spoke. "I don't like how many are still around. Let's stick together until we clear the building. It'll take more time, but if we get this place cleared, we can drive the Humvees right through those big doors tonight to hide them in the off chance anyone passes through this area. Plus, that'll give us more time to do our shopping. With this" — he gestured to the building surrounding us — "We'll need plenty of time."

A rat scurried under a boat, and I jumped back with a squeak.

Clutch's gaze snapped to mine. "What is it?"

Heat flushed my cheeks. "Nothing."

"Nothing?"

"It was a rat," I said sheepishly.

His brows rose.

I added, "It was a really big rat."

He eyed me suspiciously for a moment before returning his focus to the task at hand.

"Chicken," Jase whispered as he walked by.

"It was *really* big," I countered, but he'd already moved on to killing a zed.

We spent the next several minutes killing zeds, the entire time I kept on the lookout for rats. I hated rats nearly as much I hated zeds.

Once we finished clearing the boat section, Clutch checked in with Marco on the radio. "There are plenty of stinkers in here," Clutch reported. "It will take a little longer than planned."

"*Need help?*" came Marco's response.

"Negative. Nothing too challenging here. I'll check in every hour. If anything goes wrong, you bug out and don't look back. Protect the civilians."

Marco didn't respond fast enough for Clutch's humor.

"Tell me you'll bug out," Clutch demanded.

"*I've got it covered,*" Marco replied.

We worked our way closer to the center of the store, zigzagging through debris. We finished off any zed we came across, but as we worked our way inward, they were becoming fewer and fewer. Leaning on a table of folded shirts, a zed seemed to stare off into nothingness as though contemplating the mysteries of life. Oblivious to our presence, Griz and I approached. This one was dressed in suit. On its lapel, it had a pin with two laurel leaves crossed over a book and a shepherd's hook.

"What's that mean, I wonder," I said without thinking.

Griz's lips thinned. "It meant he was a chaplain."

I frowned. "Oh."

Griz lifted his blade and paused for a moment before finishing the deed. I turned away in haste, trying to pretend this zed never existed, and I bumped into the clothes rack. A petite zed wearing a store uniform lashed out, and I jumped back. "Shit!"

My reflexes kicked in and I swung my machete, crushing its head in a single shot. "Not frozen," I said breathlessly before yanking my machete out of the zed's skull.

"Guess there's some life left in them yet," Griz said. "Good to know."

"Be careful," Clutch cautioned.

"Yeah," I replied as I grabbed a folded shirt and cleaned the blade now coated in the thick brown sludge that had once been blood. Killing zeds had become easier over the months. Not just because I'd gained skill and became desensitized to them, but because the zeds were becoming weaker. Their bones had become brittle, to the point my machete rarely became lodged in their skulls or necks anymore.

I crept more carefully as we scoured the store for more zeds. It didn't take long for us to finish the wide-open area. With the offices in back completely burned or collapsed, we turned our attention to the restaurant on the eastern side of the store.

"Looks in pretty good shape," Jase said while the four of us stood outside the closed glass door. The area beyond the glass was draped in darkness, making it impossible to see what hid within. "Do we go for touchdown?"

Clutch and Griz stepped up to the glass pane and both looked through.

Griz spoke first. "If there's anything in there from before, it hasn't gotten out yet, which means it likely is never going to get out."

"Let's leave it for now," Clutch said. "We'll post a guard in this area to play it safe."

I looked back at all the merchandise in the store waiting to be plucked, and I grinned. Just as I was about to say *let's go shopping*, something clanged on the other side of the door.

"Ah, shit," I mumbled.

A zed's visage appeared through the glass. Then another face emerged from the darkness. More kept coming. These zeds, protected from the elements, looked nothing like the ones we'd just killed. These were *healthy* zeds, and there were at least thirty of them.

"You guys really think that door will hold?" Jase asked.

Griz and Clutch both shook their heads.

"Not a chance," Griz said.

"Son of a bitch. Let's get out of their line of sight and see if they settle down," Clutch said as we were already taking steps back.

Instead of calming, our retreat seemed to rev up the zeds even more. They pounded on the door, fighting to get past one another at us. One zed tripped as others shoved at it from behind. Its head slammed into the door, and the glass shattered. Pounding fists tore through the weakened glass. With only the metal handle bar across the middle of the door to hold back the zeds, they worked into a frenzy to get at us.

The zed that had broken the glass with its head was on the ground and crawled out from under the bar. More followed, some tumbling over the bar while the shorter ones crawled under it.

"Outside to the Humvee!" Griz shouted, and we ran.

We jumped over debris and around fallen racks. The linoleum floors had become slick with the melting snow, and we slid our way through the store. I fell hard on my knee, and stars shot through my vision. Clenching my jaw, I jumped up and forced weight on my injured leg.

"To the RP!" Clutch yelled into the radio. "The store is overrun. Get out of here!"

CHAPTER II

Griz pointed to the collapsed wall beyond the boats. "Plan B! Keep going. We can't risk the front entrance. We need to put more distance between us and them."

As we ran passed the entrance, I risked a glance behind me to see three dozen voracious zeds tumbling after us. Rats scurried under racks of clothes and counters. Fortunately, the slick floors were proving difficult for the zeds, and we were getting well ahead of them. I followed Griz as he weaved through the fallen boats and toward the open space where a huge glass door had once been used for moving boats in and out of the store.

Part of the ceiling had collapsed above the door, leaving debris piled several feet high. I stumbled over the rubble and caught myself before falling onto dangerous glass shards. Outside, the sun shone brightly enough to blind me. It took me only a second to get my bearings, and I ran toward our Humvee.

Something had drawn some of the zeds away from us and back to the main entrance. There, the loud engine of the other Humvee slashed through the area. The fast-moving distraction, with six people piled inside, plowed through the herd. Frost stood in back with a rifle and took shots at the zeds that got back up.

With them working on the herd outside, I turned and focused on the dozen or so climbing over the rubble. I unslung my rifle, took aim, and fired. A zed dropped. A shot rang off to my left, and another zed fell. A third shot joined in. We finished off the small herd in less than four minutes.

After I checked out the bodies in the rubble to make sure none survived, I turned to see Marco walking around the dead in the parking lot. I couldn't see Clutch's face, but if his slow, heavy march toward the other man was any indication, he wasn't pleased.

I hustled toward the pair as Clutch threw his arms in the air. "I told you to bug out if things turned to shit. Tell me exactly how bringing everyone into a zed swarm is bugging out?"

"I wasn't going to let you have all the fun," Marco replied.

"What part about it being a direct order didn't you understand?"

Marco pointed to the east. "My boss is lying dead

across the state line right now. I'm not like you or Griz. I wasn't some G. I. Joe Rambo before the outbreak. I was a volunteer, not a soldier, and I'm not good with following orders. Hell, before all this, I was a consultant who had just about reached Delta's Million Mile status."

Clutch wagged a finger at the younger soldier. "Someone could've died back there. That'd be on you."

After a pause, Marco spoke. "I know. If things got hairy, I would've made sure they were safe. You have my word. I'd never put them at risk."

"C'mon guys," I said as lightly as possible. "The store is just about cleared. I'd really love to do a little shopping. Okay?"

Grudgingly, they turned their attention from each other and back to the store.

It took five hours before we had the stragglers in the building dispatched and enough rubble cleared to back our vehicles inside and park them in between the boats. From outside, no one could see any sign of survivors.

We couldn't risk bandits finding us here like they had at the store on the Mississippi. We'd been exhausted and let our guard down then. It had proved to be a fatal mistake.

Never again.

The guys worked at clearing multiple exit routes, with one route to the vehicles and backup routes, one to each direction. With how prepared we were, everyone had agreed to spend as many days here as needed to sift through supplies, give the Humvees an oil change, and prepare for the long trip ahead.

I straddled an ATV, taking in the huge store surrounding me. My jaw slackened as I rested. Aside from the basic looting of cash, guns, and ammo—all of which probably happened during the first day of the outbreak—the store was relatively untouched.

I hugged myself in the shearling parka with golden cream fleece lining I'd found. I looked like an Eskimo in it. It was too warm to wear very long, but I still savored its softness and refused to take it off as I stuffed backpacks and duffels from the luggage section with my discoveries.

A smile crossed my face as I looked at the big pile of bags to my left. Everyone had a similar pile, and everyone's pile was full of similar things. Warm, *clean* clothes. Camping and hiking supplies, such as eating utensils, hydration packs, sleeping bags, blankets, and sleep pads. And even a little bit of one of the most important items: food.

Most of the snow had melted under the warmth of the sun, leaving everything damp, so I helped Hali string our new clothes on hangers to dry in the cold air.

We'd all had a good laugh at Benji's pile. He'd forgone bags and piled toys and games into a mountain. No one envied Frost as he "coached" Benji into trying on clothes and picking out the right color for a winter coat. After a lengthy debate, Frost succumbed to the boy's adamant choice on a fluorescent green coat since his grandfather had chosen a dark evergreen coat to blend into his surroundings. To Benji, green was green.

Marco and Vicki emptied the restaurant. I avoided going inside the restaurant, instead waiting at the door to haul their findings. Even with the inside door gone, the restaurant still reeked of zeds that had been cooped up inside stale air for the better part of a year.

The pair found several huge cans of tomato sauce and vegetables and several bottles of olive oil. The bags of flour and sugar had long been claimed by rodents. The little buggers had gotten to nearly everything not in a tin can. They'd even managed to chew through plastic tubs. Despite the lack of variety in food, I had no doubt that Vicki, who'd been Camp Fox's cook, would work magic with whatever ingredients she had available.

After loading what we could into our two vehicles, we quickly discovered we had a problem that was nice to have. We'd found so much stuff throughout the store that we would need to find a third vehicle.

Taking the risk for the store had proved to be well worth it. No one was injured, and we'd found enough supplies to get us to New Eden without stress of running out. We'd desperately needed this good fortune.

We took anything we could use, but we also left plenty of gear behind for any who came after. The food was another story. We took anything that could be eaten. With winter coming and no home, we couldn't afford to leave anything behind.

The surplus food we now had was crucial, since

finding gas for vehicles was becoming harder and harder with each passing day, making supply runs more and more limited. Until this month, I'd had no idea how quickly gas started to go bad if it wasn't in well-sealed containers. The Humvees could handle dirtier fuel than most modern cars, but even now, the engines pinged after the last siphoning of gas from a car on the side of the road. We added fuel additive at each fill-up, but we only had seven bottles left.

Griz was the first to point out that vehicles would be obsolete within a couple years. Everyone would be walking, riding bicycles, and riding horses — assuming horses weren't extinct by then. I dreaded the day cars became nothing more than lawn ornaments and prayed we had a permanent home, free of zeds, before the gasoline became no longer usable.

In the twilight, I glanced over to where Deb was setting down a pot filled with something steaming onto an aluminum camp-style picnic table. As if on cue, my stomach growled. I jumped off the ATV and headed straight for the food line. Jase pulled Hali to her feet.

Earlier, with Jase standing watch behind her, she had set up a cozy camp for Benji, his cot surrounded by teddy bears. The boy, oblivious to their actions, was propped against a snoring Diesel and completely engrossed with his new toys.

Jase clapped once, and Diesel shot up. A startled Benji looked around. Jase pointed to the table where Frost stood, waiting for the kid. "Dinner time, Benny boy."

Benji's face broke into a wide grin. He jumped to his feet and took off running toward his grandfather. He wasn't a fast kid, but every time food was involved, he'd come close to breaking his personal speed records. He slid into being the first in line, just like he did every meal. No one minded. Spoiling Benji was one of the few joys in this new world.

In the large soup pot was all the pasta that had survived the rats and mice. The noodles had no real sauce, only olive oil and spices found in the restaurant, but it all tasted pretty dang good to me.

Griz and Frost stood guard while the rest of us ate. Benji slurped the noodles while he fed Diesel one strand of spaghetti at a time. I twirled my noodles around my fork, savoring every bite. Jase finished first, as usual, and he always went back for seconds.

Marco tossed his Styrofoam bowl and plastic fork into a plastic bag. He stood and motioned to Frost and Griz. "I'll take watch now for one of you guys."

It was standard operating procedure to have someone stand watch twenty-four/seven. We always had at least two people guard over our group. Even inside a building like this. *Especially* inside a building like this.

Griz grabbed his dinner and sat down next to Vicki. She didn't even acknowledge him. I remembered the exact moment her personality had changed from kind and optimistic to cold and hard. It was the moment when Tyler was killed. She hadn't smiled since.

Deb burped and covered her mouth. "Excuse me," she mumbled.

Vicki had mentioned first pregnancies were even harder once a woman was in her thirties. Deb was thirty-four, and couldn't keep much of anything down. She was losing weight too quickly, and I worried how much longer she could go without losing the baby.

"Another tummy ache?" Benji asked.

Deb gave a small smile and nodded.

"Mom gives me warm milk when my tummy hurts." His face fell. He said the same thing every time he noticed Deb wasn't feeling well. I knew what Benji was going to say next. We all knew. "I miss Mom."

Diesel always seemed to notice when Benji's mood faltered, and the dog nudged the boy with his big, shiny nose. Benji scowled and wiped the slobber from his arm. The boy's features soon eased, and he rubbed the dog's ears. When he went back to his eating-slash-feeding-the-dog routine, we ate and talked about our findings as well as tomorrow's plans.

"There's a truck rental company not far from here, so maybe it wasn't destroyed," I said. "I rented a truck once to move into my house."

As soon as I said the words, a weight fell on my chest. I'd been so caught up in keeping busy that my mind didn't have the time to dwell on the past. My house, an adorable little bungalow I'd been fixing up, was likely a pile of stones sitting fewer than ten miles from here. My parent's house, not far from downtown, would've faced the same fate.

I still hated myself for not coming back for them. Not only had I left them behind, but also I never came back for them. I had planned to. In the first days, all I thought about was how I could get back into the city to find them. My dad was a doctor, my mother a nurse and a diabetic. Even though they were both retired, I knew they would've been at the hospital, helping out where they could in the most dangerous place of all.

Still, I had tried to work out a plan to make it to them. Then the news had come that the military had bombed Des Moines and all other large cities. They never stood a chance. Still, not having the chance to say good-bye—not trying to save them—would be something I would have to live with for the rest of my life.

I sensed someone watching me, and I noticed Clutch sitting in a camp chair. He motioned to the empty chair next to him. I dumped off my bowl and fork and headed to the seat Clutch had saved. I sunk into the seat, and my muscles loosened.

Clutch pointed to the night sky through the open roof. "Looks like we're going to have quite a full moon tonight."

I looked upward. The moon seemed as though it was racing to claim the sky, even before the sun relinquished its fleeting hold. "The days are getting too short. Soon the days will be shorter than the nights."

We sat as darkness bled out from every corner in the building. Small lanterns were lit, and the light licked at the dark. Without any light to mar its beauty, the moon became a brilliant pearl.

With night, came the beasts. The animals that came out of hiding after the zeds migrated. With little to fear, they searched to fill their empty stomachs.

A howl in the distance was returned by another. These weren't the coyote howls from old westerns. These howls sounded like mad men, as though the demons of the night were cackling at what the world had become, taunting us that humans were no longer the most feared predators on the planet.

The howls had become familiar, but they still unnerved me. Especially when they were the only sound of the night. Trying to ignore the distant wails, I focused intently on the moon. The iridescent pearl was stained by moon spots, and I wondered how each of those scars came to be. I mused if someone on the moon could see similar scars on the earth from all the bombings and fires.

I spoke softly. "Do you think the earth will ever be a place where we can live without fear?"

"Don't know," Clutch said. "But if we don't believe things will get better, why do we keep trying?"

"Yeah," I whispered. "I guess you're right."

As Clutch dozed off, I pulled out a small mirror and reflected the moonlight in it. The way the light shimmered and reflected in the glass would've made a pretty picture, if only I had a working camera. Instead, I focused on remembering this moment. Of the peaceful moonlit night and Clutch at my side.

Moonlight reflected off the stand of mirrors hanging nearby, all containing mirrors identical to the little one I held. A reflection beyond the stand caught my eye. I leaned forward. As I turned the mirror to move the light around, I noticed even more reflections scattered around the dark building.

Griz, nearing the end of his shift, paused to take in the reflections.

One of the reflections blinked.

I clicked the safety off my rifle. "Griz? You see that?"

"Yeah," he replied as he took a step back and did a three-sixty. "We need to get to the Humvees *now*."

I nudged Clutch, and he came awake with a deep inhalation. He grunted and rubbed his neck.

I held a finger to my lips. "Sh."

I could see his frown in the moonlight as he took in the situation. He let out the breath he'd been holding in a rush.

Slowly, I stood and walked over to Jase. A howl from inside the building woke him up before I could get there. Diesel returned with a flurry of barking. Howls surrounded us and echoed off the walls. We'd all heard the howls before.

But never in this great a number.

And never all around us.

CHAPTER III

"**W**olves!" I yelled and yanked Jase and Hali to their feet. "To the trucks!"

We had camped next to the Humvees for easy escape, so we had only a few feet between safety and the pack. However, three feet looked like a mile when countless reflective eyes were racing toward us.

Ever protective of his grandson, Frost already had Benji safely inside the Humvee with a coyote's head and the words *Charlie Coyote* painted on the hood and doors.

Deb and Vicki raced to the other Humvee—the one with *Betty Bravo*, the pinup girl Griz had painted on it— while Marco and Griz fired rounds into the dark, their gunshots echoed by yelps.

When I opened the door of Humvee Charlie, I paused to make sure Jase and Clutch were right behind me, but I found myself shoved onto the backseat, with Clutch landing on top of me and slamming the door closed.

"They're safe," he said as I crawled out from under him. I crawled across the backseat and pressed the massive Great Dane to the floor so I had a place to sit. I looked to the other Humvee to see Jase cramming Hali into the front passenger's seat.

Vicki stood at the door of the other vehicle and fired off shots while Deb climbed inside. When Marco reached Vicki, they quickly disappeared inside, and their doors shut. The last one standing, Griz laid down a burst of automatic fire while Frost pulled Benji onto his lap.

Not far from our vehicle, a wolf tore into one of Benji's teddy bears. The boy gasped and wagged a finger at the animal. "Bad dog," he scolded, his voice cracking.

Diesel cringed at the words, and I rubbed the dog's back. Benji bit back tears. Frost pulled his grandson closer, and Benji tucked his head into the older man's shoulder.

There had to be hundreds of animals in the store. They leapt over their fallen, trying to reach us. Griz stopped firing, jumped into the driver's seat, and slammed the door just as a wolf smashed against the metal and glass with a sharp cry. A wet mark of saliva remained on the glass where the wolf had slid off. Another jumped up against my window, startling me.

Diesel growled at the wolves and dogs outside our Humvees, and I rubbed the dog's fur. "It's okay. They can't us get in here."

Griz started the engine and shifted the truck into gear, which only seemed to drive the pack into more of a fury. The dogs pounded against the sides like hail on glass. Many were sickly and couldn't jump high. Some could, and their looks of determination scared the hell out of me. Some attacked the dogs nearest to them in their frenzy to get closer.

Griz pulled ahead slowly, keeping an eye on the Humvee next to us. One large but skinny dog managed to leap onto the hood, and it stood there, watching us with bloodshot eyes through the windshield. Its mouth frothed as it bared its teeth. I could hear its growl through the glass.

Griz stepped on the gas pedal, throwing the dog against the windshield, and then slammed the brakes. The dog slid off the hood, trying to claw and scratch to stay on but to no avail.

"Bad meat," I muttered.

"What?" Clutch asked.

I nodded toward the dog growling at us. "They remind me of the catfish. After eating infected meat, they're all getting sick and going crazy, like rabid animals."

Clutch watched the dog and then tilted his head. "Zeds were probably the only food they could find after the zeds killed everything else."

"Getting bit by one of these would be a bad deal," Griz added, pulling in behind the other Humvee.

"The zeds are easy prey, and they obviously have no trouble eating them. I wonder why they're trying to go for us," I said.

"I'd bet we taste better," Griz replied.

"Maybe they like the hunt," Jase said. "We'd be prime rib compared to rotten zed meat."

"They're starving," Frost said. "Most of the zed herds have moved south. And, the dogs can't get to the zeds stuck indoors. There's just not enough food left for the number of animals out there."

Once we were outside the store, the Humvee in front came to a stop, and Griz hit the brakes.

Deb's voice came over the radio. *"I know the plan was to head back to last night's camp, but we think that might be too close to be safe. Where do you think we should go?"*

"Hold on," Griz replied and threw a quick glance at us. "The only option I see is we drive until we lose our uninvited guests, but it'll burn through our gas."

Clutch nodded. "We'll get an early start on our day. Drive until we ditch the dogs. Then we come back and look for a truck to transport our remaining supplies. We'll head back here, load up during the daylight hours, and bug out before the mongrels realize what's going on."

Griz got back on the radio. "Coyote will take lead."

"Okay. We'll be right behind you."

Griz stepped on the gas, and the Humvee thumped over several bodies. I cringed. I loved animals, and even though these were after us, I knew they chased us only because they were starving. I hated what had become the way of things now: *kill or be killed*.

As we weaved around cars and down streets, animals broke off until eventually we were free of the packs. In the morning twilight, we roused zeds in our haste. Unable to get to us, they pounded against windows of the buildings and cars that trapped them, leaving brown streaks on the glass.

After four hours of sunlight, all the remaining snow had melted, leaving the world in its autumn colors once again. We still hadn't found a truck for the supplies we'd left behind. Every vehicle we checked had either no keys or gas. We tried to jump-start a truck, with no luck. We'd even tried a moving truck that had had a zed inside the cab. The stench was unbelievable. Even if the truck had started, I doubted I could've driven it.

We finally gave up and returned to the store. The building left an entirely different impression today. Yesterday, it had represented hope. Today, it represented the fact that nowhere was safe, no matter how carefully we prepared. The world was full of bloodthirsty beasts that would never stop coming.

We rushed to hook up a trailer to one of the Humvees and cram as many supplies, bicycles, and warm gear as we could squeeze into it. Clutch and Griz didn't enjoy having a trailer hinder our mobility, but they liked the idea of leaving the supplies behind even less. The dogs began showing up again—at first one or two at a time, then a half dozen or more in groups appeared. Clutch latched the trailer door closed. We left the store to the mongrels, and continued our pilgrimage to New Eden.

Marco pointed to a dot on the map. "We should try to make it here for tonight. It's the first exit we can take to where the interstate opens up again. It's also one of the places New Eden teams stop to refuel and stay when they need a place to crash on overnight trips. There isn't much in the area, so we've never had much of a problem with zeds around there. It's a good place to stop."

Clutch examined the map. Griz spoke up first. "How big is that town right there?"

"Three buildings and a gas station," Marco replied. "They've all been cleared, and the building has been fortified. Like I said, it's a New Eden way station."

Using my forefinger and thumb, I measured the distance from our current location to the dot Marco had made to mark New Eden on the map. "That's a heck of a lot of side roads to cover with only a half-day's worth of sunlight left."

Marco nodded. "I know, but I've been on those roads several times. The route is clear of any roadblocks."

"And bandits?" I asked.

"The Black Sheep are the biggest threat around here,

but we've never seen them on those roads. They avoid the Des Moines area. Too many zeds."

"Not anymore," I added. "Otherwise, we wouldn't be here, either."

"Cash is right," Clutch said. "Right now, they're probably as busy searching for food as New Eden is searching for survivors."

"We've been lucky we haven't run into them already," Griz said. "I don't want to stay out in the open."

"I know," Marco said. "I want to get back to New Eden as soon as possible."

"Coffee break's over. Let's hit the road," Clutch said. "If we stop only to look for gas, we shouldn't have any problem making it sixty klicks in five hours."

"When did you become Mr. Optimist?" I asked him with a smirk.

"Since I got myself a nice, cozy sleeping bag and pad," he said as he turned and got behind the wheel of the Humvee with the trailer hooked behind it.

We piled into our vehicles. Marco navigated and we followed, checking in on the radios every ten minutes. Every five minutes, Marco tried to reach New Eden on the radio, but either they'd changed their frequencies, or no one was in the area.

Even with the newfound rarity of zeds, it took us nearly six hours to reach our destination. Twilight had turned to darkness. Marco had us stop next door to the gas station at a restaurant with a sign that read *Marcie's*

Café: Home of Iowa's Best Hamburger.

"Mm, a burger sounds good," Jase said as he clicked on his shiny new headlamp and stepped out of our Humvee.

I turned on my headlamp and followed. I pointed to the sign on the glass door. "I think I'll have the special."

Jase gave me a look of disgust. "Meatloaf? You've got to be kidding."

"You'd love my mother's meatloaf," Clutch said as he walked past us and stepped up to the door next to Marco, who had pulled out a key hidden in the doorframe.

I shrugged at Jase. A movement in the distance caught my eye, and I squinted. "Um, guys?"

They turned, their lights blinding me.

Clutch spoke first. "What is it?"

I fidgeted. "Well, I...I swear I just saw a nun crossing the road."

Clutch frowned, and Jase smirked. "Is that a start of one of your lame jokes?"

I shook my head. "And she didn't look infected."

Their gazes—and headlamps—moved to the paved road we'd driven a few minutes earlier. I pointed to where I'd seen the woman, but saw nothing. "My eyes must've been playing tricks on me," I muttered.

Then, our lights fell on her. Sure as shit, a nun wearing full habit was standing next to a tree watching us. She shielded her eyes. "No need to blind me," she grumbled.

"Are you alone?" Clutch asked quickly as we all raised our guns.

"You don't have to worry about me none," she said as she hustled toward us. "I was just on my way back to Connie's for the night. You should get yourselves inside. It's less safe after dark."

"Keep your hands where I can see them," Clutch commanded. "And walk slowly." .

"Can you at least turn down those lights?" she replied. "I can't see a thing with them pointed at my eyes like that."

"We will once we know you don't mean to do us harm," Clutch retorted.

"Heavens, do I look like I can do you harm?"

"So you say," Clutch whispered softly. He didn't lower his weapon.

I scanned the area but saw no movement.

The nun stopped. "I figured you must be with New Eden since you knew where the key was."

Marco frowned. "We are, but I've never seen you around here before."

"Connie and I were staying at her house; it's about fifteen miles southwest of here. However, we couldn't stay there anymore. We were out looking for a new home when we ran into a few nice fellows from New Eden. They offered to give us a lift to New Eden, but we preferred to stay out here." She pointed. "They dropped us off at the house down the road, and so here we are."

Clutch edged closer to Marco and whispered, "What

do you think? She telling the truth?"

Marco shrugged. "She could be. We've cleared several houses, including the one she's in, for survivors we find but don't come to New Eden. Either by their choice or by ours."

The woman motioned to the café behind us. "Are you staying there tonight?"

Clutch kept watching Marco.

"I think she's telling the truth," Marco replied.

Clutch turned to face the woman. "We are."

"It's cold out. Connie and I don't have much for food to offer, but we still have a bit from what the nice fellas from New Eden left us. We also have a fire to keep you warm tonight. The house is quite safe. All the windows are covered. Nothing can see the fire from outside."

Clutch glanced at me, and I gave a small nod. He, too, seemed to be considering her words. She looked trustworthy enough. She was a nun, for Christ's sake — or at least dressed like one. However, that didn't mean I was going to blindly follow her.

I spoke quietly to Clutch. "If there are only two of them like she says, we have them outnumbered."

Clutch nodded and replied quietly. "They know about us already. I'd like to find out more about them. If anything sets off our instincts, we'll be better equipped to deal with it."

Clutch looked across all our faces. When he looked at Deb, he nodded. "We'll take you up on the offer. But, we'll provide dinner for you two tonight."

That Clutch had offered dinner didn't surprise me. A small part of it was to make it a fair trade, but a much larger part was because Clutch didn't trust other people's food, not unless he watched them prepare it.

She smiled. "It's settled then. You can park in the driveway, and I'll let Connie know." Without waiting for a response, she hustled up the street toward the lone house to the north of the café.

Clutch motioned us together as if we were a football team in a huddle. "We play it safe," he said. "Keep your eyes open and your ears peeled. Just because we're taking her up on her offer of hospitality doesn't mean we should trust her. No risks."

When we reached the two-story brick house, the nun and another woman stood on the front porch. As we approached, they introduced themselves.

"I'm Sister Donaldson, but all my friends call me Picadilly. And this is Connie."

I stood, frozen. Memories flooded forward as I recalled a good friend talking about his sister, a nun who'd always gone by her nickname, Picadilly. "You...had a brother named Wes?" I asked, already knowing there could be no coincidence.

Picadilly's eyes widened. "Yes. Are you from this area? Have you seen him?"

"Yes," I said and then swallowed tightly while Wes's final moments flashed through my mind...of Wes leaning over the back of the boat, of a zed lunging up and tearing out Wes's throat, of Clutch giving Wes eternal peace. I took a deep breath. "He was a good man and a dear friend. I'm sorry."

She cast her gaze downward for a long moment before looking up. "Did he suffer?"

"No," I said too quickly, afraid she'd hear the truth in my voice if I'd waited.

"Thank God for small blessings," she said softly. After another pause, she stood straighter. "Let's get you inside. There are too many things that go bump in the night to stand around outside after dark for long."

Griz and Marco did a final check of the vehicles and gear, and we entered the house with our sleeping gear and weapons. The fire in the hearth warmed my face as I crossed the foyer. The fire provided the only light except for our headlamps, yet the place felt somewhat homey. Two mattresses leaned against the wall to the left off the fireplace, with a stack of bedding to the side. A cast iron Dutch oven was propped above the flames. Several small stacks of home-canned jars and tin cans of food were on the other side of the fireplace.

Suddenly, I felt selfish we had so much stocked away in our vehicles.

Vicki carried in a cardboard box. "I'll get started on dinner."

"I'd be happy to help," Picadilly said as she begun to roll her sleeves.

I dropped my sleeping bag next to the couch. "I guess that's my cue to secure the house."

"There's no need," Picadilly said quickly. "We're safe

in here."

Connie watched us nervously and stepped closer to the stairs.

I frowned and looked upward. The light from my headlamp lit up an empty hallway and closed doors. I motioned to Jase, who was already pulling out his machete.

Clutch dropped his gear and pulled out his sword. "What's up there?"

"Nothing," Connie replied, but she didn't move.

I pressed past her and took the first steps.

Connie came up behind me. "You're guests here tonight. You don't need to raise a fuss."

At the top of the stairs, the woman moved around me and stood in front of a closed bedroom door.

"What's behind that door?" I asked, feeling confident with Jase and Clutch on either side of me.

"Nothing you need to worry about," Connie replied coldly.

Picadilly ran up the steps. "Connie's right. There is nothing here you need to worry about."

I ignored her and grabbed the door handle to find it unlocked. Before I turned, I glanced at Clutch and Jase to find both ready.

Connie grabbed my forearm. "Please don't."

I opened the door.

Inside, my light shone on a single zed sitting on the bed. His jaundiced eyes reflected the light like a cat's eyes at night. He came to his feet.

Jase lunged forward to strike at the same time Connie shoved her way into the room. "Don't hurt him!"

She managed to squeeze her way in between us and the zed, making it impossible to kill it without going through her.

She cupped the zed's cheeks. "There, there. It's all right, Henry."

The zed didn't attack. Instead, he simply stood there, watching the woman with a dull gaze. I already knew what he was.

A Zen zed.

I couldn't find the words. Clutch spoke first. "What the hell is going on here?"

"This is Henry, Connie's husband," Picadilly said. "And you don't have to worry about him."

"The hell I don't," Clutch replied. "He's a goddamn zed."

Picadilly wagged a finger at him. "You will not take the Lord's name in vain in this house."

Connie dabbed a tissue at something on Henry's cheek, and I cringed.

"Henry was never quite right after he was bit. The fever caused some brain damage and hurt his vision, but as long as you're patient with him, he's okay. He's a bit like a toddler, but he's never been violent, not once."

"How long has he been like this?" I asked.

"Since the first day of the outbreak," Connie said while still watching her husband. "He picked up Freddy from school after some fights broke out in the

45

classrooms. Poor Freddy had gotten sick, and when the fever hit, he bit Henry without thinking."

"Fred is Connie's son," Picadilly said. "He's back at Connie's house. Unfortunately, the fever hit him harder, and he got quite the mean streak. Grace doesn't seem to rain equally from God. When he got too much to handle, we were forced to move."

"These are zeds you're talking about," Clutch said.

Connie snapped around. "Look at him. He's not a zed."

A gasp behind us, and I realized we'd drawn the attention of everyone.

"He's…" Hali started.

"He's a survivor," Picadilly said before shaking her head with a sad, slow movement. "With the right medical care, I think he could recover more fully. We're trying the best we can, but honestly, we don't know what to do."

Henry stood there, rocking from one foot to the next. While he didn't look or smell rotten like other zeds did, he bore the gray pallor of someone whose heart no longer beat within his chest. He made a small moan, and Connie wrapped an arm around him.

Clutch pursed his lips. "How do you know he won't go crazy one day and attack you both? You've got a time bomb ticking in this house."

"We have to have faith," Picadilly replied.

Connie nodded. "When there's nothing else to go on, we can still go on faith."

"Before Connie and I came to be together," Picadilly said. "I was forced to break my vows. I murdered a parishioner who was attacking people in the church. I'm not proud of my actions, but I also know I had to do it. With Henry, we don't have to kill anymore. He keeps the zeds away. He even kept Fred in line until the boy became violent."

"He protects you?" I asked.

"As much as he can," the nun replied. "He moves a bit slow, but he means well. He's a bit scared right now, but once he settles down, you'll see him open up after a bit."

"Henry won't bother you tonight. I'll stay up here with him to keep him warm," Connie said.

"No," Clutch said. "It's your house. Your fire. But, I can't risk having my people stay in the same house with a zed. After we eat, we'll stay at the café and head out in the morning."

Few words were spoken through dinner. No one said anything when Connie filled a bowl of soup and carried it upstairs. By the time she returned, we'd all finished and were ready to head out.

"As long as you promise not to hurt our Henry, you are still welcome to stay the night," Picadilly said, but Clutch hadn't backed down, and I was glad. I didn't think I could sleep with a zed — or whatever Henry was — upstairs, even if he was harmless.

As we drove the several hundred feet back toward the café, Picadilly and Connie's waving forms disappeared in the rearview mirror.

Once I settled into the cold, dank café, my mind raced. I looked around the café. Memories of the two zed kids at the gas station filled my mind. They had been like Henry, likely forgotten survivors in this new world. I remembered other times when zeds had watched me and not attacked. Some I'd left, others I'd killed. Now, I couldn't help but wonder how many harmless people I'd murdered simply because they'd been infected.

I'd convinced myself that zeds felt no pain, had no conscience. It was the only way I could kill without remorse. Holy hell, if not all zeds were mindless monsters, how was I going to fight without hesitating?

My God. How many innocents had I killed?

CHAPTER IV

Minutes before we headed out the following morning, I faced a recurring debate with Jase.

"Fox Park is hidden," Jase said, his eyes pleading with me. "All anyone can see from the road is miles and miles of wilderness. I know it'll be hard, but we can make it work."

I put a hand on Jase's shoulder. "We'll make it back there. I promise. Just be patient a little longer, okay?"

Jase muttered something under his breath and went back to cramming his sleeping bag into his stuff sack.

I wanted to go back to Fox Park, too. More than anything, I wanted to return to something I knew. I also craved to be enveloped in the easy safety of New Eden. A familiar home versus trusting a man I'd known for barely a week. It was a tough choice. And I worried that we weren't making the right one.

My mood became monotone after that. We drove for hours, stopping only to refuel from the gas cans we carried onboard. Every gas station we came to had been drained, with the exception of one that looked like it had gone up in a massive explosion.

As we covered miles on the westbound I-80, I stared out the window at the landscape. Leaves had long since turned color. What few crops were planted before the outbreak were now brown and well past ready for harvesting, and I wondered if we could use it for food or seed in the spring. Most of the fields remained unplanted and were already returning to their natural state of prairie grasses and weeds.

However, the biggest difference in the landscape from that of a month ago was the distinct lack of zeds. Before the massive migrations, zeds dotted the landscape, with herds grouping around towns. These days, I saw the rare corpse, recognizable as once human only by the tattered remnants of clothing draping it. The landscape was devoid of life, with most animals being taken down by zeds or wild wolves and dogs. Before the outbreak, I'd imagined hell as a desert-like environment, full of fire and brimstone. Now, I knew exactly what hell looked like. It looked like wherever I was.

Jase and Hali were sound asleep in the front seat next to Griz, who was behind the wheel. "Do you think we're over the hump?" I asked Clutch, who sat across from me in the backseat. "That maybe we don't have to worry about the zeds coming back?"

"I think that's wishful thinking," he replied before adding, "But it'd be nice."

"Yeah, I guess you're right." I continued to watch the landscape passing by outside. I looked back inside to find Clutch watching me with concern.

"It's only natural to worry," he said, as though reading my mind. "It means you're human. Just don't let it screw with your head out there."

My brow rose. "You're telling me that you worry?"

"Of course. I'm only human."

I watched him for a moment before giving him an almost-smile. We were the lucky ones. We were part of a small world of survivors, who were still capable of thought. That was, if my prior assumption about zeds still held any weight. "Henry really came out of left field," I said.

Clutch nodded slowly. "Yeah. I didn't see that one coming. But it doesn't change anything."

"Doesn't it?" I asked.

"Believe me, if I could change the past, there'd be plenty I'd do differently." He shrugged. "But, I can't, and you can't either. We have to accept things as we see them and keep on living."

"Yeah, but what if there are a lot more zeds like Henry who can think and feel. What kind of hell must they be going through? Or, even worse, what if all the other zeds can think and feel, but can't control their urges?"

He considered for a moment. "I think if zeds had control of their senses, they wouldn't give into violence. So, no, I don't think zeds know what they're doing. I don't even think there was anything going on in Henry's head. If there was, I'd think he'd want to be put out of his misery."

I cocked my head while I considered his words. "Who are you trying to convince: you or me?"

He shrugged. "Things aren't so bad. We're alive. We've got food, and we've got a place to go." Even though he was a pessimist, Clutch always seemed to have more faith than I could muster. He reached over and gave my hand a gentle squeeze.

Then he did something he'd never done before. He didn't let go.

I sighed, my stress dissipating as I held his hand, and realized he was right. Even in this shitty world, things weren't so bad.

"We're less than twenty miles out," Marco's voice alerted us through the radio.

Clutch let go of my hand and leaned forward in between the two front seats to talk to Griz. "Do you see any good place to stop?"

After a pause, Griz pointed. "How about that machine shed on the farm over there?"

"It's worth a shot," Clutch replied.

I looked out the window and saw a small farmhouse with a couple small outbuildings, including a decently sized white tin shed.

Clutch picked up the radio. "Take the next road to your left. We'll stop at the first farmhouse."

"Copy that, but I still don't think this is necessary," Marco replied as they led us to the farm.

Clutch didn't respond.

We parked and approached the shed. The doors were all still closed, and it took us less than ten minutes to verify that the building was devoid of any life, except for a cantankerous family of raccoons. A combine harvester, a couple tractors, and three wagons filled most of the interior, but there was still room for one Humvee with the trailer. We emptied everything from the remaining Humvee, leaving only enough food and supplies to keep us fed, warm, and protected for a couple days.

Humvees were taller than most residential garage doors, making it a bit more challenging than a car to hide. When Griz and Jase pulled the metal door closed, we all looked at each other. From everyone's faces, they were as uncomfortable as I was about leaving behind over eighty percent of our "stuff." But, the alternative was too risky. If New Eden reappropriated our food and supplies when we arrived, we could be in far worse shape than not having it at all.

Everyone except for Marco had agreed we needed to play it safe until we knew if we'd be staying at New Eden. If it became our permanent home, we'd share our food and supplies. Until then, we all felt safer with a cache.

As we piled ten of us into a single Humvee, Clutch stepped in front of Marco. "I need your word that you will not, under any circumstances, tell anyone about this."

Marco scowled. "I already gave you my word. I won't tell anyone. I get it. Hell, I'd probably do the same thing if I were in your shoes."

Clutch grunted, and Jase tacked on a "we'll see."

Griz didn't have anything to say because he was busy claiming the driver's seat. Marco took the passenger seat, and Benji sat on the floor between his legs.

Somehow, we squeezed five of us into the back bucket seats, with Clutch and me on one seat, Deb and Hali sharing the other seat, and Jase on the incredibly uncomfortable hump. Behind us, in the unheated part of the Humvee, Frost sat with Diesel, and Vicki leaned into the pair for warmth...or probably because there was no other space due to all our food, gear, and weapons stacked around them.

Marco continued to try to reach New Eden on the radio, but with no success. We were still a few miles out from New Eden when movement caught my eye before the engine noise registered in my ears.

Three SUVs approached us from the west.

Marco leaned forward. "That's the New Eden flag. They must've seen us coming," his excited voice echoed through the vehicle.

The incoming SUVs flew American flags with an eagle stitched over the center.

Griz squinted in the bright sunlight. "Can you confirm? It could be a setup."

"I recognize them. It's New Eden!"

"We need to wait until we get close enough for you to verify their faces," Griz said.

Equal parts of fear and excitement fluttered through me, and I leaned forward to watch the SUVs come to a stop and form a roadblock in front of us. People with rifles jumped out and stepped behind the SUVs, using the vehicles for cover while leveling their sights upon us.

"They could be playing it safe," Clutch mused. "But I'd still make sure we can make a hasty retreat if this turns to shit."

"Already thinking the same thing," Griz said as he stopped our Humvee at least a hundred yards back in a diagonal position on the highway.

I sucked in a deep breath. "Here's hoping they recognize Marco."

Marco chuckled. "They'll recognize me. It's not *that* big a town."

Hali came awake with a stretch. "Are we there yet?" she asked.

"Almost. Assuming we don't get shot first," Griz replied bluntly.

"Not funny," the girl replied.

"I wasn't joking," he replied.

As soon as we stopped, Marco stepped out of the Humvee.

"Be careful," Clutch said as he climbed out and stood by the open door with his rifle.

"I will," Marco said. He waved his arms in the air as he approached the newcomers. A man emerged from a white SUV and met him halfway. When they embraced, I think we let out a collective sigh. Marco motioned for all of us to come out.

"Hot dog," Griz said. "Looks like they're friendlies."

Energy tightened my muscles. "We really made it, didn't we?" I said to no one in particular as I opened my door.

"It looks like it," Clutch replied, sounding just as surprised as I felt.

Our group of nine approached the SUVs. Jase looked at me and smiled. Hope flared and my lips widened into a broad smile. Likewise, I turned to Clutch, and he grinned. He embraced me and I nearly squealed. We were safe.

Marco was grinning from ear to ear when we approached. "We did it, guys. We're almost home."

"Welcome to New Eden." The man next to Marco said. "Now, surrender your weapons."

CHAPTER V

"I thought these guys were supposed to be your friends," I snapped at Marco.

Marco held up his hands. "They were. They *are*." He turned to the man at his side. "What's going on? I tried to reach you on the radio but never got a response."

"We haven't had the resources to listen on the radios lately," The man replied. "There's been a lot going on."

Marco's lips thinned. "You'll have to fill me in later, after we get these folks to New Eden. Come on, we've been on the road a long time and are beat. I gave them my word we'd be safe at New Eden."

I had to shade my eyes against the sunlight to make out the man's features. He was short, fair-skinned, with curly brown hair that had likely been much shorter and groomed before the outbreak.

The man's lips thinned. "It's nothing personal, but we've had to take new precautions since all the squadrons followed the herds south. Ever since the migration, the Black Sheep have really put a hit on New Eden. They sent in two assassins last week alone. So, you can see why we can't let anyone armed enter New Eden without quarantine and interviews."

"That's bullshit," Jase said at my side. "We're obviously not bandits. Look at us. Half of our group is women. We even have a kid with us. Have you ever seen bandits like this before?"

The man scowled. "And one of the assassins was a teenaged girl. Listen, I get that you're not happy. That's fair. But, it doesn't change the rules. I won't negotiate on this. If you want to enter New Eden, you have to surrender your weapons until you're cleared."

Clutch took a step forward. "And how long will that take?"

"Since Marco led you here, probably two days at most," the man replied. "The choice is yours. I'll give you five minutes to make your decision."

The man tilted his head at Marco. "In the meantime, you can fill me in. Where is the rest of your squadron? Why did they send you ahead?"

Even though we'd all gathered around Clutch, no one spoke. We all watched Marco.

"I'm all that's left," Marco said after a long pause. "The Black Sheep had ambushed their community." He pointed our way. "We moved in to help, but things went bad. There's no one left. Everyone's gone."

The man placed a hand on Marco's shoulder. "I'm sorry for your loss. I hope your squadron was able to put just as much a hurtin' on the Black Sheep."

"We did, but one managed to get away." Marco took a deep breath. "And, these folks say he was missing three fingers on his left hand."

"*Hodge,*" the man said, the name dripping with hatred. "That son of a bitch just won't die. Well, I guess we couldn't expect to be that lucky. At least you got the rest. Not that it helps the pain. Good people were lost, and the news is going to hit New Eden hard. Especially since the capital had ordered all but one of our remaining squadrons to the south."

"South?" Marco asked. "Why?"

"A lot's happened this week. I'll fill you in once we reach town. You've been through enough and probably want to sleep in a safe place tonight."

"Do I ever," Marco said quickly. "Give us a moment."

The man nodded and took several steps back.

Marco joined us. "How about it? You guys ready to give New Eden a shot?"

After a moment of internal debate, I shrugged. "We didn't drive all this way for nothing. I'd say we give it a shot."

"Oh, what the hell," Griz said. "We didn't come all this way for a Sunday drive."

Others chimed in before Clutch spoke loudly. "We've

come a long way. And, we all could use a place to kick up our heels for a bit. Marco's like us. He's a survivor, and I believe him. New Eden is worth a shot. All right. We've had this debate a hundred times. This is the last vote. New Eden or Fox Park. Each person has to make his or her own decision." He lifted a hand. "All in favor of New Eden, raise your hand."

One by one, the hands went up. Benji was watching Frost, and his small hand shot up as soon as his grandfather raised his hand, like always. Jase and then Hali grudgingly lifted his hand after all other hands rose. It was unanimous.

"Okay," I said, not really knowing what to say. "I guess it's settled. New Eden, it is."

Marco grinned at us before waving Justin back over. "You guys won't regret it," he said. "New Eden is good people.

The man stepped over, followed by several others. "So you've decided?"

Clutch made eye contact with each of us one last time before speaking. "We have. We'll follow you to New Eden under the condition that we can each retain a weapon for self-defense."

"That's not our policy," the man replied.

"Where we came from, we'd let folks keep knives," Jase said. "You can't leave folks completely defenseless, not in this world."

"No guns," the man said after a moment. "Not until you're cleared."

"No guns," Clutch echoed.

"Fair enough." He motioned to their SUVs. "I'll ride with Marco in your vehicle. You'll ride with my folks and follow us to New Eden."

"What are you going to do with our Humvee?" Griz asked. "Because I've got a lot of hours with her and would hate to see her go."

"We'll park it—*her*—until you're done with quarantine, at which time she's all yours again."

"Including everything inside?" Griz countered.

"Including everything inside, as long as it doesn't pose a risk to New Eden citizens. Marco's been with us since the beginning, and I trust his judgment. If you don't mean to do harm to anyone in New Eden, you'll have nothing to fear from us."

He then called to his men to collect our weapons. "The name's Justin, and I serve as the mayor of New Eden, the safest place in the Midwest. You have my word. You'll be safe there."

He motioned to Marco. "Marco, you can fill me in on what's happened in the past month."

We'll see, I thought to myself as I gave up my rifle. Sunlight glistened off the barrel as I handed it over in exchange for the promise of safety. I was relieved we stashed most of our supplies, but I had a tough time believing Marco would keep his word. After all, New Eden was his home. Why wouldn't he tell them?

I didn't have long to dwell on the situation, because the short drive felt like it took only seconds before we came to a fenced-in small town flying a huge American flag with an eagle stitched over it.

New Eden.

We had arrived.

AMBITION

CHAPTER VI

New Eden was the exact opposite of Camp Fox in one manner. Whereas we had protected ourselves through seclusion, New Eden broadcasted their location to anyone for miles. Like most of Nebraska, the small town was surrounded by flatlands for as far as the eye could see.

The New Eden flag proudly flew at the front gate. The size of the flag reminded me of ones I'd seen while eating breakfast at Perkins restaurants, and I realized that was probably where they'd found it.

A mishmash of fencing at least ten feet high—layers of wire, wood, and poles—closed off New Eden from the rest of the world. When we pulled up to the gate, we were all asked to step out of our vehicle. I took a deep breath, feeling better that Clutch, Jase, Griz, and I were still together.

As Justin's men led us through the gate, I could now see the town, which looked like it had been an old, broken-down, small town before the outbreak. There were wood guard towers erected inside the fence. Every tower was manned, and every guard kept a wary eye and semi-raised weapon pointed in our direction. Everything was exactly as Marco described it except for one thing: there were none of the military vehicles and soldiers Marco had spoken about. If we wanted, I had a feeling we could've rammed through the gates in our Humvee, and they could've done little to stop us.

People emerged from around buildings. None looked too thin, and most looked relatively clean. Only a couple people could've passed as beggars. A medium-sized dog galloped forward to sniff Diesel. Diesel sniffed back, and they did a friendly "nice to meet you" doggie dance around each other.

"Buddy's harmless," a man who looked about my age said as he approached. "Unless you're a zed, then he turns into the Terror of the Plains. The rest of the time, he just trots wherever he feels like around town and startles the feral cats. But, they're the bosses around town. They keep the mice away." He walked alongside us. "The name's Charlie. I'd offer my hand, but we have a twenty-four hour quarantine period for travelers on the off chance you're infected and turn. I'll be one of your hosts tonight."

Justin stepped out of our Humvee, and we all watched as Marco pulled the vehicle into a garage to be locked away during our quarantine. As Justin approached us, Charlie spoke. "You'll want time to get settled in. I'll stop by later."

Justin motioned to town. "Here's New Eden. Well, sort of. This is the edge of town. The real town starts another block in. You'll get the tour after your quarantine is up. For your first night, you'll be staying in the building right over there." He pointed at a small brick building with a U.S. Postal Service emblem etched into the glass door.

He motioned for us to follow, and he started walking. Several guards kept their distance but made it clear they were herding us toward the building. I swallowed and took the lead, checking to make sure the rest of our group was right behind me. People stood around, watching us.

Justin held open the glass door, and I cautiously stepped in. Inside, six beds filled nearly the entire space. When Clutch entered, I saw him take in the whole place—no doubt searching for weaknesses, surveillance, and whatever it was he always looked for. As for me, I looked for places that would be safe from zeds, bad guys, and animals. Beyond that, I didn't know much else to look for.

"We don't have enough beds for everyone. We'll see if we can't scrounge up some mats, but at least it's only for one night," Justin said. "Truth is, we haven't come across any groups larger than four in months."

"Believe me, we've slept in worse conditions," I said.

Justin motioned around. "You have free run of this building, but you can't leave. There are guards stationed outside every wall. There's a single toilet and sink right down the hall. It's not much. What you see is what you get."

My eyes widened. "You have running water?"

"Yes. We also have electricity, and somehow natural gas is still pumping through the lines, but blackouts are common. We're still working on a better long-term solution."

"Impressive," Clutch said at my side.

"Supper will be brought in just before sunset. I have a couple errands to take care of, so Charlie and I will be back to talk with you later."

Justin waited until everyone was inside before he stepped out, meeting Marco on the way. Justin gave him a smile before leaving.

Benji started to jump on a mattress, burning more of that never-ending supply of energy eight-year-olds possessed. Frost sat down on the floor next to the boy's bed.

Clutch and I stood off to the side as people claimed beds for the night.

Some things never changed. All the men waited for the women to choose beds before claiming theirs. Jase quickly claimed the one next to Hali, though he tried to look all cool about it. I was planning to unroll my sleeping bag on the floor, but I sensed eyes on me and noticed both Griz and Clutch were motioning me to take the last bed. I shrugged with a smile and then jumped onto the mattress. "If you insist."

Marco sat on the floor next to Deb, and I frowned. "Why are you in here with us, Marco? Guilty by association?"

He looked up. "Standard operating procedures. Anyone who's been outside for more than a day has to stay in quarantine overnight."

"We just can't get rid of him, can we?" Jase muttered, and everyone chuckled.

Truth was, I was happy to have Marco with us. Someone with a foot in our world and a foot in New Eden's. Especially since as long as he was with us, the less chance he had to tell others about our secret cache. Although, I supposed he could've told Justin about it already.

Whether Justin knew about our other Humvee and supplies, he gave no hint when Charlie and he returned a couple hours later with bowls and a stockpot filled with something steamy that smelled of carrots.

"Potato and carrot soup," Charlie said as he set the pot down. "We don't have anything fancy around here, but it gets the job done."

Justin started handing out plastic bowls, cups, and spoons. "Marco had said you've done a pretty good job in regards to eating balanced meals, and I can tell. You can't understand how much hope it gives me to see that you're not only healthy but thrived out there."

"*Thrived* is a strong word," I said.

"You have a pregnant woman, a child, and none of you are sick. That alone is a miracle. Many people here will be excited to hear about you. Most folks who arrive at New Eden's gates look half-starved and a day away from getting turned into zeds. Nevertheless, we're always happy to see any survivors make it here. In fact, the capital has announced that's our primary directive: to save and rebuild."

"Hm," I said as I thought through it. "Shouldn't the primary directive be holding off zeds?"

"We don't have to worry about zeds anymore."

I frowned. "The herds will be back in the spring. We have to be ready for them."

Justin shook his head. "No, they won't."

"What makes you so sure?" Clutch asked as he handed me a bowl of soup and sat down with a second bowl for himself.

"They won't be back because we nuked the South."

I jerked back. The spoonful of soup I was about to eat splashed off the spoon. I barely registered the gasps around me. "You—"

"—bombed the South?" Clutch completed the question for me.

"As in nuclear warheads?" Jase added.

Justin replied. "Yes, the government dropped nuclear bombs on the south to wipe out the herds. Any remaining zeds will be dead soon enough, because the capital ordered all available resources to head south to finish off zeds that escaped the kill zone. Marco's squadron would've been sent south as soon as they returned. So, you can see why zeds aren't our primary issue now. They're nearing extinction."

"No more zeds," Hali said softly.

"But we released nuclear warheads on our own soil," Griz said.

Justin stammered. "Well, yes. More accurately, what's left of the United States, Canadian, and Mexican governments released warheads on U.S. and Mexican soil."

"But, there would've been survivors down there," Vicki said with a frown. "How many innocent survivors were killed?"

Justin answered. "When the herds started to cross into Missouri, the capital sent every plane and bus south to save survivors before the herds reached them. From what I hear, they pulled out over ten thousand total, which is a lot better than the alternative. With the numbers in the herds, it's safe to say the herds would've found anyone alive down there."

Marco had mentioned some part of the government had survived, but I hadn't realized they had control over that much firepower—let alone that many resources—that they could support taking on that many survivors. I hadn't even imagined there could be ten thousand total survivors left in the world. Hearing the number sent a strange sensation through my body. That number, coupled with the idea of the zeds going up in flames...It almost felt like...*hope*.

Justin continued. "We'll clean up the zeds in this area as we come across them, but we have to first focus on pulling in survivors before winter hits. Every province has been charged with rebuilding the country. New Eden may be one of the smaller provinces, but we have to pull our weight, just like everyone else. Unfortunately, all we have left is the New Eden security force and part of one squadron. So, every able-bodied man will be a huge benefit to us."

"How'd the government contact you?" Clutch asked. "Camp Fox was on the radio every day trying to reach someone, and this is the first I've heard of it. We were never contacted by anyone in government—no military, no politicians, nothing."

Justin shook his head. "They didn't find us by radio. They use drones to fly over the country and take pictures. They map out all survivors sites and reach out to any settlements of significant size. They said that for the longest time, they were losing more sites than they were finding. There were too many zeds spread everywhere for them to provide rescue support. It wasn't until the migration started in Canada that they started planning Operation Redemption: eradicating the zed threat and building our new country."

"It's crucial we find survivors quickly," Charlie said. "There are so many more deadly risks besides zeds out there."

"Like dogs," I said.

"And bandits," Vicki muttered coldly.

Charlie nodded. "Yes, but there are even far worse threats out there, which we have no control over."

"Like what?" Jase asked.

"Winter, for one," Justin replied. "Most folks in the freeze-zones don't know how to survive without electricity. Outside of New Eden, I expect we'll lose many survivors this first winter to cold and starvation. Then, there's dysentery and all the diseases that come with that. It was a miracle you made it here. Marco told me the route you took here, from the Mississippi River to Highway 20, onto I-380, and then across I-80."

"Yeah, so?" I asked, confused.

"There's a nuclear plant down between Highway 20 and I-380. Its reactor melted down last week, probably within a day after you drove through."

"Holy shit," I muttered, but no one else spoke.

"That's probably going to happen to every nuclear power plant in the world. Without maintenance—and most of these have had no maintenance for nearly a year—it's only a matter of time."

"You made it, but most won't make it on their own. They need our help."

"And you have enough food to take on more?"

Justin grimaced. "It's not easy, but we'll make it work. The capital has distributed rations and has promised to send more. But, we have to be able to rely only on ourselves."

"That's smart," Clutch said. "It's never a good idea to put all your eggs in one basket, especially when that basket involves politicians."

Justin smiled. "Marco told me a couple of you were in the military, so you may have a bit more experience with politicians than I have. I sold insurance before this. I could get you the best rates for your auto, house, or boat. I loved what I did. I went home each day knowing I was doing my best to ensure people were protected so when disaster struck, they'd be back on their feet in no time. In a way, I still have the same job, except it's more important than ever. If we don't get people back on their feet after this disaster, they'll die, and we'll never get the chance at building a new country. It's going to take every single one of us working hard day in and day out to rebuild this world so our children can thrive. It won't be the same world as before, and maybe that's a good thing. But, if New Eden is a sign of things to come, it's going to be worth it."

Justin was about to say more, but an armed guard stepped inside, and looked straight at him. "Thea's looking for you."

Justin stood. "Duty calls. Charlie will answer any more questions you have. Please remember, you are not to attempt to leave this building under any circumstances. We don't mess around inside the fence. Security's orders are to shoot-to-kill anyone and anything that may pose a risk to us. With that said, I hope you make the best of the situation. You are safe within these walls, so sleep well."

Not waiting around to take questions, Justin left with

the guard.

Charlie chuckled. "Funny when Justin talks about sleeping, since he never sleeps. He'd have to stop working for five minutes first."

"And, Charlie sleeps enough for both of them," Marco joked. "From what I hear, your wife complains you're out like a light the moment your head hits the pillow. That's no way to please a woman."

"I can assure you, Sarah has never been disappointed in my husbandly duties," Charlie replied quickly.

"That's because she's never been with a real man," Marco added.

Charlie raised a brow. "Just because you're popular with the local sheep, doesn't make you a man."

"Ha, ha," Marco replied drily before flipping the other man the bird.

"I think a few more of my brain cells killed themselves," Jase said.

"Not to interrupt this fascinating conversation," Hali said, "but, what happens next? Once we're done with quarantine?"

"Finally," Griz said, "someone says something intelligent."

"Your quarantine will end at three p.m. tomorrow, once you each have a physical exam. Marco vouched for you, so Justin is bypassing your interviews. He said it's clear you're not bandits. I'll give you a tour, and if you decide to stay, you will be assigned homes, and you'll sign up for jobs. You may not get your first pick, but I can guarantee there's something for everyone."

"Sounds fair enough," I said. After all, the system mirrored what we'd had at Camp Fox.

Charlie stirred the stockpot. "It's almost curfew, and I need to get home to Sarah before she starts to worry. Whatever leftover soup you have will be your breakfast, and you can get drinking water from the sink. Any last thing before I head out?"

No one needed anything, so Charlie left, and I heard the lock click in place. Griz went around and turned off all the lights except a small lamp. He turned and eyed Clutch. "What do you think?"

"I think we're safe here for the night. Tomorrow, we'll see."

I could see Griz shrug in the faint light before he turned off the lamp, leaving us in darkness, with only moonlight from the window.

Clutch went to lie on the floor. I tugged his arm, and he crawled into the small twin-sized bed next to me. I lay in his arms as I tried to clear my mind of nuclear bombs, zeds, and winter.

"What about the zeds like Henry? What if they can recover?" Deb asked softly, to whom, I had no idea. "If they went with the herds to the south, they would've been killed too, along with other survivors, like us. What if we lived a couple states farther south?"

When no one answered, I spent the next couple of hours pondering her questions until at some point my mind mercifully drifted off.

Charlie Martel and his wife, Sarah, made excellent tour guides. After cold soup for breakfast and a light lunch of applesauce and flatbread, the couple proudly granted our freedom from quarantine and led us outside.

Charlie spoke. "If you decide to stay —"

"And we hope you do," Sarah interjected before handing out business cards to each of us. On the front read, *Charles Martel, Chief Operating Officer, S&C Technologies.* Scrawled across the back of each business card were handwritten numbers one through fourteen, but several numbers were already punched out.

"These are your ration cards," Charlie said. "Every Sunday, everyone gets ration cards. Each card has fourteen punches, which comes out to two meals per day. How you use those punches is completely up to you, but once they're used up, you're waiting until Sunday for your next card. Since this is Tuesday, we already took off what would've been the last two days' worth of rations."

"How do we get new cards?" I asked.

"You'll take a job," Charlie replied. "Everyone who takes a job gets a weekly card. Any exceptions must be approved by Justin."

"Rations are available in the general store. Over

there." Sarah pointed. "It's about two blocks from your house."

Charlie added, "Justin has house number Twenty-Six set aside for you. Most survivors are assigned rooms in other houses. We try to fill up each house before starting with an empty one. But, Marco said you'd all prefer to stay in the same house if possible. Twenty-Six is a three-bedroom bungalow. But, it should fit ten of you fine."

"Ten?" Deb turned to Marco. "You're staying with us?"

"Yeah," he replied. "I used to stay in the squadron house number Three." He sighed, "It doesn't feel right now — "

"I'm glad," she said.

"You're one of us," I added.

He smiled. "Thanks."

"How about house keys?" Clutch asked.

Sarah shrugged. "Sorry. We don't have any keys. We only found keys in a couple houses. And, we don't have the ability to make keys. So, pretty much all the houses remain unlocked, but I suppose you could put a chair against the door or something if it makes you feel safer."

"Hm," Clutch replied.

As we walked through the neighborhood, I observed how busy everyone seemed. Two men were pushing wheelbarrows full of food into the general store, where a short line had already formed. I was surprised at how normal everything seemed. One woman was pruning a rose bush. Two kids were on swings that creaked with every back-and-forth movement. Many of the houses reminded me of my small bungalow in Des Moines. Old, nothing fancy, and needing some TLC. Even before the outbreak, this town looked like it'd been struggling.

"You can't even tell any herds passed through this area," I said.

"Oh, they came through here, all right," Charlie said. "It was the first time we had to use the missile silo. We stayed down there for a full week before we risked coming out."

"We quickly learned that the silo wasn't ready for long-term occupation," Sarah added. "Justin has doubled efforts to improve the structure and better equip the silo. Our goal is to have it ready by winter in case our power goes out or it's as bad a winter as folks up north are saying it could be. Below ground would be much warmer and safer if we need to hibernate."

Charlie motioned to a woman covering a garden with leaves and mulch. "We're expecting an early winter. Justin's contact in the capital says they already have a foot of snow on the ground."

My eyes widened. "Where's that?"

"Saskatchewan. Canada, the northernmost parts of Mexico, and the U.S. have merged into one nation. They're still working on names, laws, and all that, but we needed each other to survive."

"We're Canadian now?" Jase asked.

Charlie shrugged with a smile. "Yeah, I guess so."

"I'm not so sure about that," Hali added with a grin

as she enunciated "about" as "aboot."

"I guess hockey is the new national pastime," Griz added.

"Well, the healthcare program can't get any worse," Clutch mumbled.

We laughed, and Charlie ushered us along the tour.

When we turned onto a street of small houses—most reminded me of the pillbox-style houses from the 1940s—Hali frowned. "Why do you cram everyone inside these small houses?"

Charlie's brows rose. "What do you mean?"

"We drove by a new housing development a few miles back. Why don't any of you stay there?"

"Two reasons," Charlie replied. "One, we only have enough resources to defend this two-square-mile area. We won't leave any residents unprotected. And two, the missile silo is within the fence. It's our fail-safe. In case of any emergency, all residents immediately evacuate to the silo."

"We practice twice per week," Sarah added. "Every Tuesday and Thursday. We've gotten the entire population of four hundred and sixty four souls into the silo and sealed in nine minutes and twenty-eight seconds. Justin thinks we need to get it down to five minutes."

"Agreed," Clutch said. "If the fences were breached, you could easily be overrun in under ten minutes. What are your backup plans?"

Charlie frowned, and then shook his head. "The silo

is it. We've been working non-stop at getting it back into shape. It hadn't been used in forty years. A good part of it was full of water, and some of the floorboards had rusted through. We've got it dried out, and we store our food in there for winter. The government flew over and dropped seven pallets of food about three weeks ago, so we're sitting pretty decent for the winter now."

"Let me guess," Griz said. "That's about the same time the bandits upped their game."

Sarah nodded. "Most of the bandits are hungry and scared, like us."

Charlie continued. "The difference is we got Justin and they got Hodge. Two leaders with very different approaches. Under Hodge, they first tried to offer "protection" in exchange for access to the silo, but Justin saw right through their bully tactics and refused unless they became New Eden residents. A few joined right up, but it didn't take Hodge long to make an example of anyone who tried to leave his group. Soon after, the assassination attempts on Justin started. According to the last assassin we questioned, they think if they kill Justin, the rest of us will fall in line."

They're probably right, I thought to myself. Without Tyler and Clutch, Camp Fox would've crumpled against attacks. Though, in the end, their leadership hadn't mattered. The Black Sheep had still managed to take nearly than everything and everyone from us.

Charlie led us to a small brick house. "This is Justin's home and where most of New Eden business is handled. Come on in. Justin wanted to talk with you."

I was surprised that Justin lived in one of the smaller houses. There was nothing special about it. And, other than the New Eden flag hanging near the door, nothing indicated the house was different from any other down the street.

"Why did you change the American flag?" I asked.

"Justin figured it would be good to give New Eden a symbol. Since there's no longer a United States, we were all born here and wanted to keep the stars and stripes. We voted on the eagle as a symbol of our strength, and we ended up with the New Eden flag. Who knows, maybe it'll become the new state flag once all the dust settles."

As we filed through the door, I found Justin sitting at a large oak dining table. Two men sat next to him, both completely focused on the stacks of paper in front of them. A cat lay on a chair, seemingly oblivious to us.

As· soon as Justin caught sight of us, he stood. "How's the tour going? I hope Charlie and Sarah are answering your questions."

"They did," I said. "Thank you for the hospitality."

Justin smiled. "Oh, it's not only to be nice. I'm hoping you all decide to become New Eden residents. We need all the people we can get. From renovating the silo, to managing the food and supplies, to securing the town and surrounding area, we're extremely short-staffed." He looked at Clutch and Griz before continuing. "Your experience would be invaluable here. Anyone with military experience served on our squadrons, and between the one we lost and the two the capital has taken control of, we have essentially no forces to scout, forage, and bring in survivors. We have a state trooper who runs our security forces behind the gates, and his teams have been running double-duty lately. So, you see how much I hope you decide to stay here with us."

"New Eden is a good place," Marco added. "I'm proud to call it home. We work hard here, but that's because we're building from scratch."

"Thank you, Marco," Justin said. "He's right. I know New Eden can become a sanctuary for all as long as we work together to make that happen."

Pride seeped through his words, and I wondered if he hadn't bitten off more than he could chew. "That's a bit ambitious, don't you think? How can you possibly support such large numbers of people?" I asked.

He shrugged. "I believe the only way we can rebuild is to move beyond surviving day-by-day. I believe we need a vision so we don't get lost. Perhaps it's a bit lofty, but I know we can get there. So, are you in to help rebuild the world?"

Clutch spoke first. "We need some time to mull it over."

"Fair enough," Justin replied. "You have probationary residency for two weeks. That should give you enough time to recuperate from your journey and get to know the folks and culture of New Eden. Then, you'll either have to leave or pledge residency to New

Eden." He smiled. "And, I have no doubt you'll all fit right in. Now, if you'll excuse me, it seems that status meetings don't stop for the apocalypse."

We were shuffled back outside in a small flock, where we stood in a circle in the front yard. "Why's a pledge so important? We never had people do that to stay with Camp Fox," Jase said. "It's not like we're applying for citizenship or something."

"You very well could be," a man's voice said from behind.

I turned around to see a haggard old man approach. Unlike everyone else I'd seen, he looked like a beggar. As he approached, I wrinkled my nose. He also smelled like a beggar.

"Come on, Romeo. Don't scare them," Marco said.

The man muttered something and wandered off.

"Romeo?" Hali asked.

"A nickname," Marco replied. "He's harmless enough. Believe it or not, he was a successful businessman before the outbreak, but the stress screwed up his head. Sure, what he said could be true. The country we knew is gone. Who knows what will form out of the ashes. But, more important, Justin believes in the ceremony. He thinks the pledge helps people feel like they're joining something special, like they made the A-Team."

"If we're the A-Team, I'm B.A. Baracus then," Jase said.

"You don't have nearly enough bling," I said,

pointing at the small gold cross he wore around his neck.

Marco rolled his eyes. "I was talking about sports. You know, the A-Team, B-Team, and so on."

Jase waved him away. "I'm still B.A. If a beggar gets a nickname, I think I deserve one, too."

"That's not how nicknames work," I said. "You can't pick your own. Take mine. Clutch came up with it the first day we met."

"How mushy," Jase said drily before he held up his ration card. "I don't know about you guys, but B.A. is hungry and going to get some food."

"Me, too," Hali said, and several others then chimed in.

"I'll bring you through the line the first time," Marco said. "It's pretty easy, but there's a process you follow."

Clutch held his ration card to Marco. "Grab me some chow. I want to walk around some more."

"I'll go with you," I said.

"Count me in," Griz added.

Clutch nodded and turned to the others. "Be at the house before dark. That gives you about one hour to grab grub, give or take."

Both Jase and Hali gave matching salutes. Griz and I held out our ration cards, and I held onto mine before Jase took it. "No stealing rations, hungry man," I said.

He smirked before tugging it away. "B.A.'s no thief."

As the rest of our group headed off to the ration line, I called out, "Calling yourself B.A. isn't going to make the name stick."

Whether Jase heard me or not, he didn't acknowledge.

I smiled. What an odd family we made. Even though I worried about each of them, I couldn't imagine not having them around. "We've got it pretty good," I said softly.

"Yeah," Clutch replied. "Now, let's secure the house."

Griz nodded. "I was thinking the same thing."

One hour later, we had gone through our new house from top to bottom. Someone had brought in enough mattresses for all of us, and I worked on setting up the bedrooms while Clutch and Griz talked through house security and escape plans. The house had only one bathroom for ten people. Rather than seeing that as a detriment, I squealed at the luxury. We'd gone months without electricity. Maybe Justin was right. To survive, we had to focus on something bigger than living day-by-day.

As twilight settled in, Clutch and I sat on the front porch, sipping tea, and watched people return to their houses for the night. Other than lights in many windows and a pair of security guards who walked the streets, the town seemed empty.

That was, until the howling started. This pack sounded bigger than the one that had surrounded us in Des Moines. I worriedly eyed Clutch.

"The fences must keep them out," he said and

pointed to the security guards. "They don't look worried."

We were a block in from the fences, but every now and then, I could see a dark shape move outside the fence. After several minutes, there was an electrical *zap*, followed by a yelp. After a couple more repetitions of the same sounds at different parts around the town, Clutch frowned.

"They're searching for a weakness in the fence."

I shivered.

Of all moments, Romeo came jogging down the street, yelling something that sounded like verses from the Bible. As he passed our house, he pointed toward the darkness outside the fence. "It's a sign of the apocalypse. 666. The mark of the beast is now here. First we had wars, then we had the plague, and now the beast has arrived."

One of the security guards blocked Romeo's path. "C'mon, Romeo. You know the rules. Get on home now. We need to keep things quiet at night." The guard glanced our way. "No need to worry. Everything's safe."

Romeo giggled and bolted around, and the two guards followed in what almost looked like a game of tag.

After they disappeared around a corner, I turned back to Clutch. "Well, that was interesting."

"Yeah," he replied softly.

A cold wind blew through my coat, and I leaned into

Clutch. He wrapped an arm around me, but after a moment, he bristled and pulled away.

"You know, with the zeds gone, we might be safe here. We can start fresh. *You* can start fresh. You don't need me anymore."

I looked at him and cocked my head. "What do you mean?"

"This thing. Us." He motioned from me to him. "It can't work."

My brows rose. "Really?" My eyes narrowed, and I crossed my arms over my chest. "Why the hell not?"

Clutch took in a deep breath and seemed to struggle to find words. Finally, in a rush, he spoke. "We both know you can do better than me. I'm no good for anyone. There's something inside me that's…broken. I was broke before all this happened. I'm not going to get better. This is who I am. I don't want to bring you down with me."

"Do you have feelings for me?"

"That's not the point. It's about what's best for you. There's something hollow inside, something I lost in Afghanistan. And, I never found it."

"So what? You have issues. Hell, we've all got issues. There's not a single person left in this world who isn't dealing with some fucked up shit in their heads. Sure, you were in the minority and had PTSD before the outbreak. But, by now, everyone has been pushed beyond their breaking points. None of us can be who we were before."

"But there are others who aren't as fucked up," he said, sounding utterly helpless.

I came to my feet, cupped his cheeks, and looked down into his eyes. "I accept you exactly the way you are. We'll deal with your nightmares and shit together. But, you have to meet me halfway. You have to accept yourself first."

His brows tightened when I bent down and kissed him. He didn't kiss back, but at least he didn't pull away.

I straightened. "You don't have to be with me if you don't want to be. Don't run away because you don't think you're worth it. I know you're worth it."

I didn't wait for a response. I headed inside and up to bed.

Clutch never came upstairs.

CHAPTER VII

For the first time in weeks, I awoke feeling fully rested. I would've slept later except for the forgotten sound of a toilet flushing snapped me from dark dreams.

I stood and stretched. The small scar—the one shaped like a bullet hole on my calf—burned just like it did every morning until the muscle loosened. Once my old wound quit sending tiny spears of fire through my leg, I headed out into the hall and ran into Deb exiting the bathroom with a hand over her mouth.

I frowned. "Morning sickness?"

She nodded, swallowed, and then turned right back around and disappeared into the bathroom again.

I shook my head slowly and went down to the kitchen to make her some tea, one of the few foods not counted against our weekly rations. It took another ten minutes before she reappeared. Back when Deb announced she was pregnant, Doc had estimated she was about four months along since she had started to show. That was a month ago. Deb was losing weight with every passing week since there were fewer and fewer things she could stomach. Vicki had said it was normal for certain women to be sick throughout their entire pregnancy, but I had seen the worry even in her eyes.

I watched Deb as she slowly took a seat at the table and rested her head on her crossed arms.

When she didn't move, I spoke softly. "How are you doing?"

She raised her head ever so slowly and took a deep breath. "As well as can be expected for being knocked up after the end of the world."

I winced. "When you put it that way..."

She slowly leaned back. "Sorry. I'm not trying to be a Debbie Downer — "

A sharp burst of laughter escaped before I could muffle it.

"The name fits," she said with a shrug. "After everything we've been through, I should be thankful to be in a real house with real electricity and an honest-to-god working toilet. I'm tired of being tired and sick and cranky. I blame it on the hormones. Those prenatal vitamins are awful for nausea. The smell of oatmeal makes me sick, yet I would kill for a breakfast burrito with jalapeños right now. Go figure."

I handed her a cup. "I'm running low on jalapeños at the moment, but how about some tea? It's the real thing."

She grimaced before reaching out for it. "Not quite the same, but it seems to be one of the few things I can keep down."

While Deb and I sat in silence, sipping our tea, I heard the rustle of others getting ready for the day. Vicki was the first to make an appearance. She poured herself a cup and then waved as she headed to the door. "I'll see you after work."

Deb pushed herself to her feet. "I should be going, too."

I put my hand on her shoulder. "Rest. They'll understand."

"Late for my first day? I don't think so."

"Trust me," I said. "They know you're pregnant. They'll understand."

She watched me for a moment and then sunk back into her seat. "Thank you."

Clutch walked stiffly in. He eyed us both before heading to the teapot and pouring himself a cup. Whereas my calf ached, Clutch had to deal with an entire body that had taken more abuse than most bodies were made to handle. Dislocated joints and vertebrae, broken bones, and too many years of treating his body like an ATV were taking their toll. Headaches, stiffness, pinched nerves, and aches plagued him. Especially in the mornings.

After several long sips of tea, he turned around to make eye contact. "Ready to head?"

It was just like Clutch to pretend last night never happened. I pursed my lips. "I just need to grab my coat," I replied before turning back to Deb. "Need me to pick you up anything?"

She glanced at me hopefully.

"Anything except a breakfast burrito?" I added.

She sighed. "If that's the case, then, no."

"Is it morning already?" Jase said as he dragged himself down the hall with his eyes still closed, impressively not walking into anything.

"The sun's been up for ten minutes," Clutch said.

We both smiled, and Jase scowled. Even with an unpleasant expression, Jase looked more refreshed than he had in a long time. For being the opposite of a morning person, he woke up without his usual grumpiness. He hadn't even snapped at Clutch or me yet.

It made me realize just how exhausted we'd been. A single day at New Eden, and the difference was palpable. There was optimism in the air that I hadn't felt since we'd first arrived at the river barge. I hated to be too hopeful, especially when I didn't yet trust Justin or the people of New Eden, but I couldn't help but think New Eden could become *home*.

A place where Clutch, Jase, and I would be safe. Together.

"Are you all right?" Clutch asked.

I snapped back to reality. "Yeah. Let's get to work."

The next nine days were a blur of working, eating, and sleeping. We each worked ten-hour shifts doing menial jobs around New Eden. The first three days, I helped clean all the public facilities. The men were tasked to help transform an old drugstore into a community center.

The only adult member of our group who didn't work was Deb. Marco paid a visit to Justin on the first morning. That evening, Justin had made it clear, in no uncertain terms, that Deb was on bed rest until she had written permission from Dr. Edmund, New Eden's one and only physician.

Surprisingly, Benji was required to attend school. Diesel was even allowed to accompany the boy as long as the dog didn't distract the other six students. Since Benji had loved school before the outbreak, he had awakened before everyone else for his first day of school.

When all ten of us were together, the topic always returned to whether we'd stay at New Eden. Winter was lurking around the corner. We still had enough time to make it back to Fox Park, but we had no idea what we'd find there. New Eden seemed safe, but we were the outsiders here.

We all knew Marco was staying. He'd made it clear, just like he'd made it clear he wanted us—especially Deb—to stay.

On the second night, Frost said he was staying. He had Benji to think of, and he was convinced New Eden was the best place for the boy.

Deb's announcement came the following night. She was terrified of having a baby on the road and wanted to stay at New Eden at least until the baby was born. Here, she had a roof over her head, a semblance of medical care, and a perception of safety. Marco was ecstatic—he had a knack of always showing up whenever Deb needed something. Justin was especially happy that Deb would pledge allegiance to New Eden. Hers would be the first birth at New Eden, and everyone treated her as though she was the Virgin Mary.

On that same night, Vicki said she'd stay with Deb.

Jase announced he wanted to return to Fox Park at the first sign of spring, but he said he'd go wherever we went. He firmly believed the park was where we belonged, and Hali agreed. The teenagers had formed a fast friendship during her early days at Camp Fox—notably, right after her father tried to sell her for their safety.

As for the rest of us, we were still undecided. I had no doubt Clutch would go wherever I went, and vice versa. Despite our issues, Clutch wouldn't give up on me. I knew it.

Griz was tight-lipped, which was rare for him. He'd formed a fast friendship with Marco, but as a Ranger, he was a kindred spirit with Clutch. I suspected he'd go wherever he believed he could do the most good.

Tension around our indecision grew with each passing day. We craved to return to Fox Park...but we needed the safety of New Eden for the winter. Unfortunately, Justin gave us ten days, not a season, to pledge fealty. Then again, it wasn't like they could keep us here if we wanted to leave in the spring. Or, could they?

On the tenth day, while I was delivering lunches to the seven patrol officers on duty, Justin found me. I'd been trying to avoid him after Clutch told me Justin had cornered him the day earlier. I was one of those people who, before the outbreak, had always said 'yes' to everyone. It didn't matter if it was a party at someone's house, a request from a charity, or asking for a helping hand, I had always been the sucker.

As Justin and Charlie approached, I looked for a way out. I'd finished my last delivery and had a lunch break. I couldn't pretend I hadn't seen them. We'd already made eye contact. I looked to the left and to the right but saw no chance for escape, only a cat watching me from its perch on a window.

Charlie smiled and nodded toward the animal. "The cats keep the mice away. Luckily, they don't get sick like the dogs do. They've never gone after the zeds. There must be enough mice to keep them content."

Justin handed me a steaming mug. "I thought you might like some hot cocoa."

"Thanks," I said when he handed it to me.

"I ran into Clutch yesterday," Justin began.

I nodded. "He mentioned it."

He continued. "Today's your tenth day at Camp Fox. Have you reached a decision yet?"

I frowned. "Don't we have until tomorrow morning to give you our answer?"

"You do. I was wondering if you were on the fence. If so, I was going to see if we could answer any questions to help you make your decision."

"You've been more than fair to us," I said after a moment. "If we choose not to stay, it's not because of how we've been treated here. New Eden is a good community. You're good people."

Pride beamed through Justin's smile. "We try to do our best with what we have. We may not have much choice in what's thrown at us, but we do have a choice in how we cope. Free will may be the one thing that saves us."

"We have incoming!" someone shouted, and I twisted around to the front gate.

Justin ran toward the guard who'd yelled, and I jogged behind him. Already, two more guards were racing toward our position.

The first guard pointed to at least four vehicles in the distance. "It's still too far away to make out if I've seen any of those vehicles before. I can't tell if it's Black

Sheep or friendlies right now."

"Call in all reinforcements," Justin said. "If they're launching a frontal assault, they won't find us to be easy prey."

"I've got it," one of the men said and took off.

"Give me a gun," I said. "I can help."

Justin watched me for a moment and then nodded. "Charlie, send all nonessential personnel to the silo. Arm anyone, including the Fox Group, who wants to be out here with us."

Charlie nodded and then took off running.

The newcomers slowed as they approached, and I counted five—not four vehicles as I'd originally thought. They were older trucks and cars, because older vehicles seemed better equipped to handle deteriorating gasoline. The old blue truck in lead had a long stick with a white sheet tied to it.

"They're here in peace," Justin said, though he didn't sound exactly confident.

A dozen armed guards lined up behind the fence's concrete pillars, showing a clear display of force. By the time the vehicles came to a stop, another fifty men were running toward us with weapons.

Clutch handed me my rifle. My hands instantly remembered the weight and feel of the weapon. It took me only a couple seconds to check to see that it was still fully loaded. I saw he had his Blaser rifle, and I smiled. "Just like old times, huh?"

He smirked. "Just like it." Then he noticed Justin, and

his face hardened. "What's your protocol for dealing with threats?"

Justin nodded to the vehicles. "They're flying a white flag. We give them a chance to state their case. If they show us no hostility and don't pose a threat to New Eden, we'll allow them to come in under quarantine conditions."

"And if they pose a threat?" Clutch asked.

"Then we refuse them entry."

"That's all?" I asked.

Justin frowned. "No. We used to have one of our squadrons follow them to ensure they left. Showing we outman and outgun them has always been enough to scare off bandits. Let's hope that's enough today if these guys mean us harm, because we're running desperately low on firepower."

Clutch muttered something under his breath. "We'll have to ramp up New Eden's forces."

"We're a town, not a military installation."

"There's no difference, not anymore," Clutch said.

Jase and Griz came running toward us. They were covered in sawdust and still wearing their work gloves. Before reaching us, they paused and grabbed rifles off a stack of guns on an ATV parked nearby.

"Sit rep?" Griz asked when they met us.

"The situation is five vehicles flying a white flag," I responded quickly. "We don't know if they're friendly yet."

"So they haven't shown any signs of aggression?"

Griz countered.

"They haven't shown their hand yet," Clutch said, and then he nodded toward the newcomers. "But it looks like we'll find out soon enough."

Two men stepped from the blue truck. They held their open hands in the air as they approached, one with a limp. Both men were terribly ragged, with soiled clothes and matted hair. One man lowered his arms to hold his ribs, but the other nudged, and he raised his hands again. No other people stepped out of the remaining vehicles.

"Jesus," I said. "These guys are in rough shape."

Justin moved toward the gate, and we each took a position behind vehicles, barrels, and poles, aiming our weapons at the newcomers. He glanced back at us as though making sure we were ready. Then, he turned back to the pair of newcomers. "Stop right there. That's close enough."

The men did as they were told and stood ten feet from Justin, with only the wire gate between them.

Justin spoke first. "Welcome to New Eden. Put any weapons you might be carrying on the ground."

"We don't have any on us," the taller of the two men said. "We left them in the truck."

Justin nodded to one of the sentries. Charlie opened the gate for the sentry to squeeze through and walk up to the two men, careful to stay out of our line of fire should the pair be violent.

The sentry checked the one who'd spoken, then the

other, shorter man. He stepped back and held up a small revolver he'd taken from the second man. He tucked the revolver into his belt and backed off to the side, keeping his own firearm leveled on the newcomers.

Justin shook his head. "Lying isn't a way to earn trust."

"I need to protect myself. I wasn't planning on using it," he said.

"We need your help," the taller of the two men said.

"We got no place to stay. We were run out," the second man added.

Justin held up a hand. "I'll hear your case, but only when I know you don't intend to cause trouble. So, here's how it's going to work. I ask the questions. You answer them. Do you understand?"

They nodded. The shorter man spoke again. "Will you let us in then?"

Justin wagged his finger. "Tut, tut. Didn't you listen? *I'm* the one asking the questions. And, if I happen to not believe you or don't like your answers, you will not be allowed entrance."

The taller man punched his compatriot in the arm. "Shut up, you idiot. You trying to get us killed?" The smaller one glared and clenched his fists but didn't speak. I kept my rifle leveled on him.

"Let's start over," Justin said. "How many are in your party?"

"Nineteen. No, twenty-one counting Jim and me,"

the taller man said.

"Where are you coming from?" Justin asked.

"North of here," the man replied after a pause.

Justin narrowed his gaze. "Exactly how far north? That's Black Sheep territory."

The pair fidgeted, and I inhaled. "They're bandits," I said.

Justin glanced at me, and he gave a tight nod before turning back to the newcomers. "Black Sheep aren't welcome here. You can turn around and leave now."

The taller man tamped the air. "I ain't going to lie and try to deny it. Yeah, we were Sheep. But, we ain't Sheep no more. Once Hodge disappeared, we started to break apart. Then, we were attacked by some group of crazy survivors. After that, the mutts started to pick us off one by one. We got nothing. We're starving and about out of gas. If we stay out here, we're gonna die. Please, let us in. I never did anything wrong against New Eden, I swear it on my momma's grave."

Marco walked up to stand by Justin. "When did Hodge disappear?" he asked the Black Sheep.

"A month ago, maybe," he replied. "I don't know for sure. He took some guys out east to clear the river but never came back."

I smiled and glanced at Clutch. He caught my gaze with the same look. *Hope.*

I had shot at Hodge a few weeks ago but was sure I'd missed.

His gang had attacked us in the middle of the night.

We'd set up camp in the middle of a massive sporting goods store on the banks of the Mississippi River. Our security had been lax that night. Hours earlier on that same day, we'd survived having our last home burn to the ground and were exhausted. We paid dearly for our mistake. Nearly all of Camp Fox was murdered; leaving only nine of us to remember.

Hodge had been the only bandit to escape, and I carried the shame of letting him get away. Now, the possibility that he hadn't survived lifted a metric ton off my chest.

"Let me get this straight," Justin said. "You guys fell apart and now need help from the same people you've stolen from and tried to kill. Did I get that right?"

Neither answered for a long time, until finally, the taller man spoke. "We're hungry."

"You should've been making friends rather than enemies," Justin said. "Let me guess. Those 'crazy survivors' that attacked you fought back because you attacked first."

"It wasn't like that," the shorter man named Jim said. "It was self-defense."

"I find that hard to believe," Justin said. "Since twice in as many months you people tried to kill me and take over New Eden. I imagine you got what you had coming. Now, if you don't leave, you will be arrested or shot."

Jim's face darkened into red, and he burst toward the sentry standing outside the gate. I fired a shot, but the taller man jumped in the way, and the bullet meant for Jim hit his compatriot in the chest. He went down. More shots fired from around me. Before I lined up a second shot, Jim had somehow managed to get behind the sentry, who he now held at knifepoint.

The bandits' vehicles, except for the empty lead vehicle, raced toward us. Shotgun barrels poked out from their open windows. I homed in my sights onto Jim's left eye, the only clear shot I had. Even then, if my aim was even the slightest off, I would be killing one of Justin's men.

"We have nowhere else to go. You gotta take us in!" Jim yelled.

I fired.

Jim collapsed, and the sentry ran toward the gate. Charlie grunted as he pulled it open.

The four vehicles were nearly upon us, but their driving was erratic, causing their shots to fly everywhere. As soon as the sentry was through the gate, Charlie pushed it closed. Instead of running away, once he latched the gate, he slid down. As he turned around, I noticed the red stain widening on his shirt.

"No," I gasped before yelling out, "Charlie's down!"

A sentry ran for the injured man, but gunfire forced him back. As the vehicles approached, we all focused our efforts on the occupants within. Windshields shattered. One SUV drove off the road and crashed into a tree. Of the three remaining vehicles, the first one slammed into the gate. Metal wire screeched and buckled under the impact, but the gate held. Charlie had managed to pull himself a few feet away; inches closer, and he would've been killed in the crash.

The other two vehicles stopped to the side and laid down fire while the first SUV backed up. With a loud clank of shifting gears, it launched forward. Blood splattered its broken windshield the second before impact. The driver's foot remained on the gas pedal. Metal cried as the SUV tried to force itself through the layers of wire fencing and wood boards.

Clutch ran past me, and my eyes widened. Crouched, he weaved through gunfire and stopped at the bumper of the SUV, on our side of the gate. He raised his rifle and shot through the fence at the vehicle's occupants. The engine immediately slowed but the SUV still pressed against the gate.

Metal clanged, and the top part of the gate fell inward. Clutch grabbed Charlie and pulled him clear, and two other people carried the injured man away. I focused on laying down cover fire, and I saw at least one of my shots find its target when one of the passengers dropped his shotgun and collapsed over his open door. Gunfire slowed, and then stopped from the two vehicles.

"Cease fire!" Justin yelled, waving his arms. He motioned to the sentries who'd been on duty.

I continued to scan the area as three men moved to the gate and pushed their way through the bent door. One pulled the dead driver from the SUV that had rammed into the gate and cut the engine. He held up his thumb.

Justin turned to the other two vehicles peppered with bullets. "Lay down your weapons and step out slowly. Any sudden moves, and you will be shot."

No one emerged, and I took advantage of the silence to swap magazines. After an endless minute, Justin nodded to the trio on the other side of the gate, and they moved slowly to the closest vehicle. With two holding their rifles, the third man checked the entire vehicle. He stepped back and shook his head in Justin's direction, and they moved to the last remaining vehicle.

I was careful to scan the area, to make sure there was no one else sneaking around, but everything seemed quiet. It was the eerie kind of silence that followed a gunfight, where my ears were ringing like after a music concert, yet everything felt muted.

At the last vehicle, the sentries dragged out a man who showed no resistance. His eyes were closed, and I couldn't even tell if he was conscious. Two of the sentries dragged him back to the gate and through the small door.

Justin met them inside, and I moved closer.

Justin came down on a knee. "Why did you attack?"

The man's head rolled weakly. "No — where else — to go."

I swallowed, knowing the feeling all too well. *Desperation.*

"If you hadn't shot at us, we wouldn't have shot at

you," Justin said.

The man struggled and lifted his hand, only to drop it, and his last breath puffed from his lungs.

Everyone stood around, and then someone cheered. The sentries chanted out, "New Eden!"

Justin joined in. "It's over. New Eden is safe. Anyone who attacks New Eden will suffer the same fate."

I didn't join in. I'd never found anyone's death a time for celebration. Not Hodge's. Hell, not even Doyle's. There were too few of us left. With every death, I knew humanity was taking one step closer to the brink.

Clutch stepped up to me, and I looked into his eyes. "How's Charlie?"

His lips tightened. "We'll see."

I sighed. "Is there no safe place left in this world?"

Clutch didn't answer. Jase and Griz walked over.

Jase slung his rifle over his back. "It feels good to have my rifle back."

"Yup," Griz said without looking up from reloading one of his mags.

I spotted Justin watching us. He didn't come closer, but I knew what he was thinking. I chewed my lip before speaking. "We've got a decision to make. Stay or go?"

Griz clicked the mag into his rifle. "These guys sure could use our help. Even today, it was sheer luck they didn't have more casualties."

"They need our help. But, do they deserve it?" Clutch asked.

I thought for a moment. "Of all the roads we could've taken, and all the places we could've ended up, somehow — a full state over — our paths still managed to cross. I don't believe in coincidence. I think we're meant to be here, at this time."

Clutch breathed heavily and then nodded. "We should stay."

I turned to Jase and Griz.

"You know where I stand. I'm in," Griz said quickly.

Jase shrugged. "It's cold out there. We have electricity and food in here. I'm in. What have we got to lose?"

TEMPTATION

CHAPTER VIII

Two weeks later

All of New Eden gathered around us, and I found myself fidgeting. My breath circled in tiny wisps of fog in the freezing morning air, and I hugged myself to keep from shivering.

Justin held up his right hand, and the conversations hushed. "Repeat after me."

The nine sole Fox survivors raised our hands.

"As a citizen of the New Eden province ..."

"As a citizen of the New Eden province," we answered in chorus.

"I pledge to defend and support our province, with all that I am..."

"I pledge to defend and support our province, with all that I am..."

"With the highest level of integrity and honor, I give this oath of fealty."

"With the highest level of integrity and honor, I give this oath of fealty."

Justin smiled. "Welcome to New Eden."

Cheers erupted. Someone patted me on the back, and we found ourselves swarmed by people welcoming us into the community. I glanced to Clutch at my side, and he wore a genuine smile. He wasn't exactly a people person, yet there was no mistaking his demeanor. He looked at me, and I returned his smile. He shrugged, and I knew why he was happy. I sensed the same happiness.

We belonged somewhere.

It wasn't Camp Fox, but it still felt good. *Safe.*

Even Jase looked happy, though he was a consummate extrovert and handled attention like a fish in water. He still wanted to return to Fox Park, but like everywhere we'd been, he'd quickly acclimated to New Eden. It seemed the younger the person, the more easily they adapted to change, and it made me wonder what we lost as we aged.

Justin made his way down the celebratory line and stopped in front of me. His smile was wide as he held out his hand. "New Eden is lucky to have you."

I accepted his hand. "We're lucky to have New Eden."

He shook Clutch's hand next. "We have the start of something good here. I know it. We'll talk more later. I need to get back and send your names to the capital. We keep track of all citizens. Seeing the lists grow gives everyone hope."

"What's the number up to?" I asked.

"Four hundred and seventy-three at New Eden, counting you. We're one of the smaller provinces. Colorado has the largest with nearly ten thousand. Over eighty-seven thousand across the new, combined country. We're hoping to have found and tracked at least a hundred thousand by the first of July."

"You think that many made it?" Clutch asked.

Justin nodded. "I'm sure of it. The problem is we're all scattered right now. We need to pull together to build a foundation."

"How's the rest of the world looking?" Clutch asked.

Justin shrugged. "Australia was the least hit. They're still at twenty-plus percent, and they're the ones who reached out to us and are connecting the rest of the world. They're still trying to get data on Europe, Asia, and Africa. Now, if you'll excuse me…"

He bowed out and headed down the street.

"A hundred thousand," Clutch said softly.

"Yeah," I added, just as softly. "The human race might have a chance after all."

"Why the long faces? Today's a big day."

I looked over to see Sarah pushing Charlie in a wheelchair.

I frowned. "Shouldn't you still be in bed? It's been less than a week."

"That's what I told him," Sarah said. "But, Charlie will never miss a party."

Charlie waved a hand. "Oh, I'm fine. Just a little tender."

"You were *shot*," I said.

"And, the bullet missed everything that needs to keep working," he countered.

"Still," Sarah added. "You have to be careful. There's only so much medicine lying around."

"I know, I know," Charlie said in a rush. "Enough about me. Have you picked your new roles? Today's your last as free agents."

Clutch chuckled next to me. "By picking new roles, you mean signing up for jobs?"

Charlie shrugged. "Roles, jobs, whatever you want to call them. But, seriously. Have you picked your role yet? It's important to select the one that's the best fit for you. It won't feel as much like a job if you enjoy it."

"So you say," I said with a smirk.

"Well, whatever you picked, I hope you enjoy it," Sarah said before placing a hand on Charlie's shoulder. "We need to grab on to any joy we can find nowadays."

Charlie held her hand, and they gazed into each other's eyes. She then backed up the wheelchair, and the pair departed without another word.

The crowd had thinned. People had returned to work or home.

"I suppose it's time for us to head to work," I said.

"See you after dinner," Vicki said, and I waved to her

and Deb as they walked away.

Last night, we'd each settled on our roles, which we'd start today. We were all assigned the first shift since we were newcomers, though I suspected we'd each be assigned different shifts as we earned their trust.

Once a school dietary aide, Vicki volunteered to help with rations. Deb volunteered to serve as a medical aide after she went for a prenatal checkup with New Eden's only doctor and saw he had no help, but a waiting room full of patients with jammed fingers, splinters, and minor cuts. Dr. Edmund likely had agreed so he could keep a close eye on her health.

"Be careful," Hali said, eying Jase.

"I always am," Jase replied with a grin.

She jogged to catch up with Vicki and Deb, since their workplaces were all in a close vicinity to one another. Hali signed up as soon as she found out New Eden had no one to manage the distribution of clothing and non-perishable supplies.

Frost and Benji had long since disappeared. Frost, with his general contractor experience, had signed up for silo renovations, while Benji had full school days.

The rest of us had signed up for security. When we arrived at the security building, Justin, along with another man, was already waiting for us.

"Already report us to the capital?" Clutch asked, and I noticed a hint of something hard in his question.

"All done," Justin said, sounding pleased. Then he looked to each of us: Clutch, Griz, Jase, and me. "I was hoping a couple of you would choose the squadron. With you, we have a full team again."

He pointed to a SUV parked near the gate, where Marco leaned against the side of the vehicle and waved in our direction. "The squadron is meeting in about ten minutes from now. Clutch and Griz, they're expecting you. Clutch, since you're the senior-ranking military vet here, Marco proposed that you command the squadron."

Clutch pursed his lips. "A sergeant isn't exactly senior ranking. There's a reason sergeants aren't commanders."

Griz chuckled. "Yeah, they're too cranky to be one."

Clutch flipped him the bird. "It's yours. You're the only other soldier in this place."

"Oh, hell no," Griz said. "I might have more of a personality, but the last thing I want to do is babysit amateurs. That's up your alley."

I scowled. "What's that supposed to mean?"

Griz smirked.

"This is important," Justin said, not giving Griz time for a witty comeback. "After losing Marco's squadron to the Black Sheep and the capital claiming our other squadrons to locate survivors in the south, it's crucial we keep our only squadron running in tip-top shape. This is our only crew equipped to travel out of New Eden."

"You can count on me," Clutch said, any humor gone from his voice.

"Well, that covers the squadron then," Justin said.

My brows rose. "What, you're not letting Jase or me serve as scouts?"

Justin watched me for a moment before turning to Jase. "Jase, I'd like you to meet Zach. Zach runs the New Eden security forces, and you'll be on his team."

Zach held out his hand. "Welcome to the force."

Jase didn't shake it. Instead, confused, Jase looked from Clutch to me and then to Justin. "But, I'm with these guys. We work together."

Justin spoke first. "I know you're more than capable to have survived out there for so long, but it's New Eden policy to not allow anyone under the age of eighteen to serve on the squadron. It's safer within the fence," Justin said.

"That's bullshit," Jase said. "I'm as good as anyone else out there."

"I'm not doing this to be difficult," Justin said. "I can't break policy for you. You—the youth—are our future. If we don't work toward our future, we won't have a future."

"The force isn't some place for lackeys," Zach said. "Our job is as important—if not more so—than the squadron's. We're the last line of defense for New Eden. These people are trusting their lives to our ability to keep them safe. We take out any danger that comes up to our fences as well as handle any problems within the fences. We also serve as backup support to the squadron. So, you see, it's not going to be a walk in the park. You'll see plenty of action, I can guarantee it."

Jase frowned.

"Give the force a shot," Clutch said. "Maybe they'll reconsider later."

"We have more guns and more ammo than the squadron," Zach added. "Marco mentioned you were pretty good with a motorcycle. We have ATVs on the force, but I happen to have a Honda 250 bike sitting in the garage that's yours as a sign-on bonus if you want it. I won't ever lie to you, we're in desperate need of personnel. You won't be treated like a kid here, I swear it."

Jase's frown disappeared as he tried not to look excited. "Well, I suppose I could give it a shot."

Zach smiled and held out his hand again.

This time, Jase shook it.

"What about me?" I asked with narrow eyes.

Justin's lips pursed. "Just like we have a rule in place to protect our youth, we have a rule in place to protect our women. Have you considered an administrative job? Marco said you're good with numbers. I could use help with the supplies tracking."

"That's bullshit. You don't need me behind a desk." I pointed. "You need me out there. I can fly over the area and identify problems before they get close."

Justin shrugged. "We don't have an airplane anywhere near here."

"I can find one. Then, all I'll need is a fuel tank and a decent mechanic."

"Two things we have in very short supply," he countered.

I pursed my lips. "Okay, then. If I stay on the ground, I can still help. I can take down a zed from over a hundred meters away."

Clutch spoke first. "She's right. Cash is the best sniper around. You'd be doing New Eden a disservice by not leveraging her talent."

"Unfortunately, we're running desperately low on ammunition," Justin said. "We're down to our last boxes, and we've cleared every known armory and supply store in the area. None of us will have any ammo before long."

Exasperated, I nearly rolled my eyes. "Fine, Then use me to scout for supplies, survivors, and trouble. Just because I'm a woman, I'm just as capable in my own right."

It was the first time I'd seen Justin uncomfortable. "Look at it this way. Men survivors outnumber women over three to one here. Any loss of a woman or child kills morale. It makes sense for women to choose the safer jobs, and we have plenty of openings —"

"No," I said, and took a deep breath. "Listen. I'm not trying to be difficult. I'm only trying to be where I can provide the most value."

"Cash..." Justin said.

Zach cut in. "C'mon, Justin. You know how short-staffed the force is. And, Cash has been out there, with these guys, for months. I'd be glad to have her on the force. It's safer than the squadron, but she can still make a difference."

I bit my lip. While I wanted to be outside the walls—with Clutch—I also didn't want to burn my shot with Zach's force. It would be better than shuffling paperwork. I didn't enjoy our team being split up, but I knew we'd have to make concessions at New Eden. After all, we were the newcomers here and had to abide by their rules. Not that it made things sit any easier in my gut.

Justin finally relented. "Fine, fine. Cash and Jase will serve on the security force." Then, he wagged a finger at me. "But, you will both be careful and do exactly what Zach says. I will not have you risk your lives unnecessarily."

"I got it," I said, trying not to frown, holding back the sting of disappointment of being judged just because I had tits.

Justin looked over each of us and then clapped his hands together. "We're all set. Let's get to work."

When Zach had said we'd see plenty of action, what he'd meant was that our days would be filled with hotheaded disputes and fiery tempers. My first day on the job, Mary stole from Jim's garden, the meal rations weren't enough for Ron's 260-pound frame, and Diesel caught a rabbit that Saul intended to eat. The second day, I learned most people used up their ration cards a day early, and they all believed they deserved extra rations for working.

My partner was Zach. Even though he chose me because I was the only woman on the force and he was being protective, he wasn't a bad partner. He had far more patience than I did, but he didn't take bullshit from anyone. Not even Bryn, the pretty woman who'd been caught at least five times before stealing from people's houses. We caught her pilfering canned pumpkin from house twelve. I would've kicked her out of New Eden after the second time. But, Justin was too protective of any women in New Eden. And everyone knew it.

"It's the ones like her who will make it so no one can trust anyone," I grumbled after Zach locked Bryn up for the night.

He shrugged. "She's a hard worker. Justin says as long as she's adding more value to New Eden than taking away, she stays."

"Locking her up overnight and giving her a free meal doesn't do any good. She gets the same punishment after each offense, and she keeps on stealing. You need to up the ante each time. Make the punishment worse until she decides to be a team player or leaves New Eden."

"What would you do?"

I thought for a moment. "I'd start by pulling her

rations the next time she steals. Then, I'd try humiliation, such as those public stocks they used in the Middle Ages. After that, I'd send her outside the gates."

"Remind me not to get on your bad side."

I chuckled. "If you think that's bad, you're lucky you can't read my mind as to what I'd really do." A cold wind blew, and I shivered. "It's hard enough the way it is to survive out here. We don't need interminably selfish people to make it worse."

I envied Clutch, Griz, and Marco. The squadron of twelve men hit the road each day and was home in time for dinner. While the only excitement we got was taking out every zed or sick animal that reached the fence. The zeds were easy. Most had rotted enough they moved slowly in the cold. When the temperatures dropped about ten degrees below freezing, they couldn't move at all. Easy to take out with a quick stab.

The animals were another story. Between them and the zeds, the landscape was depleted of meat, making us walking around in New Eden look like a feast in their starved gazes. I could've sworn the damn things were taunting us. Running up to the fence, barking to get our attention, and then running back off into the surrounding woods. By day, they'd come out one or two at a time. By night, they numbered in the dozens, as they searched for weak spots at our fences. Our job was to scare them off. Kill them whenever we could. I hated that part of my job more than anything else. Not only because I was killing something that had once been a domesticated animal, but also because those dogs scared me a lot more than I was scaring them.

Zach pointed to the two men headed our way. "Our shift is done, and not a moment too soon."

I rubbed my gloved hands together. "Good. It's downright freezing out here."

"It looks like a storm could be finally rolling in," he added as we walked to the force's headquarters, which was next door to the quarantine-slash-jail.

I glanced at the overcast sky blanketing everything in gray. "It's looked like that for three days now."

"Yeah, but the wind's picked up. I bet something's headed our way." He stepped inside and held the door open for me.

I paused. "What month is this? Are we still in November?"

"Yeah," he replied. "Thanksgiving is next week already."

I sighed and entered. "Well, I guess we're lucky to have gone this long before Mother Nature reared her ugly head again. When we got hit last month with snow already, I was expecting a hell of a winter ahead of us."

He nodded. "I was, too. Luckily, she's been focusing on Canada so far."

"Let's keep it that way."

When the next shift stepped inside, we quickly chatted and made notes in the daily log before heading our separate ways. The wind picked up, and I found myself jogging home. A block from my house, I found

Jase walking home from his shift on the other side of town. Poor Jase was stuck with the deadbeat on the force, leaving Jase to do all the heavy lifting. A couple days ago, I'd found Jase walking his shift alone, his partner no doubt taking another "break."

We met in front of the house. "You don't look so hot. Are you feeling okay?" I asked.

He wiped his red nose. "Just tired. I didn't sleep great last night. And, this cold weather doesn't help."

I put a hand on his shoulder. "I'll make you some tea. Hopefully you'll sleep better tonight."

He sniffled. "Yeah."

"So, how'd Dick ditch you today?"

His partner's name was actually Richard, and he went by Rich, but we quickly decided that "Dick" fit him better.

Jase rolled his eyes. "Dick was a no-show. Caught the flu."

My brows rose. "And exactly how could Dick catch the flu in a fenced-in town?"

He shrugged.

I shook my head. "Gotta give the guy credit. He comes up with a new excuse every day. I bet he's faking it. I haven't heard any rumors about a flu going around. Geez, I hope he's faking it. The flu would be miserable to catch. It's not like we get sick days or time off around here."

"You're telling me," he said and took the porch steps one at a time.

I frowned. Usually Jase leapt up the steps to get inside and eat. That he was practically dragging his feet today worried me.

Someone coughed daintily, and I froze. In slow motion, I stepped inside. Hali was lying on the couch. Several wadded tissues peppered the floor. Jase had sat down next to her and was rubbing her arm.

Vicki came in from the kitchen, carrying two steamy mugs. She gave me a knowing look before handing Jase and Hali a mug. I followed her into the kitchen.

"The flu's here," she said as she rinsed dishes in the sink. "Hali's got it. Benji's been in bed all day. You know how kids are. He probably picked it up at school and brought it home."

I let out a deep breath. "How's everyone else?"

"Okay for now." She turned around and leaned against the sink. "But, I can tell I'm more tired than normal. I'm going to bed after a bit to try to fend it off. How are you doing?"

"I feel fine."

"Good," she said. "Deb is staying at the clinic. Marco's with her. They're quarantining her to make sure she doesn't catch it. It's probably your run-of-the-mill flu bug. Deb accused Justin of being overly careful. I have to admit, I'm siding with Justin this time."

The sound of familiar, heavy boot steps on the porch pulled our attention to the foyer.

"I'll put more tea on," Vicki said.

"I can do it," I said. "Get some rest."

After a moment's hesitation, she nodded. "Thank you," she said and headed up the stairs.

I put on the water to boil, and heard Clutch enter the kitchen. He came up behind me, and I leaned back and into his warmth. "I was beginning to wonder where you were."

"We were at Justin's," he said and reached around me and grabbed a handful of walnuts and pumpkin seeds from a bowl under the cabinet. "He had us scout the Omaha suburbs today."

I turned around. "Why?"

He popped some nuts in his mouth and chewed. "Justin wants New Eden to have a Thanksgiving feast. He thinks it's important for morale. Lincoln's closer, but it was more heavily bombed. And, we did find a store in Omaha that hadn't been destroyed."

I frowned. "But, the cities are too dangerous. We learned that when we tried to camp in the store by Des Moines. There are way too many things that want to eat us in cities."

He shook his head. "The zeds won't be a problem. The temperature's dropped enough that all the ones we've come across lately were popsicles. As for the dogs, except for the sick ones, the packs seem to come out only at night. They're still too skittish to come out during the day."

"Still..." I cautioned. "There could be a lot more of them around the larger city."

He flashed one of his rare smiles and ran a thumb

over my cheek. "It'll be fine. The superstore we found isn't too far into town. It should be an easy in-and-out. But, we have to move fast. If we don't hurry and grab what we can, other survivors will get to these stores first. And, once we run out of gas, getting supplies out of the cities will be infinitely harder."

"I know," I said, frowning. "But, I still don't like it. Besides, how are you going to make it into Omaha, raid a store, and make it back here in one day? The squadron is too small to unload a store. You need more help."

"We'll be fine. The squadron is heading out first thing in the morning. We're taking all three haulers. We'll be gone for two nights."

"You need more hands," I said. "Jase and I—"

"Have to stay here," he interrupted. "Without the squadron, New Eden only has the police force to protect it. And, Justin mentioned there's a flu bug going around. You and Jase need to be careful."

"You're the one who needs to be careful."

His smile widened. "I always am."

CHAPTER IX

The temperature hovered at ten degrees Fahrenheit the morning the squadron headed out. An inch of fresh snow covered the ground. I went with Clutch and Griz to see them off. Marco had stayed the night with Deb, and I could see he was reluctant to leave her when he dragged his feet to the gate at dawn.

As the squadron loaded up, I grabbed Clutch's jacket, pulled him down, and kissed him solidly on the lips. He wrapped his arms around me. Someone whistled, and I ignored it. When I let go, Clutch looked rather pleased with himself. Typical guy expression. I held up three fingers. "Three days. You better be home in three days, or else I'm coming to get you."

He chuckled. "We'll be back with time to spare. I don't plan to get on your bad side."

I stuck out my chin and tried not to smile. "Damn

straight."

"Where's my kiss?" Griz asked, holding out his arms.

I grinned and walked into his embrace. I kissed his cheek as he squeezed me half to death. When he let me go, I scolded, "Be careful out there." Without waiting for an answer, I spun on my heel and walked away, though once I was around the building, I stopped and then watched them drive through the open gate from my relatively hidden place.

After the gate closed behind the loud trucks, my heart pounded. While I'd grown accustomed to Clutch heading outside the fence every day, worry chewed at my nerves when he wasn't home at night. Since the outbreak, I could count on two hands the number of nights we'd spent apart.

The first few times, I'd worried about how I could possibly get by without him. Then, my fear had switched gears. Somewhere along the line, my feelings for Clutch had morphed into something deep and tangible, and I constantly worried about what could happen to him out there. I wanted to be there to protect him, even though he was more than capable of taking care of himself.

After the gate closed behind the trucks, I hustled into the force's HQ, a small brick building that had once been Justin's insurance office.

It was freezing inside. It was New Eden policy to not use precious energy to heat any building no one lived in. Even then, the force checked out every house every week to make sure energy wasn't being wasted. With the exception of the medical clinic, thermostats couldn't be set higher than sixty degrees, which felt balmy to me after being outside most of every day.

"Just the two of us so far?"

I jumped and turned to see Zach. "Jase caught the flu."

He frowned. "Rich, Steve, and Jack all called in sick. I haven't heard from anyone else yet. That flu is spreading fast."

"It makes sense. We're all working long hours in cold weather and not getting enough nutrients. And, we're all in a relatively enclosed environment. Any virus that passes through is going to hit us hard."

"You're starting to sound like a doctor."

I shrugged. "My dad was one. My mom was a nurse. I guess it's in my genes."

"Why didn't you go into medicine?"

"I didn't like dealing with people, and I used to get queasy at the sight of blood. So, I went the actuary route, though it wasn't exactly the best career to prepare me for all this. Justin said you were a state trooper before the outbreak"

He chuckled. "I was a volunteer reserve officer. For my day job, I worked in a factory. I assembled modular components for wind turbines."

"That'll come in handy if we can put up a wind turbine in New Eden."

He shook his head. "Afraid not. I'm in the same boat

as you. My skills are pretty much worthless nowadays. I worked on the RF module housing. The other ninety-nine percent of a wind turbine's components is beyond my expertise."

"Well, aren't we the pair?"

He grinned. "Yeah. The fate of New Eden is in the hands of a number jockey and a windmill monkey." He motioned toward the door. "Shall we?"

I glanced at the icy window and cringed. "Let's go defend the hapless citizens of New Eden against...well, the hapless citizens of New Eden."

Two days later

Justin, Zach, myself, and five other people stood around Charlie's bed. Sarah sat in a chair next to him, biting back tears while she held his hand and crooned her love for him.

I fidgeted. I'd never been any good around the dying. Probably because most of the time, the dying had been bitten, and I needed to be there to bring them permanent death after they'd died the first time. Today was different. Charlie had caught the flu, and it wasn't even a bad flu as flus went. Only the run-of-the-mill flu that made its victims achy, sniffly, and coughy. Jase, Vicki, and Hali had all returned to work already. But, to the weak and infirm, the flu was always dangerous.

Charlie had been still healing from his gunshot when the flu struck. It had knocked him down hard, and he'd quickly become bedridden. Earlier this morning, the doctor announced Charlie had pneumonia, and there was nothing that could be done. After that, Sarah had demanded the doctor return to the clinic to help those who could be saved.

Charlie's breaths rasped in lungs filling with fluid.

Zach and I stopped during each of our daily rounds. A line of people cycled through the house, giving their regards to Sarah and their final good-byes to Charlie, though both seemed oblivious to anyone in their home.

As a coughing fit wracked Charlie and Sarah let out a sob, I swallowed the lump in my throat. Charlie was a good man. My lip quivered. "It's not fair," I said softly, turned on my heel, and walked from the room.

Inside the hall, I took a deep breath. The cool air helped, but still a weight pressed upon my chest. Everyone died — that was a part of life — but the world had become nothing but death. Picking us off one by one. What hope was there if we were going to die, anyway?

I leaned against the painted wall, and stared blankly at the picture at the end of the hall. It was a print of a famous painting — The Birth of Venus. It fit in with the tapestries and clay pots, all that remained of the house's original occupants.

A wail erupted from within the bedroom, and I

clenched my eyes shut.

Footsteps entered the hallway, and I heard the door quietly close. "It's over," Zach said softly.

I opened my eyes and rested my head against the wall. Everyone who knew Charlie loved him. I couldn't fathom him ever having an enemy. "Losing Charlie will be hard on New Eden."

The corner of his lip curled almost into a smile before dropping again. "It will be hardest on Sarah."

I remembered her swollen, red eyes, brimming with loss. "Yeah."

We stood there for a long minute before I pushed off from the wall. "We should continue our rounds."

Zach thought for a moment and then nodded. "I could use some fresh air, anyway. We'll check on Sarah later. She's got plenty of company right now."

We headed outside and continued our long, cold walk around the western half of New Eden. Even wearing my arctic coat, ski mask, stocking hat, and gloves, the cold bit at our fingers and noses, and we took indoor breaks every thirty minutes to prevent frostbite. As we did every day, we took a full hour to walk through the first floors of the silo. Our job was to make sure everything was secure, but truthfully, there was an inherent security to the silo, and the more stairs I descended, the safer I felt. Especially when Clutch was still away. He'd be home soon, probably even before I was off duty.

Knowing Clutch would be safe within the New Eden

fences tonight, the heavy weight on my chest began to lift. Justin was right—a Thanksgiving feast would be a perfect event for New Eden—symbolic of making new friends and a new life together. Everyone was excited to see what Clutch's squadron would bring back from Omaha. Even though half of the town was still recovering from the flu, the impatient excitement in the air was palpable.

By sunset, my muscles trembled with adrenaline. I had to force myself to slow down to keep with Zach's casual pace.

Zach fought back a smile. "The squadron will be back before too long. Why don't you head home?"

I glanced at my watch. "We still have twenty minutes left on our shift."

He shrugged. "I can handle the daily log. Go on, I'm sure Clutch, Griz, and Marco will be starving by the time they get back."

I eyed him for a moment before pulling him into a big hug. "Thanks. I owe you one."

"I'll see you in the morning."

Zach headed toward the HQ, while I turned and headed the opposite direction. The nightly howls had begun, and I could see many pairs of eyes reflecting moonlight from the other side of the fence.

My pace picked up with every block, pausing only when I passed Charlie and Sarah's house. I stood there for a long moment before deciding to check in on Sarah to see if she needed anything. I bounded up the steps and didn't bother knocking. Inside, the house was nearly empty. On the table sat a variety of food and gifts dropped off by various friends and neighbors throughout the day. I continued down the hallway and into the bedroom. The bed now lay empty, and I suspected Charlie's body was now at the clinic, which also served as the town morgue.

A lone woman sat in a chair reading a leather-bound book. She looked up when I entered. "Hello, Cash."

I couldn't remember her name. I knew she worked with Vicki, but I'd never talked with her before. "Where's Sarah?"

She motioned to the bathroom. "Taking a bath. She wanted some alone time."

"Oh," I said. "I guess I can stop back later."

"She should be out any time. She's been in there ever since they took Charlie away."

"Okay," I said. I stood there, twiddling my thumbs, and waited for Sarah. After a minute or two, I sensed a gaze on me, and I looked at the woman. "What?"

"Is Marco your brother?" she asked.

"What?"

"Someone said he was your brother. I was wondering. I think it's pretty cool he found you out there. What are the odds?"

I rolled my eyes. "He's not my brother. He's Mexican. I've never even been to Mexico. Just because we're both of Hispanic descent doesn't mean we're related."

She shrugged. "Sorry."

I glanced at my watch. "How long can Sarah stay in there?"

She laid the open book down on her lap. "I don't know, but she's been in there for ages already. Two, maybe three hours? Everyone else left a long time ago. It seemed wrong to leave her alone, so I stayed."

"I'm glad you did." As minutes passed, a sense of foreboding formed in my gut. "Any sounds?"

She thought for a moment. "She ran a bath when she first went in, but after that...no, I can't say I've heard anything."

I walked over to the bathroom door and knocked. "Sarah? It's me, Cash." No response. I knocked louder. "Sarah, open up."

When I heard nothing, I tried the handle, but it was locked. My heart pounded at the silence on the other side. I ran my fingers along the woodwork above the door and found a long, hexagonal-shaped key. I slid it into the keyhole, and the lock clicked. "Sarah, I'm coming in."

Still nothing.

I glanced back at the other woman who was now standing, her eyes wide.

I took a deep breath and opened the door. Sarah lay in the bathtub, staring at nothing. The water was murky with red. One arm was in the water, the other strewn over the side of the tub, a still river of blood puddled on the floor below it. It took several seconds for the scene to register in my brain, and my lips quivered. "Oh, Sarah, *no.*"

A gasp behind me. "Sarah!"

I turned in time to barely catch the woman as she collapsed.

She pressed her face against my chest and cried. "I should've known," she whimpered. "I sat out there while she...she..."

"You couldn't have known. No one could've known," I said, stroking her hair while staring at Sarah's lifeless body. I didn't bother checking for a pulse. The amount of blood and her pallor told the entire story. Sarah had chosen not to live without her Charlie and taken matters into her own hands.

"I don't understand," she said. "Sarah couldn't hurt a fly. Why would she do that to herself?"

I didn't answer.

"It's not right," she mumbled and continued crying.

When her sobs slowed to a simmer, I helped her up, walked her down the hallway, and sat her on the couch.

She shook her head. "I've lost two husbands. One to cancer, the other to those creatures outside the fence. It tore my heart out each time, but I survived. If only Sarah could've seen that things would get better."

The front door opened, and I turned to see Zach step inside. He grinned. "I figured you were heading home." His smile dropped abruptly. "What happened?"

"It's Sarah," I said. "She—she's in the bathroom."

Zach headed down the hallway with intent and returned a minute later. Somber, he looked across our faces. "Cash, can you go get Justin and Doc Edmund? I'll stay here with Izzie."

I nodded and turned as though in a haze. "Yeah, sure. I'll be right back."

I barely remembered running to Justin's house or to the clinic. But, I ended up back at Charlie and Sarah's house with both men a few minutes later. They quickly took control. Justin made calls on the portable radio he always carried, and the doctor went immediately to check on Sarah.

I didn't stick around. I numbly walked to my house. I could no longer find the quick walking pace I had before. All the excitement I'd been harboring had been muted.

I shut the front door, and the shrill howls were muffled by the walls. I was glad to find the living room empty, with everyone else in bed still recuperating. I sat down in a recliner and leaned back.

And waited for Clutch to come home.

The following morning

"Still no word from the squadron?" I asked for the third time in an hour as I drummed my fingers on Justin's desk.

Justin didn't look up from the papers he was working

on. "Not yet."

Jase stepped from behind me and leaned on Justin's desk. He had a tissue in one hand, and his nose was still red from being sick. He'd quickly recuperated, but the flu had left him in a rather cranky, groggy mood. "Don't tell me there was no Plan B? You know, in case they got stuck somewhere?"

Justin's lips tightened before leaning back. "I'm sure they had some alternative plans worked up while they were on the road. But, we didn't work on any additional plans in case they didn't return. It seemed to be a straightforward plan. Low risk."

The front door opened, and cold wind hit my cheeks. Justin lunged forward to keep his papers from blowing away. A man walked in. He removed his scarf before I recognized him as one of New Eden's handymen. He crossed his arms over his chest. "They're not back, are they?"

Justin sighed and dropped his pen. "Not yet."

The man stomped a couple steps closer. "I told you that they never should've left. We've lost our last remaining squadron, and it's your fault. You were greedy to demand a Thanksgiving feast, and now look what's happened."

"Calm down, Folsom," Justin said. "The squadron is probably running late."

"Late? You mean like Smith's squadron? Or Martin's squadron? How many more men have to die before you learn that we shouldn't send our squadrons out there?"

I winced at the man's biting words and flashed a glance at Jase, who seemed as uncomfortable as I was to be in the same room as this pair.

Justin seemed oblivious to the remark and gave the man a calm gaze. "Those were extenuating circumstances. The zeds are no longer a serious issue, and the Black Sheep have been broken and disbanded. It's safer now."

"Safer?" the man balked. "How about the wild dogs? How about all the bandits we don't know about? You keep sending men out to die, when we already have everything we need to survive within these fences."

"You're only thinking of the status quo. We don't have enough if we grow our numbers," Justin replied quickly.

The man waved him off and headed back to the door. He opened it, letting the cold wind blow in. He faced Justin one more time. "I'm raising a vote of no confidence at the next council meeting. Your dictatorship has killed enough men."

With that, he left and slammed the door shut behind him.

I watched the man walk outside the window and disappear down the sidewalk. Outside, the day was a dark gray, with the sun hidden by layers upon layers of clouds. It was almost as though something were casting a giant shadow over us. It was exactly as I felt.

Justin sighed. "Sorry about the interruption."

"He's not exactly one of your cheerleaders," I said.

Justin chuckled drily. "Folsom voted for the other guy."

"Ah," I said. "And, I'm guessing the other guy is campaigning again."

Justin shook his head. "My opponent was Randy Smith."

Jase elbowed me, and I shrugged and gave him my I-didn't-know look.

"Smith's squadron was overtaken by zeds near Lincoln last summer," Justin continued.

"Sorry," I muttered.

"It's okay." Justin smiled weakly. "I'm sure there are at least a dozen folks out there right now who want to be running this place. But enough about politics. Now, if you don't mind, I have more papers to read and sign."

I took a step back but didn't leave. I eyed Jase, and he returned a hard look. I nodded and then turned back to Justin. "Clutch always keeps his word. The squadron missed their deadline, which means something is up."

"We don't leave our people out there," Jase added.

Justin closed his eyes for a moment. "And what exactly do you propose?"

I began. "I—"

"We," Jase interrupted.

I smiled. "*We*—Jase and I—will look for them."

Justin stood. "No way. Absolutely not. There's no way I'll let a teenager and a—"

"Woman?" I finished for him, my brow raised. "Really, Justin, the times have changed. Jase and I are scouts. We know how to get around out there."

"Besides," Jase said. "We're new to New Eden. If something happened to us, it wouldn't be as bad as if something happened to Zach or you."

Justin shot a hard look. "You're wrong. You would be sorely missed." He grabbed his radio and barked a command. "Send Tom to my house." He set the radio down without waiting for the response. He eyed us. "If you go, I'm sending Tom with you."

I shook my head. "Jase and I can move quickly on our own. We're used to being out there. And, we don't want to put anyone at risk who doesn't need to be."

"Tom is with the squadron. He had the flu the morning they headed out, but he's doing much better now. If anyone went, I'd prefer it would be only Tom. The squadron may already be lost," Justin said. "It doesn't make sense to lose more people searching for them."

"Bullshit," I snapped. "It makes a hell of a lot more sense than sitting on your ass and signing your name a hundred times."

"This is important—"

"Oh, buy a rubber stamp already," Jase added drily.

"We're going, and we don't need your approval," I said. "The last time I checked, all citizens had the right to pass through the gates at any time."

"You're not prisoners here, but if you're gone for more than a day, you'll have to sit through quarantine again."

"Fine," I said.

"Fine," Jase said.

Tom strolled in at that moment, and the redhead with a full beard paused to take in the full scene before walking for Justin's desk. He reminded me of an easygoing lumberjack, and I suspected he even wore a plaid flannel underneath his brown coat and coveralls. Hell, he could've been mistaken for a model on the front of a maple syrup bottle. "What's up, boss?"

"Thanks for coming, Tom. Are you up for a little trip?"

He smiled like he already knew what Justin was thinking. "Sure. I could be ready to head out in thirty minutes."

"Cash and Jase have their minds made up to go and look for the rest of your squadron. You were involved in the planning. I want you with them."

Tom nodded. "I'm fine with that. We'll just be driving, so it should be safe enough. To be honest, I was planning on heading out to look for them today, anyway." He thought for a moment, then eyed Jase and me. "Are you sure you're up for heading outside the fence? We could be gone until dark."

"We're good," we replied simultaneously.

Tom shrugged. "If you're good, I'm good."

Justin's eyelids became heavy, as though he were physically drained. "What's the plan?"

"Easy," I said before anyone else spoke. "We'll take a single vehicle with enough fuel to get to Omaha and back. We'll follow the same route the squadron took."

"We'll need the map Clutch left with you," Tom said to Justin.

Justin ruffled through his papers.

Clutch had talked me through his mission the night before he left. Whenever we planned a mission of some kind, we talked through it together. It helped us think of risks or gaps we hadn't covered.

Last night, when Clutch didn't return home, I couldn't sleep. I tossed and turned in bed and checked the front door every ten minutes. The night's silence was broken only by the howling of the wild packs. I had tried to draw Clutch's route from memory, but the truth was, I always had lousy navigation skills. Jase, on the other hand, had a gift for navigating. There was a reason I always took him when I flew over the Fox Park area. But, unfortunately, Jase had been down with the flu when Clutch went through the squadron's plan and route. If Jase hadn't gotten sick, we would've had a map drawn from scratch and been on the road already.

When the night had given way to a cloudy morning and Clutch hadn't yet returned, my heart had felt like someone had dropped a hundred-pound weight on it. I'd already made up my mind and was packed to go by the time Jase made an appearance in the kitchen. Though, he'd evidently had the same idea, since he met me in the kitchen fully geared up. "I'm ready," was all he said, and it was all he needed to say.

"Ah, here it is," Justin said before flattening a map on

the table. He pointed to a line drawn with blue marker. "This is the route they were taking both ways, and these dots are the general area of the big-box stores they were going to check out." He tapped on two X's on the map. "The interstate is blocked here and here." He continued to speak as he drew lines along smaller highways. "If you run into trouble, I recommend you take these roads. We know they're clear."

Jase took the map, folded it, and stuck it inside his coat.

Justin looked at Tom. "Is your radio fully charged?"

"I had it on the charger all night," he replied.

Justin nodded. "Okay, then. Report in every hour until you're out of range, which is roughly twenty miles. And, as soon as you're back in range, you better report in."

"I know the routine," Tom added.

"I know," Justin said, sighing. "And, take the F-150. It'll be the best for the trip."

Tom turned to Jase and me. "How soon can you be ready? You'll need food and warm gear to get through a couple days. I'd like to get on the road as early as possible."

"We're ready now," Jase said.

Tom smiled. "All right then. I left my bag at my house. We'll head out in thirty minutes."

We turned to leave, and Jase paused, glancing back at Justin. "Don't worry. We'll bring the squadron back with us."

I kept silent, praying that when we brought back the squadron, we'd be bringing back our friends and family and not a truckload of corpses.

PRUDENCE

CHAPTER X

The day was cold, but the sun shone brightly. Cold enough and bright enough that two rainbow sundogs appeared on either side of the sun, haloing the brilliant star like celestial gems. I shaded my eyes and slid on my pair of aviator sunglasses.

There was a strange nostalgia about being back on the road. While being on the constant lookout for trouble was exhausting, I found it easier to breathe in the open space. Especially now that any zeds we came across stood frozen in place like statues in a Tim Burton film.

With most zeds having made what I hoped was their final pilgrimage south, I wondered if the worst was over. The fence kept out animals easily enough, but it never could've kept out the herds of zeds. If the capital hadn't nuked the south, it would be a matter of time before the herds had killed us all.

Had it only been nine months since the outbreak? It seemed like ages ago. Yet, it had taken only a sliver of the years I'd lived to see the world decimated.

Jase coughed and popped a cough drop into his mouth. Even though he'd recuperated, it seemed the junk in his chest would linger longer. It was the same with everyone who'd caught the bug, and I worried how many of those cases would turn into bronchitis or life-threatening pneumonia.

Spring couldn't come soon enough. I remembered the feasts my mother would prepare for each seasonal equinox. It was a tradition that had been passed down through her family for generations. I remembered the dates of the equinoxes as much as the dates of any holiday. After all, they were a holiday in my family. I frowned. "What's today's date?"

Jase shrugged. "I don't know. Why?"

Tom concentrated. "Is it November 24? No, maybe it's the 25th" His lips tightened. "I can't remember. Thanksgiving is in two days. That's all I remember."

"I'll find a calendar," I said. "It's important to keep track of dates."

Jase rolled his eyes. "You're such a nerd."

I poked my tongue out at him. He grinned and turned away. Tom drove us in silence for the next hour while I stared hazily out the window. Hints of snow bunched in the shallow crevices of the plowed fields. Dozens upon dozens of unmoving, white wind turbines stood watch, silent scarecrows in the endless fields. No sign of the squadron, let alone any remnants of humanity.

Movement ahead caught my eye, and I squinted to make out the shapes. Ahead of us in the ditch were several furred shapes. They were tearing into something. When I saw a piece of blue clothing, I sighed. "Just a zed," I muttered to no one in particular, hoping that was true.

"I can't imagine they taste good," Jase said.

I nodded. "Eating diseased meat can't be good for them."

"They're starving," Tom said. "It's hard to imagine. In a single day, there were so many dogs and other pets abandoned by their caregivers. They were suddenly forced to hide from something that looked like their masters and search for their own food. I'm amazed as many survived as they did."

The dogs looked up as we passed by and cocked their heads, as though they were trying to remember the sound of engines. They didn't look healthy. Their fur was matted, and their eyes glassy.

"What will happen when they run out of zeds to eat?"

I swallowed. "I'm guessing they'll either turn on each other or starve to death. Either way, it won't be pretty. Poor things."

"Sometimes I'm glad Betsy didn't make it," Jase said softly, fingering the small gold cross he wore around his neck. "If something happened to me, I wouldn't want her out here, living like this."

I remembered the day he showed up at Clutch's farm, cradling his injured dog, which had been attacked by Jase's zed father. The small collie had sacrificed herself to protect Jase from his own father and had paid the price.

"It's hard to believe," Jase continued. "All these dogs were someone's pet at one time."

"Yeah," I said, hoping he'd move on to another topic.

"I never see any small dogs. They must've been killed by zeds or the packs in the early days."

I thought of my parents' adorable Shih Tzu, Peaches. How the little fur ball would curl up in my lap within five minutes of my being in the house. She was the sweetest thing, always happy to see me. And, boy was she smart. That little dog somehow knew my mom needed her insulin even before my mom did.

"I'll try to reach Clutch again," I said abruptly and ran through all the channels we used on the radio. After a few minutes of hearing nothing but static, I rummaged through my backpack and pulled out a can of Spam and some crackers. We'd taken all our rations for the remainder of the week to play it safe.

When we'd left this morning, we'd said no good-byes. Instead, Jase and I had dropped a note on the counter before we'd made our way for Justin's house. By then, we'd already known that we were either leaving to search for Clutch, Griz, and the rest of the squadron or getting arrested.

I grabbed a spoon and popped open the can of salty meat. "I'll eat an early lunch, and then we can switch seats, Tom," I said before scooping out a sliver of the meat and squeezing it in between two stale crackers.

Tom didn't take his eyes off the road. "I can eat and drive."

"Tut, tut," Jase scolded from the backseat. "Clutch hasn't ground that rule into you yet?"

"Which rule is that?" Tom asked.

"Everyone needs to focus on his one job. The driver focuses on driving. The passengers focus on looking out."

"Cash is eating while looking out," Tom countered.

I nodded. "But all I have to do is sit here and look. You have to be ready to slam on the brakes or crank the wheel in case something happens."

Tom smiled. "And what do you think is going to happen out here? Any remaining zeds are too slow. The Black Sheep are gone, and the roads are clear."

I shrugged. "You never know. You have to be ready for anything. Or, like Clutch says, you always have to keep a step ahead." I found myself thinking back to everything Clutch had taught us. I knew I wouldn't have lasted the first day of the outbreak if he hadn't taken me with him to his farm. He'd saved my life, Jase's life, and that of so many others.

Still, he didn't think he was worth anything. Idiot.

"One time," Jase began, "Cash and I were flying over

this one small town, looking for survivors, when we came across this flat-roofed building. Some folks had run out onto the roof. We turned to drop the official Camp Fox goody bag—some food and directions to Fox Park—when they started to throw bricks at us. For real. They even had a big slingshot set up and everything. If Cash hadn't banked hard right then, we would've been clobbered."

I chuckled drily. "Yeah, we didn't always get the welcome mat rolled out."

"But, you tried to help. That's what counts." He slowed down. "I'm getting hungry. Here's a good spot to refuel and switch. At this speed, we'll be to Omaha within a few hours."

"We'd be there already if Tom could drive faster than thirty," Jase said. "I think I just got my first gray hair."

I smirked but didn't say anything. Tom wasn't comfortable driving fast. Safety was more important than speed. Even though every fiber of my being wanted to rush into Omaha to find the squadron.

I dumped the empty Spam tin into a plastic bag, glugged a long drink of water, grabbed my rifle, and looked outside at the flat Nebraska fields, with only the interstate dividing the land.

Tom shifted the truck into Park and cut the engine.

When he went to open the door, I grabbed his arm. "Hold on."

He glanced back at me. "What?"

After a moment of scanning the wide-open space

around us, I relaxed. "I'm used to zeds running out from every direction to eat me. I guess I'm not used to the quiet yet."

"It's okay," Jase said. "I had the same gut reaction, too. It's weird, not expecting zeds anymore."

"There are still plenty out there," I cautioned. "We still have to be careful."

"But they're frozen stiff by now," Tom said as he opened the door and stepped outside.

I couldn't open the door without scanning the area one final time. This particular section of the interstate had no cars on it. The roadblocks of crashed cars seemed to be centered at the cities and towns. Weeds grew tall in the shallow ditches and as bold tufts in the unplanted fields. Something could hide in there.

"Cash, it's all clear," Tom said.

"I know," I said and pushed open the door. Frigid air blasted my face.

Jase followed. He stayed near me, and it grated on my nerves to know that he felt the need to protect me, when it was supposed to be the other way around.

Tom was already up on the truck bed and unraveling the fuel hose and portable pump. He connected it to one of the three, 55-gallon drums of gas we brought along with us. He handed me the clear plastic hose. I slid my rifle over my shoulder and grabbed the end of the hose. Jase stood watch while I opened the gas cap and slid the hose in. "Ready," I said.

Tom started pumping. At first, a slow trickle of gas

ran through the hose, and then more and more came. Tom continued to manually pump for a tedious ten minutes, and I listened to the gas going into the tank. Jase walked casually around the truck, doing a full circle every couple of minutes or so.

When the sound of the gas gurgling in the tank changed, I held up my hand. "It's full."

Tom stopped pumping and wiped his brow. Even in the freezing air, he was sweating from pumping gas. Once I shook out the last drips from the hose, I pulled it from the tank and handed it back to Tom, who unhooked the pump and rolled everything back up.

He jumped off the back of the truck and rubbed his hands. "We're all set."

I nodded and headed back to the truck.

"Shotgun," Jase said as he butted in front of Tom at the passenger door.

"After you," Tom said rather sarcastically before stepping back, opening the back door, and climbing in.

I strapped myself into the driver's seat and started up the truck. Immediately, warm air belted out from the heater, and I savored the heat on my skin. Jase picked up the map from the dash and studied it. A quick glance to the backseat showed Tom biting into some kind of tortilla wrap. I shifted the truck into gear and slowly picked up speed.

Before the outbreak, I'd had a lead foot. Two speeding tickets a year was my average. Now, I never drove above fifty-five for two reasons. One, the faster I was going, the less time I'd have to react; and two, driving any faster would hurt the gas mileage. Even though I was anxious to find Clutch, I would've been stupid to rush. For all we knew, they hadn't even made it to Omaha.

Tom spoke in between bites. "It's kind of peaceful out here with nothing to remind us of the outbreak."

"Yeah," Jase said before taking a bite of his own lunch. "If you don't count the complete lack of anybody on an interstate except for us."

"I don't miss the chaos of what life was like before," I said. "But, I sure miss a lot of the conveniences we had."

"It's like Mother Nature forced a reboot," Tom said. "When people knocked the world out of balance, she sent in a disease to knock things back into line."

I considered his words for a moment. "You're assuming the outbreak wasn't man-made."

"You're assuming it was?" Tom asked.

I shrugged. "No. Maybe. I don't know. I remember there was a lot of speculation in the first days, but no one came out and said, 'this is the cause.'"

"I think the worse assumption," Jase started, "is to assume the outbreak is going to reset the balance. This isn't Star Wars, and there's no 'force' out there to help keep a balance," he air-quoted. "You've seen what the virus is doing to animals that feed on the zeds. The virus has only one goal, and that goal is to destroy. It's the Grim Reaper of viruses."

"Wow," I said. "When did you become the

philosopher?"

A red light came on the instrument panel, and I frowned. *Check engine.* "Uh oh," I said. "Tom, you don't happen to be car mechanic by any chance?"

"I didn't own a car until I was out of college," Tom replied. "Why?"

"What's wrong?" Jase asked.

I tapped on the instrument panel, even though I knew that did no good. "I think that last batch of gas was bad or had water in it. Either way, the engine isn't happy about something."

"It still sounds okay. Maybe it's a fluke," Jase said.

"Fingers crossed," I added.

Tom leaned forward to look over Jase's shoulder at the map. He pointed. "Take the next exit. If we need to swap vehicles, we should take a county road. There would be more houses, so hopefully, a better chance for finding a vehicle. If the battery is dead, we should be able to swap in the truck's battery. Then we'll be good to go."

My muscles tightened as I gripped the wheel. It took only three miles before the engine started to make a clacking sound, metal pinging on metal in a regular rhythm.

Jase pointed. "There's the exit. Now, if only we can keep this beater going until we find new wheels."

Evidently, the truck didn't relish being called "beater," because the very next second the engine sputtered and died. Several lights blinked on the instrument panel. "Shit," I said. The truck's momentum slowed without power. My heart pounded with every foot of ground it covered. I found myself leaning forward, to edge the truck farther down the road, but it crept to a stop on the inclined exit ramp.

"Da da da dun," Jase chanted ominously.

I scanned the area around us for a house, danger, anything.

Tom spoke. "Robert Frost once said in a poem something like, 'I have taken the path less traveled by, and that has made all the difference.'"

"Yeah, but Frost never said if that difference was good or bad." I grabbed my rifle and my binoculars and stepped outside. I walked around to the back of the truck and climbed onto the bed and then onto the roof. Cold wind blew through my jeans. Shading my eyes against the sun, I made a count of the buildings in the area.

Jase climbed up next to me, and the roof dented in. "At least we have some options." He pointed. "I'm thinking we go for those two houses across the road from each other."

"I was thinking the same thing," I said, looking through the binoculars. "Both have all their garage and building doors closed. We could get lucky."

"But the house to the north is closer," Tom said from the ground.

"True," I said and hopped down. "But, there's not enough sunlight left to hit all three houses today. With two houses, we have twice the chance of finding a vehicle we could use."

"And twice the risk for trouble," Jase added.

"I thought you said you wanted to check out that pair of houses first."

Jase gave a weak smile. "I thought we *should* check them out first. I didn't say I *wanted* to check them out first. I *want* to stay in the truck and call AAA, but their service has really gone downhill this year."

"Well, I say let's grab our gear and hit the road. I don't like standing out in the middle of nowhere," I said and walked around the truck and grabbed my backpack. I rummaged through it and grabbed a ski mask, stocking hat, and gloves.

In less than fifteen minutes, we had the truck pushed back onto the interstate and parked under the overpass, the best camouflage we could think of to minimize its appearance in the unlikely event someone passed through this area.

Jase, Tom, and I walked up the exit ramp and turned left on the small highway. The pair of houses stood about a mile away. Close enough to see their garages were closed, but too far to see any signs of violence or danger.

We kept Tom at a quicker pace than he was clearly used to, but he didn't complain. I hated being out in the open, especially in an area I wasn't familiar with. We had no idea what could be hiding within any of those buildings or behind the small cropping of trees. I felt like a sitting duck.

At our quick pace, we reached the pair of houses in ten minutes. We slowed as we examined each one. "Which one do you want to try first?" I asked, looking from the white-and-brick ranch on the right to the blue two-story on the left.

Jase held up a finger. "Eenie meanie miney moe, catch a tiger by its toe. If it hollers, let it go, eenie meanie miney *moe*." He pointed to the house on the left. "The Smurf house, it is."

"All right," I said, rubbing my cold fingers. "Using a startlingly brilliant display of deductive reasoning, Jase has made the call. The garage is detached, so I'd say that's a great place to start."

Jase and Tom nodded, and we walked slowly up the driveway, expecting something to jump out from behind the building at any second. I watched the house as we walked by it to the garage, which was set farther back from the road.

"Cover me," I said and tiptoed onto the porch. The big oak door stood open, a screen door the only barrier between us and anything inside. I could already smell the rank odor of one or more zeds inside. A blend of putrid disease and decomposition. I stayed to the left of the screen door and threw a quick glance inside. Chairs were knocked over. I backed quietly off the porch.

"I'm pretty sure the house still has its occupants, so we should keep it quiet."

Jase was already slinging his rifle and pulling out his

machete.

"They should be frozen," Tom said.

"You want to bet the farm on that?" I asked as I swapped my rifle for the machete I had strapped to the front of my backpack. "No need to draw any unwanted attention if we don't have to."

Jase put a hand on Tom's shoulder. "I don't know about you, but between Cash and me, we have thirty-five rounds of ammo left. I'd prefer to save those until I really need them if I can."

Pride swelled in my chest. In a matter of months, Jase had transitioned from a high schooler to a man. To see him morph into a leader gave me hope for his future. If anyone could make it in this world, Jase could. With everything he'd lost, what would've broken most seemed to have honed him. Out of us all, Jase still had the strongest connection to his humanity. Clutch had always been jaded, and I was certainly jaded. But, Jase…he was the best of us.

We spread out as we approached the garage. It was an older building with no windows, not even small ones in the doors.

Jase reached the door first. He put his ear up to it. After a moment, he looked to us and shook his head. I took off my sunglasses and nodded to Tom. "Get your flashlight ready," I whispered. I stood to Jase's right and held up three fingers. Two. One.

Jase pulled the door open and jumped back. I stepped forward, ready to swing the machete at anything that moved. Nothing came forward from the dark. The air was cold but fresh. A beam of light shone from over my shoulder, and I could see a single compact car sitting under a layer of dust.

"It's clear," I said and stepped inside.

Tom followed, and he shone his light around the small garage. The undisturbed dust showed no signs of recent activity, so I relaxed my grip on my machete.

Paint cans and boxes sat on open shelves. I walked past them and opened the car door. The keys were in the ignition, and I sat on the seat. Holding my breath, I turned the key but nothing happened. No lights came on, not even a growl of an engine trying to start.

I looked at Jase and Tom, frowned, and shook my head.

"This car won't work," I heard Tom say from behind the car. "Two flat tires."

He kicked the side of the car, and I cringed at the noise.

Jase popped his head in the door. "Geez. Can you make a little more noise next time?"

"Oh, sorry," Tom said sheepishly.

"Let's check the other garage," I said, not bothering to shut the driver's door.

Jase was still standing watch outside.

I slid my sunglasses back on. "See anything?"

"Not yet," he replied. "Maybe we're far enough out of any towns that there isn't anything out here."

"We can hope," I said.

As we walked down the driveway, Tom slowed near the house. "I wonder how all the people who were at home during the outbreak became infected."

I shrugged. "Maybe a loved one brought the virus home. Maybe a neighbor. Maybe they also ate the infected food. Given enough time, it seemed as though the infection found a way into every house."

We crossed the highway and approached the ranch. This one had an attached garage, with two grain bins and a white tin building in the yard to the left. The building reminded me of the stocked Humvee we'd hidden before we entered New Eden. We really could've used that vehicle today.

A doghouse stood next to the garage. A corpse that was nothing more than fur and bones lay inside the kennel. A chain attached to the doghouse was still connected to the dog collar. I swallowed and looked away. I always hated seeing reminders of how the virus killed things even outside its reach.

"Poor thing," Jase said softly.

I continued forward to the garage. This one had windows in the garage door, making it easy to peer inside. "Shit."

"What is it?" Tom asked from behind me.

"The garage is empty." I turned around and frowned. "I guess we have to check the bigger buildings."

None of us delayed in walking past the kennel. As we passed the grain bins, I made a mental note to check it for grain that we could use. Staring at the metal, vivid memories of the first innocent I killed filled my mind. She had been a young girl who'd been hurt worse than any doctor could fix. Her tears still haunted my dreams. When I put the barrel to her temple and pulled the trigger, I killed more than her. I killed something inside me that day.

My innocence.

When we reached the big building, I clenched my eyes shut briefly to squeeze away the vision. When I opened them, she was gone, and I sucked in a deep, cold breath to ground me.

Like the garage, this building also had windows in it, and had shrubs planted around it. I imagined it had been a meticulously maintained place by its proud owners, but weeds and grass had overgrown and given everything an unkempt appearance.

Jase jogged up to a window. He spun around, his eyes wide. "Hot dog. You guys have got to see this."

Tom and I cramped in around him and looked through the window. Sitting under a stream of sunlight sat a pristine, 1950s Chevrolet truck.

Tom whistled. "Now, that's style."

"If we can keep anything running, it'd be that," Jase said.

Tom's brows rose in disbelief. "An old truck? Why?"

"The old stuff isn't as finicky with gas. Fewer computers, I guess," Jase replied. Not staying around to converse, he hustled to the door and peered through the window. "Everything looks clear. You guys ready?"

I couldn't help but smile. He sounded like a kid at Christmas. I walked over to him. "I'll take the door. You can be first in."

His grin widened. He threw a glance back at Tom and lifted three fingers. He quickly counted down to one, and I threw the door open. Jase jumped inside, and Tom followed.

The windows let in enough light that we didn't need flashlights. I stood watch at the door, looking from outside to inside and back outside again. After a few minutes, Jase jogged over to the yellow truck and waved me inside. "All clear."

After one final look outside, I stepped inside and shut the door. The air smelled lightly of a car shop. Oil, rubber, and gas. On the walls hung various hubcaps and Chevy signs. A large chevron was painted across the center of the floor. Clearly, the truck's owner was an aficionado and loved this truck dearly.

Tom continued to walk around the shop, inspecting various items, and I watched Jase. He opened the door and sat gingerly onto the leather seats. He ran his hands across the dash. "This baby is a work of art."

"Yeah, but can this work of art start?"

He held up a hand. "You can't rush perfection."

After long moments of cooing words to the truck, Jase turned the key. The engine moaned but didn't catch. After a couple attempts, the engine moaned less and less as what little juice the battery had left was now gone. Jase patted the dash before stepping out. "The good news is she's full of gas and ready to start. We don't need to change batteries. She just needs a jump."

"But we don't have any electricity," I said.

Jase shook his head. "Don't need it. The battery from the other truck should be enough to get us going."

"There are some garden supplies in back," Tom said. "We could use the wheelbarrow to transport the battery. It will be easier than carrying it a mile."

"We have about two hours until sunset," I said as I checked to make sure the door locked. "We need a secure place for the night."

"Why can't we keep going? Omaha can't be more than an hour or two away."

"Which puts us getting into a town full of who knows what after dark," I said. "We can't risk moving at night. And, I think this is as good a place as any for tonight."

"I'd rather be out there searching for the squadron," Tom said.

"If you drove faster, we could be in Omaha by now," Jase countered.

"We're here for the night," I said. "Bundle up. It's going to get pretty dang cold in here, colder than it is already."

"Never fear," Jase said. "I saw one of those propane heaters on a shelf. That'll keep us toasty."

"That solves one problem," I said. "But the bigger problem is all these windows. If we use any light whatsoever once the sun sets, we'll be in a fishbowl.

Anyone or anything in the area couldn't help but notice. Maybe the house will be easier to hide in."

Jase shrugged. "But, we've already cleared this shop. We can do what we used to do. We get settled in early so when the sun sets, we go dark. And, we rotate shifts through the night."

I smirked. "You really want to stay in here, don't you."

He grinned. "Heck, yeah. I don't want to leave this girl all alone."

I sighed. "Okay. Let's get this building secure for the night. When the sun sets, we go dark. Tom, you take first watch. I'll take the midnight shift, and Jase, you get early morning. As soon as the sun rises, we'll grab the battery and get Jase's new baby up and running."

It took the full two hours to prepare for the night. We had to clear things from the floor so we wouldn't trip in the dark. We set up a tin wire with tools tied onto it at the door to serve as a noisemaker in case someone managed to open the door without us noticing. We had to set up the propane heater—which was full of propane, thank God—and our bedding for the night. Jase, of course, quickly claimed the front seat of the truck. I unrolled my sleeping bag on the bed, while Tom set his bag on a camp chair he'd found somewhere.

We ate together as the sun turned from bright yellow to deep gold to finally a reddish glaze before disappearing. I tried to reach Clutch on the radio again, but we were still too far away, their batteries were dead, or they couldn't answer. I prayed for either of the first two options.

As I lay down to squeeze in a few hours of sleep before my shift, I felt the silence. There were no dog or wolf howls. It was a sound I'd grown accustomed to at New Eden. A constant reminder that danger trolled outside the fence. But here, even within sixty miles or so of Omaha, there was nothing but silence.

I fell asleep fast and hard.

I woke to the sunlight peeking through the windows, and I jerked up. I looked around to get my bearings. Tom sat in his chair, snoring softly. Jase was a tangle of limbs on the front seat. I jumped onto the concrete, ran to the door, and winced when my calf reminded me it didn't savor quick movements in the morning. Luckily, outside, nothing had changed. I double-checked to make sure the door was locked before going to each window and looking outside.

Once I was comfortable we were alone, I walked over to Tom's chair and kicked him in the leg.

His eyes blinked open. "Wha — what it is?"

"Why didn't you wake me? No one was on watch this morning."

He rubbed his eyes. "Oh. I must've dozed off. Sorry."

"You're sorry?" I opened my mouth and then closed it, glaring at him. "What if something happened last night? What if someone or something attacked?"

"Nothing did."

"If something did, we would've been sitting ducks."

"But, there's no one around here. We're safe in here."

"There's no such thing as *safe* anymore." I spun on my heel and stuffed my bedding into my backpack.

Jase had wakened, and he looked around, frowning. "Why'd you let me sleep through my watch?"

"I didn't," I said. "Tom fell asleep, and I slept straight through the night."

Jase scowled in Tom's direction. "Dumbass."

Tom held up his hands. "I said I was sorry."

I slung on my backpack. "Let's go get that battery so we can get back on the road."

Tom had the common sense to stay quiet during our walk back to the truck. He pushed the wheelbarrow. It squeaked relentlessly, adding a headache to my already frustrating morning. The good news was that the truck was exactly as we'd left it. The bad news was the battery took us longer than we'd planned to charge the old Chevy. Once Jase got the truck running, he found an oil leak, and the two men spent the next ten hours improvising a solution. By then, it was dark, and we stayed a second night. Tom fell asleep again, but I hadn't let myself sleep, so I was ready.

When Tom woke the next morning, neither Jase nor I had any interest in talking with him. I opened the shop door, Jase started up the Chevy, and we piled into the front seat. We drove back to our stranded truck and loaded one of the drums of gasoline onto the back of the Chevy. When we pulled away from the truck, I squinted at the house to the north. "Stop," I said and rolled down the window.

Jase hit the brakes.

"What is it?" Tom asked.

"Give me a minute." I rummaged through my bag and pulled out the small pair of binoculars. I zoomed in on the house the opposite direction of the two houses we'd checked out. "There are horses with saddles in the yard."

"You sure?" Jase asked.

I nodded and handed my binoculars across Tom to Jase. "See for yourself."

"We should stop and talk to them," Tom said.

Jase and I both stared blankly at him.

"What?" he asked. "It's the right thing to do."

"Yeah, if you want to get us killed," Jase said.

"It's not the smart thing to do," I said. "We have no idea how they would greet strangers. From personal experience, you've got about a ten percent chance they're going to welcome you with open arms."

"Cash was an actuary in a past life. She knows," Jase added.

"We have a mission already," I said. "We have to find the squadron and bring them home. No detours. It would be nice to be back to New Eden before Thanksgiving is over."

"So far, this Thanksgiving sucks," Jase said and hit the gas. He didn't stop until we reached the outskirts of Omaha. The dead city showed its gashes from being bombed. Splintered buildings stood in the distant city center. Only the suburbs remained somewhat intact, and many of those buildings had burned or collapsed.

With every mile, more and more stranded and crashed vehicles filled the interstate. But, unlike Des Moines, I saw no zeds standing outside. Only remnants of bodies. Lots and lots of bodies. I examined the map in between glances out the window. "We should see the store any time now."

Tom pointed. "There it is, a Costco."

Jase took the exit ramp. Vehicles had been pushed out of the way far enough for us to weave through a narrow path. The first zed I found was sitting in the driver's seat of one of the cars. The zed's hand gripped the steering wheel as it stared at us with lifeless eyes, but it made no movement.

"See? Frozen solid," Tom said.

I grabbed my binoculars. Frost-covered minivans, SUVs, cars, and trucks were parked outside the store. "No sign of the squadron's vehicles," I mumbled.

"They must've continued on to find another store," Tom said.

My eyes narrowed. "Someone blocked the main doors." In front of where the main doors should be, a semi-truck and trailer sat, obscuring any sign of entrance.

"There." Jase pointed up.

I followed his direction, and saw a man waving down at us from the roof of the building. I could see his wide grin, and my heart leapt. "It's Clutch."

I rolled down my window and waved back, squealing in delight. Clutch motioned to the back of the store, and I nodded. "He wants us to go to the back entrance."

"They must be parked behind there," Tom said.

Jase gunned the engine and sped around the corner. "Now, *this* is Thanksgiving."

Something wasn't adding up. "Why are they still here?"

When we turned the next corner, it started to make sense. "Where are the trucks?" Tom asked.

Jase put the truck into park. When he went to open his door, I yanked his arm. "Wait."

He turned to me, confused.

I pointed to the row of shrubs outlining the parking lot. "Look."

Hundreds of glistening eyes peered out at us.

CHAPTER XI

The steel door to the back entrance opened a crack, and Griz's face appeared. "Pull up as close as you can to this door," he said. "That way, you can get inside without getting pounced."

Jase reversed and pulled the truck up to the entrance, leaving only a few feet in between the driver's side of the truck and the steel door. He cut the engine and grabbed the keys. I grabbed my bag.

Griz threw open the door, and it dinged into the truck. "Careful," Jase said as he opened his door and jumped inside. Tom slid across the seat, followed last by me. I heard movement behind me, and I shoved forward, falling into Tom and onto the floor of the store as the door slammed shut.

I looked up to see a hand reaching out. I grabbed it, and Griz tugged me to my feet and into a hard embrace.

"It's good to see some friendly faces around here," he said.

"Now, we can get out of here and back home," Marco said.

"Hey, Marco." I gave him a hug.

Jase waved. "Polo!" Marco waved back.

"What happened here?" I asked. "Where are your trucks?"

"That's the question of the day," Griz replied. "We just about had them loaded, and then some asshats blocked the door and took off with our trucks, like we were a drive-through window."

"We tried to reach you by radio," Jase said. "You guys had us worried."

"Batteries are dead," Griz said. "Hard to believe, but there's nothing to recharge them in here. You'd think a giant store like this would have generators, but not a single one left on the shelves, and the store's backup generators were bone-dry."

Solar stake lights were lying down all the aisles, bringing light to the shadows. Three men came around a corner, and I ran toward them. Clutch barely had time to stop before I jumped into his arms. He lifted me, and I hugged him. When I pulled away, I gave him a halfhearted glare. "You see? I told you I'd come after you."

He smiled. "I figured as much." Then, his smile faded. "But, you shouldn't have come. It's dangerous out there."

175

I shot him a hard look, and he lowered me to my feet. "Which is exactly why we came for you. You don't think we'd leave you guys out here to die, do you?"

Jase came up and slapped Clutch's shoulder. "It's good to see you, man. What do you think of my new truck?"

Clutch's brow rose. "A 1957 Chevy? She's a beaut. How'd you come across her?"

"Long story," I said. "Jase can fill you in on the drive back. Speaking of which, what needs done so we can hit the road?"

"We've been waiting out the hungry mouths outside," Clutch replied. "Once we knew the bandits weren't coming back, we switched gears to finding new vehicles. Unfortunately, that turned out to be much easier said than done."

"That's an understatement," Griz said. "We didn't get more than five feet out the back door before a pack of mangy dogs came at us. Within an hour, there were probably two hundred of the buggers out there. Although, a city the size of this, there's bound to be thousands of dogs that managed to get free and survive. Anyway, we moved to the front of the store and cut through the back of the big rig. The bandits left it running when they used it to block the doors. But, by the time we cut through the box to get to the cab, its fuel tanks were dry. We'd already burned our ammo to clear the store, so we've been waiting for the dogs to find something more interesting. But, they're persistent and ornery little bastards."

"Why'd you have to kill the zeds inside?" Tom asked. "They should've been frozen through and through."

Clutch chuckled drily. "The ones outside may be frozen, but the ones inside still had plenty of life left in them. The building's insulation must buffer enough of the cold, and they must still generate enough body heat that the temps need to drop more to stiffen them up."

I grimaced, though I'd feared as much. "So, we still have all the zeds trapped inside buildings to deal with."

"At some point, yeah," Clutch said. "But, if we wait until the temps drop more, we can take them one building at a time, like we did this one."

"Except we won't have any ammo to do this to all the buildings," I countered. "We'll have to get creative."

"And, we will. Later. Right now, we need to send out recon to secure us some transportation home," Clutch said.

"I'm guessing you already have a plan," I said.

Clutch nodded. "An easy grab-and-go. Bring our transportation to us and load up. We've collected over twenty sets of keys from the shoppers still in the store. At least a couple vehicles in the parking lot should still have juice. But, the damn mutts are between us and our wheels."

"We figured they'd get hungry and leave," Griz said. "The numbers are already down quite a bit. Within a week or so, they would've been gone." He grinned. "But now we don't have to wait for the flea-bitten mongrels to leave or eat each other."

"We'll head out in ten," Clutch said. "Griz, Marco, and I will take the truck—"

"I'll drive," Jase inserted.

Clutch watched the teenager for a moment, before giving a tight nod. "Okay. Jase will drive. The rest of us will ride in the back."

"Isn't that too dangerous?" I asked. "Can't the dogs jump up and reach you back there?"

"They could," Clutch said. "Except all of them are half-starved and many of them are sick. We should be able to block the few that can get up that high." He pointed at me. "Do you have ammo?"

"Not much. A little."

"How much is 'a little?'"

"Thirty-five rounds."

He frowned. "That's enough. I want you covering us from the roof in case this heads south." He looked around. "Everyone else, be ready to defend a perimeter at the back door and load up. We're not going to stick around this shithole once we have transportation."

A guy named Jack led me to the roof, while everyone else stayed below and prepared for what Jase called Operation: Carjack.

On the flat, empty rooftop, frostbite posed the only danger. I walked the edge of the roof until I found the right spot overlooking the parking lot. I settled onto my stomach and set up my rifle. Below, I didn't see any dogs, though some of the ones waiting out back were bound to follow the truck.

The sound of the Chevy's engine cut through the frozen air, and I focused on waiting for the truck to enter my line of sight. Once it did, I watched Jase drive the truck, with three men standing on back. Clutch stood with his sword drawn. Griz and Marco each had machetes, and Griz had added an axe to his collection.

Behind the truck followed a dozen mangy dogs. Most were large, but there were a couple mid-sized ones, though I couldn't make out any particular breeds. The procession reminded me of the Pied Piper plan we'd used several times against the zeds. Only this time, we *didn't* want to be followed.

The truck drove slowly, and I watched Marco dump a bag full of keys onto the roof of the truck. He picked them up, one by one, holding them out toward the parked cars. When the lights flashed on a red minivan, Marco thumped the roof, and the truck pulled to a stop, making a tight 'T' with the van.

The dogs circled the truck. I could hear their snarls from my position. None had jumped yet, but I had no idea how they were going to get from the truck to the van. Then, Marco jumped off the truck and onto the hood of the van. A dog lunged at him, and I fired. The dog fell back with a yelp. This incensed the other dogs, and their growls grew in volume.

"Nice shot," Jack said, and I ignored him.

Marco wiped the windshield and looked inside. He

gave the truck a thumbs up. Jase pulled away slowly, and Clutch and Griz yelled out at the dogs. Nearly all snapped around and followed them, leaving only two who seemed to be concentrating on Marco. He looked up at me, and I fired twice. Each shot took out a dog. Marco jumped down and was inside the van in no time.

The van's engine turned over and engaged, and I breathed a sigh of relief. I wanted this to be over. I hated killing animals, especially what had once been pets. There was something horribly wrong about it. The poor things were only trying to survive. We had done this to them. We had raised them as pets and then abandoned them. It only made sense for them to return to their wolf roots to survive. It made me think of Diesel. He'd be one of these dogs if he didn't have Frost or Benji to look after him. He could've been one of the dogs I'd just shot.

I squeezed my eyes shut and opened them. The truck stopped at a green SUV. This time, Griz jumped onto the hood. Fewer dogs followed Clutch's voice this time. They were learning. After I killed five dogs, at least one of which I could've sworn was a gray wolf, Griz climbed inside the SUV, and started it up.

All three vehicles — the Chevy, the SUV, and the minivan — headed back around the building.

The remaining dogs attacked their fallen comrades. It was a kill-or-be-killed world now. My shooting wasn't perfect today; they weren't all kill shots, and the injured dogs screamed in agony as the others tore into them. I couldn't get any clear shots on the poor animals. The bile rose in my throat, and I jumped to my feet. Without looking back, I crossed the roof in time to see the three vehicles form a tight semicircle around the back door.

For the second time, I got down and aimed my rifle. Now, nearly all the dogs cautiously stepped toward the vehicles. Their bristled fur and growls made it clear they weren't coming out to play.

The doors popped open, and the men ran inside. Thankfully, none of the dogs managed to get around the cars before the back door closed, so I didn't have to shoot anything else. I yanked open the access door and jogged down the stairs to find men stuffing items into shopping carts. It seemed about half of the carts were filled with beer.

Clutch shook his head. "This mission is a scrub. We don't have space for the supplies. We'll come back next week with a plan and better equipment."

"We should get the semi-truck going then," Tom said. "Take what we can now."

Clutch pursed his lips. "Good luck finding diesel. Besides, we don't know when those guys who left the truck will be back. We have no ammo and no plan to hold them off. We need to get back to New Eden and regroup. Our lives are more important than this stuff." He motioned around him. "We have three vehicles and fourteen people. Do the math. Take what you can, but what doesn't fit will get left behind."

There was some grumbling, but no one outright argued against Clutch's plan.

He continued. "When it comes time to move, you'd better move. I don't like the look of those dogs. Be careful out there. If you get rabies, game over."

"The dogs will eat anything," Jack said from behind me. "To buy us time to load, we should shoot a few. Give the rest something to keep busy with."

Shock sent me jerking around. "You can't be serious."

"It's a good idea," Clutch said. "We can use the distraction."

I hemmed for a moment. Finally, I spoke. "Why don't we throw them some food from here? There has to be something in here that we can feed them. They're starving."

"They're also sick. Their aggression could trump their hunger," Clutch said.

I narrowed my eyes.

"But, we can give it a shot," he added, and turned to the squadron. "Hey, Tom. Where was the dog food you came across earlier?"

"It's over by the shop area," one of the guys said.

Clutch held out a hand. "Then go get it."

He jumped, grabbed an empty cart, and headed in the direction he'd pointed. Two other men rushed to follow.

I took a seat and shook my head. "Why didn't you guys try feeding the dogs before? Maybe once they had food, they would've moved on."

Griz chuckled. "A city girl like you never had strays

before, huh."

I frowned. "No. Why?"

"The food would attract anything hungry in the area," Griz said. "And once they got hungry again, they'd be back for more."

"This diversion will work one time," Clutch said. "It'll keep the ones here busy for a few minutes, but at the same time, it's going to draw in a shitload more."

"Oh." I stared off for a moment. "We can try something else instead."

Clutch shook his head. "No. It's a good plan."

Ten minutes later, we had hauled ten fifty-pound bags of dog food up to the roof. I didn't carry a bag, but followed them up the stairs. Outside, we all stood along the roof edge, looking down.

"Here goes nothing," Griz said, and dropped his bag. It fell the thirty-foot drop and exploded when it hit the ground.

A dog crept forward, and then three more followed. They sniffed the food before scooping up mouthfuls of the kibble.

I couldn't help but smile. "It's working."

"Bombs away," Jase said, and dropped his bag. The remaining bags dropped, and soon, all the dogs in the area came to enjoy the feast.

"That should buy us a couple minutes," Clutch said. "Let's get out of here."

We all jogged toward the stairs. "Thanks," I said when Clutch had me go before him. "It means a lot."

He didn't say anything, but I could see in his gaze that he understood. There was enough death out there already. Anything we could do to leave one fewer scar on our souls was worth it.

"Move it, move it," Clutch ordered, and we all rushed toward the back entrance. "Head to your DV!"

Several men had full carts, and I had no idea where they were going to find room for everything. Three vehicles for fourteen people? They must've figured we had clown cars sitting out there with bottomless trunks. Not wanting to get blocked behind their carts, I squeezed between them, and Clutch did the same. Jase managed to climb over the carts, and Griz and Marco shoved their way through.

All I took from the store was a bag full of mini first-aid kits, two paperback novels, and the insert I broke free from a religious photo frame. It had the Prayer of St. Francis of Assisi. When I was a little girl, my mother used to sing that prayer when she washed dishes. Clutch carried a single bottle of whiskey. I didn't see what Griz had stuffed into his backpack.

Clutch had his sword drawn, and I situated everything so I could hold out my machete. He peeked out the door, turned back to us, and nodded. "It looks good. Time to bug out. Watch yourselves out there." He yanked open the door and we rushed forward. Several dogs eating outside the semicircle froze and ducked, as though expecting us to attack.

We didn't. Clutch opened the Chevy's door and

shoved me in, coming in behind me. Griz and Marco jumped onto the bed. Jase, who'd refused to give up the keys, quickly hopped in and shut the door. As he started the engine, I twisted around to see men climb into the other vehicles. We'd planned who would ride in which vehicle earlier so everything would move smoothly.

But, rather than climbing in, the others were busy unloading five shopping carts. Cases of beer were thrown on the roof of the mini-van. I saw movement come from under the SUV.

"Watch out!" I yelled through the glass, but no one looked up.

"God damn it," Clutch muttered. "Move, move!"

Jack didn't notice the dog creeping out from under the green vehicle until it was too late. The dog—it reminded me of a black Lab—lunged and knocked Jack onto his back. He screamed out. Someone swung a bat, and the dog was knocked away with a yelp. It limped but came at Jack again. He was pulled inside, and the door slammed shut the instant the dog made its second attack into the door.

"Lead us out of here," Clutch said, and Jase popped the truck into gear.

The vehicles were tight together, and it took Jase several turns before he was able to drive away. He winced every time the bumper hit the concrete wall or the minivan behind us. He gunned the engine but slowed down quickly to weave around the rapidly increasing number of dogs around us.

I kept watch behind us, to make sure both vehicles were following, and—more important—to make sure both Griz and Marco were safe. They had to be freezing out there, but they were both adamant about climbing on the truck rather than squeezing in the other vehicles to make the getaway faster. If only the others were as fast, Jack wouldn't have been attacked.

I wondered how Jack was doing. If he was seriously injured. I was hoping the dog hadn't bit through his clothes. If he caught rabies, there would be little anyone could do. Clutch thumbed the radio a couple times, but no one responded from the other two vehicles.

"They must not have their radios plugged in," I said. "It won't be too long before we can pull over and talk to them."

He plugged the radio back into the lighter, and dropped the radio on the dash.

Jase picked up speed once we made it onto the interstate, but he kept it slow enough that Griz and Marco didn't get knocked around too badly. Any dogs that followed drifted off, and soon we were leaving the skyline of a destroyed Omaha behind.

Griz and Marco were tucked low into the bed of the truck and snuggled together. I almost laughed until I realized how cold it must've been for them back there. I turned back to Clutch and Jase. "How much longer before we can stop? The guys will freeze back there."

"Go ten more klicks before we slow down," Clutch

said. "That should be enough distance between us and the packs in the city."

Jase cocked his head.

"Drive seven more miles," Clutch added.

"Why didn't you say so?" Jase said.

"I did," Clutch answered.

They bantered for the full seven miles before Clutch pointed to an exit and overpass. "Take us up there."

"Yes, sir," Jase said with a hint of sarcasm.

He took the exit and came to a stop in the middle of the overpass. Clutch zipped his coat up, and I opened the door and slid out. From this vantage point, we could see for miles in every direction.

Griz and Marco climbed stiffly out of the back, and I could hear their teeth chatter from where I stood. I rubbed Griz's arm. "Why don't you guys sit in the truck for now? Warm up until we figure out who's riding with whom."

"Now, that is the best thing I've heard all day," Griz said through chattering teeth.

Clutch walked around the overpass, his eyes shaded against the sun, and scanned the area around us. I watched the approaching vehicles. When the SUV stopped, I walked over and opened Jack's door. He sat inside, grimacing, with boxes and bags piled on him and the others.

"How are you doing?" I asked.

"Dog got its teeth into my arm," he said.

"Do you need stitches?" I asked.

"It's not bad," he said. "It barely broke the skin. Hurts worse than it looks."

I sighed. "Well, let's hope it didn't have rabies." I held out one of the first aid kits I'd picked up at the store."

"I don't need it," he said. "I already cleaned it up."

I shrugged. "Suit yourself."

I turned away and saw Clutch pulling things out of the minivan. "C'mon, we need to be able to fit two more in here. And who the hell grabbed a baby seat?"

Clutch went to throw the big box, but Marco sprang from the truck. "That's mine." He grabbed the box from Clutch. "It's for Deb."

Clutch's lips thinned. "Strap it to the roof or something. It takes up too damn much room."

"Hey guys," Griz said, and we turned around. He stepped from the truck and pointed down the road to the north. "Recognize anything?"

I searched the road but only saw a few derelict vehicles that were covered in ash and grime.

"Son of a bitch," Clutch muttered. He jogged over to the truck and stood behind the hood, staring at something in that direction.

I pulled out my binoculars and ran toward him. I looked through them, moving across the landscape. "What do you see?"

"Let me see those," he said and took my binoculars. He looked through them for a minute.

I stared in the same direction and then finally spotted

it. "Holy shit. Are those our trucks?"

"Yeah," he replied and handed me my binoculars.

In the distance, I could make out a church — St. Dominic's according to the stone sign up front. Tucked nearly behind the church were, sure enough, our trucks. Their beds were still filled with supplies. We never would've seen them from the interstate; someone had hid them carefully. But, they hadn't planned on us coming up on this overpass.

Clutch turned around to face the rest of our traveling companions. "Load up and regroup below this overpass. Let's see about getting our trucks back."

"But, it's too dangerous," Tom said.

I patted Tom's shoulder. "Look at the bright side. You said you were disappointed not getting to go to church on Thanksgiving. Here's your chance."

CHAPTER XII

We moved in without waiting for the sun to set, figuring that if the thieves were halfway decent at surviving, they would've seen us long before we ever saw them.

Clutch was as hardheaded as they came, but he was also practical. We weren't going after the thieves, only our four missing trucks. The thieves had carried no guns when they'd stolen our trucks, so Clutch figured they had no ammo. Still, the plan wasn't without risk.

The plan was as simple and safe as we could make it: drive cautiously up to the trucks, check each truck for its keys, and drive off, all the while keeping an eye out for trouble. If the thieves tried anything, we were going to hightail it out of there.

Jase drove the Chevy. We'd emptied out the bed, leaving the drum of gas and extra supplies with the

other vehicles under the overpass. Now, four men—
Clutch, Griz, Marco, and Tom—rode in back, with each
one going for a specific truck. I rode in back with them
to look for any signs of trouble and to lay down cover
fire if things turned messy.

I searched for movement as we approached the
parking lot. Other than seeing some candles lit inside
the church, I saw nothing. The parking lot was open,
with few trees or shrubs to hide danger.

We didn't *need* the trucks and supplies. We could
find more of both, but finding supplies wasn't easy or
risk-free. The squadron had loaded all the canned food
from the Costco into the trucks before they'd been
stolen. To find as much food, we'd have to find another
large store. Finding stores that hadn't been destroyed,
looted, or infested was like finding needles in haystacks.
Simply put, going after these trucks was safer than the
alternative.

More important, it was a matter of honor.

Jase pulled in slowly, the engine a notch above idle.
That I saw no one worried me. They had to have seen us
or at least heard the truck. Noise carried more now
without the constant hum of traffic, jets, television, and
phones. My ears had become more sensitive to sound in
the past several months.

Still, the only sound I could hear was Jase's truck.
The only movement I could see was us. As soon as I
started to wonder if the thieves weren't around, I
noticed a figure move within the church. I homed in my

scope to count six people inside the glass doors, watching us.

"We have at least a half dozen people inside the church," I announced. "They're standing inside the entrance."

"I have them," Clutch said, soon echoed by Griz and Marco.

"None have rifles. I see only spears and blunt weapons," Griz said. "These don't look like high-risk bandits. But, keep your eyes peeled for any of their friends."

It was hard not to stare at the people staring right back at us, but I forced myself to scan the bushes and under the trucks for snipers.

Jase slammed on the brakes, and I nearly went flying over the roof.

"There are nails all over the ground," Jase yelled. "They could pop my tires."

I looked forward to see the concrete glistening with metal. They were trying to cripple us, to either send us limping off, scared, or to chase us down and finish us off on the road. Worse, I didn't know how we could possibly make it far with the trucks since there was a field of nails between them and the road.

Clutch tapped the roof of the truck. "Stay here, Jase, but be ready to hit reverse and haul ass out of here if I give the call."

He set down his sword, stood in the truck, and faced the church. "We've come for our trucks. You stole items that didn't belong to you, and we're taking it back. No one has to get hurt. Don't show any aggression, and we'll take our trucks and be on our way. You can have everything else in the store. I'll give you ten seconds to respond. "

On the other side of the glass door, the figures moved, and I could hear a murmur of voices talking over one another. After a moment, the door opened, and an older man stepped outside, though he was quickly flanked by a young man wearing a gray SMSU sweatshirt and gripping a bat. Since he had the weapon, I narrowed my scope onto his chest. In small letters, above and below the acronym, his shirt read *Southwest Minnesota State University*, and I frowned.

It couldn't be possible. I'd been there. After the herds passed through.

The older man spoke. "We meant no ill will, but what you took from the store belongs to no one and everyone. You claimed it because it sat on shelves. We claimed it because it sat on the beds of trucks. There's no difference."

"Like hell there's no difference," Clutch said. "We laid claim the moment we sweat on that cargo. We'd earned it, fair and square."

"Clutch," I said to his back, and he cocked his head slightly to show he was listening. "These guys might be from Marshall."

Clutch stiffened. "How do you know?"

"Look. The kid's sweatshirt," I replied. "SMSU."

The older man began to say something, but Clutch cut him off. "Where are you from?"

The man frowned. "Why does that matter? Regardless of where we're each from, we all have rights to what's in that store."

"Where'd the kid get that sweatshirt?" Clutch countered. "Are you bandits? Did he take it off another survivor?"

The younger man visibly bristled. "It's my shirt. I'm a freshman at SMSU. We ain't bandits, you son of—"

"'Aren't,' Nathan," the older man said, placing a hand on the student's shoulder. "We *aren't* bandits." Then, he turned back to us. "I'm Professor Dominic Caler. I served on the faculty at SMSU. Nathan here was one of my students. Southwest Minnesota State University is a small university in Marshall, Minnesota."

"I know exactly where it is," Clutch said. "I was there after the herds passed through."

The man stood straighter. "*After* the herds, you say? Did you find survivors?"

Clutch shook his head. "No. We went there to look for survivors, but the herds hit it pretty hard."

The professor's eyes narrowed. "Now it's my turn to ask if you're bandits. Why else would you travel so far north unless you'd heard of a group of survivors to raid?"

"We're not bandits. A few of us are from Fox Park," Clutch said as though it would mean anything to the professor. "You happen to know a guy named Manny?

About this tall?" He leveled his hand at his shoulder.

"Yes, I'm familiar with him."

"Manny had a small group with him. They had gone out looking for supplies when the herds hit and couldn't get back to their families at Marshall. They went south to stay ahead of the herds and joined up with our camp."

"I spoke with Manny's people during the first few hours. Many of them had family stuck in Marshall. They would've gone back for them."

"We had a pilot at the camp," Clutch said, referring to me. "She flew a few of us, including one of Manny's guys, to Marshall. But, when we got there, all we found was infected."

The professor's lips pursed. "We were last there about a month ago. It took us awhile to move around the herds and make it back, but we made it. When we saw the community center had been opened up, I'd hoped everyone had come out and connected with other survivors, but we haven't been able to track any of them down yet. We're still looking. We'd only planned to stop here to recuperate and restock for a week before heading back out again."

"Where's Manny now?" the professor asked.

I swallowed.

Clutch shook his head slowly. "I'm sorry to give you the bad news, Professor. We had a bad run in with some bandits. They took down nearly our entire group, including Manny and all of his people."

"That is bad news, indeed," the professor said. "And that sort of news seems to be all we hear nowadays."

"I tell you what," Clutch said. "Since you're from Marshall, we'll leave you two trucks and take two trucks with us. But you have to help us clear these nails."

"That is an acceptable deal. However, you must secure your weapons. I give you my word my people will do the same. My people will not raise a hand against you unless you threaten one of ours."

"You've got yourself a deal," Clutch said. "But, you try to hurt one of mine, and you won't like what happens."

The professor smiled. "Trust is earned in small steps."

Clutch had Jase cut the engine, and we left our larger weapons in the back of the truck. We still wore our side arms, knives, and whatnot. Clutch also hadn't mentioned that we each carried a radio and would call for backup the second shit went south.

The SMSU kid—his name was Nathan—found a couple brooms inside the church. This Marshall group was smaller than I'd expected. Where Manny had a dozen with him, I'd only seen four so far with this group. Aside from Professor Caler, the other three were college students. Peter had no interest in meeting any of us. He was thoroughly closed off from the rest of the world and had his nose buried in a book the entire time we worked at brushing nails away. Joachim, on the other hand, didn't trust us. He kept a safe distance and watched us from the corner of his eye. With his skepticism, he was probably the best equipped of his group to survive in this world.

The professor talked the most of any of them, though when I got closer to him, I noticed how frail he was.

"Cancer," he said when he caught my expression. "I gave cigarettes too many years of my life, and now they're demanding more."

After we cleared a path for the trucks, Nathan took the brooms back.

I caught Clutch and Griz looking out at the sky. I strolled over to them. "It's getting late," I said.

"We're going to have to hunker down soon or else we'll get caught in the dark," Griz said.

Clutch glanced over at the church, his lips tight.

"You're welcome to stay the night," the professor said, walking over. "You need a shelter for the night, don't you?"

"We should hit the road," Clutch said. "We'll find a place."

"The church offers plenty of room. We've already set up our camp in the undercroft. You can have the nave."

"The what?" I asked.

"We're in the basement," he replied, not sounding like I was an idiot for asking what was probably obvious to Catholics far more devout than I ever was. "You can stay where mass would've taken place, if you so choose. The pews should make adequate beds. I saw two other vehicles earlier. I imagine they would also stay."

"Give us a minute, and I'll check with them," Clutch said and turned away.

"Certainly," he said and headed into the church.

Clutch looked at me. "Where's that place you three stayed at on your way to find us?"

I thought for a moment. "A little over an hour from here, I think."

"That would put us there after sunset," Griz said.

"There was another group less than two miles up the road," I said. "I suspect they knew we were in the area, but we didn't stop to chat."

Clutch frowned. "I don't like going into a situation with an unknown quantity. Even though we don't know this group much better, my gut says we can trust this guy. What do you think?"

"I'm with you," Griz said. "If they were bandits, one of them would've given off a suspicious vibe by now."

"I agree," I said. "I get why they took our trucks. It's what most would do. I think they're just trying to get by."

Clutch nodded. "We'll stay the night. Let the others know. We'll run a double security detail to play it safe."

One hour later, we had camp set up within the church and had Jack slouched in a pew. He'd lost his color and was sweating profusely, and we all worried the infection he'd picked up from the dog bite was rabies. When the professor found out, he frowned. "I wish we could help, but we have no antibiotics here. There's a veterinary clinic a couple miles to the north, but we've already been through it. There's nothing but empty shelves and dead animals inside."

"Hang in there," Clutch said after checking Jack's bandage. "We'll get you back to the clinic tomorrow, and they'll get you fixed up."

Jack winced and leaned back. As he rested, we moved the rest of our weapons inside, despite the professor's complaints. He could complain all he wanted. It was one item which Clutch — or any of us — refused to negotiate.

Our trucks, including the two we'd reclaimed, were backed up to the church in case we needed to make a hasty exit. The only thing that stood between the doors and the trucks were two large concrete statues of lions, and they weren't going anywhere.

The Marshall survivors totaled seven — eight if you counted their small dog named Boy — but we'd only met six of them so far. Bonnie and Hugh had come upstairs only because Professor Caler had asked them introduce themselves before they quickly returned to the basement. They were skittish and tended to stay to themselves. I was glad they didn't stick around. The only member of their group we hadn't met yet was "taking some much-needed rest after a long night."

We'd carried in two boxes of food to have a bona fide Thanksgiving dinner, if canned meat and gravy, instant potatoes, and canned cranberry sauce counted. We set out the food across the altar. I'm sure the professor saw some kind of symbolism in it, but it was really the easiest place to put everything.

Boy, the black-and-white dog that had been adopted by the Marshall survivors, anxiously sat as the lone guard of the feast. I think if he could've reached the altar, he would've pulled everything down. But he was a small mutt, and despite trying over and over again, he couldn't jump high enough.

While the food heated on small makeshift stoves, Tom walked around the pews, collecting bibles.

"What are you doing?" I asked. "We don't have room for all those books."

"They're not books, they're bibles," he replied. "And we don't have enough at New Eden."

I didn't bother arguing with him. I figured he'd find a way to fit boxes of bibles onto the trucks regardless of what I said. So I returned to the altar.

My stomach growled at the smell of warm food, and I inhaled the aroma. When I bent down to steal a spoonful of gravy, Jase slapped my hand. "You have to wait, just like everyone else."

I scowled at him before turning away. "I saw you sneaking a bite," I mumbled.

"I was tasting it for flavor. A chef's prerogative."

Professor Caler was examining the spread on the altar. "We're missing wine. I'll see what I can find in the priest's quarters."

"I'll help out," I offered.

The professor snapped around faster than I'd seen him ever move. "No, no, that's quite all right. I can manage."

I frowned at his sudden stubbornness and glanced to Jase.

He frowned before watching Caler disappear around the corner. "He must be hiding the good stuff back there."

"Or something," I murmured.

He stood and lifted the steaming pot with both hands. "The feast is ready."

"Woot!" I cheered and cleared a spot for the stew of meat, gravy, and vegetables Jase had mixed together from a couple dozen cans. That stuff alone was better than we had, but the coup de grace was the *spice*. They'd found boxes of salt, pepper, and seasonings at the store. I couldn't remember the last time my food had been seasoned with anything except some fresh-ground herb we'd found. I was more excited for this Thanksgiving feast than any other Thanksgiving in my life.

The professor carried food to the three members of his team staying in the basement. Everyone else sat around the altar, on the steps, or on pews, and ate. It felt like a real Thanksgiving, with old friends and new acquaintances sitting together around a feast.

All the church's candles were lit. We didn't bother covering the windows, since it was cold enough the zeds were frozen, and the church was far enough off the main roads that no one would see the light unless they were going directly by the church.

The seasoning was strong, nearly overpowering the stew, but I still went back for seconds — and thirds. The church wine the professor brought out was the worst I'd ever had, but I still had another glass.

Clutch took tiny sips from his bottle of whiskey, and I knew the only reason he was showing moderation was to stay sober. Once we were back within the safety of New Eden's fences, I knew that bottle would empty fast.

"Time for a toast," the professor said, and we all raised our glasses. "Here's to new friends and new starts."

"Cheers," we all said.

As everyone ate, drank, and conversed, the professor looked at Clutch. "I have a doctorate in human psychology. I consider myself a respectable judge of character. And, I believe you and your group are decent people."

Clutch nodded while he chewed.

The professor continued. "Our group used to be four times this size. We ran into trouble a little over two weeks ago. Some men who called themselves the Black Sheep demanded a toll for traveling through their territory. What they demanded, we couldn't pay. They attacked, and we defended ourselves. We fended them off, but our losses were terrible. You've met Bonnie and Hugh. They both lost their spouses, and struggle to get by. We wandered for two days until we reached Omaha. The sun caught off the stained glass windows of this church just right to catch my eye. It was a rainbow drawing us in. And, we've been here ever since."

"You were lucky," Clutch said. "We avoid churches. Just about every single one we found was full of zeds."

The professor chuckled. "Everywhere is full. Even hell is full."

Clutch raised a brow. "Hell is full?"

"A young girl told me that once." He motioned around him. "She said, 'Hell has to be full. That's why all the dead are now walking the earth.'"

Clutch shrugged. "It's as good an explanation as anything out there."

"So where are you going after this?" I asked.

The professor thought for a moment. "I'd like to say we'll continue our search for Marshall survivors, but I've seen the hopelessness in my friends' eyes. I'm afraid if we continue our search, it'll kill them. All they've seen is death. It's all they know now. Until we met your group today, I must admit, I was beginning to feel the same despair."

Clutch chuckled. "Was that before or after you ran off with our supplies?"

The professor smiled. "Would you have shared if we'd stopped and introduced ourselves?"

Clutch shrugged and then bore a smirk. "Maybe. If you'd asked nicely."

"Well, forgive me for my false assumption. I had mistakenly believed you would kill my people rather than share."

"That's generally a safe assumption nowadays," Clutch said.

"However, we did leave a full-sized tractor-trailer there for you. We already had your trucks. You couldn't give pursuit. We could've taken our truck, but we chose to leave it so you wouldn't be stranded."

"That didn't work out as planned. Since you blocked the doors with the trailer, I'm not sure how you expected us to get to the cab in time. And, with how quickly it ran out of gas, it had under a quarter tank of diesel in it when you left it running."

"We were perhaps a touch overly cautious in that we didn't want you to chase us," he said. "We only wanted to delay you until we could make it to the church. We had no intention of stranding you at the store. After all, you make an intimidating lot in your brown and green clothes and carrying swords and machetes."

The professor watched me for a moment. "You don't have the look of a soldier, yet you dress like one."

I shrugged and looked down at the hunting clothes I'd found at the sporting goods store in Des Moines. "They have lots of pockets and they hold up."

"I, on the other hand, am having a harder time each day 'holding up.'" He came to his feet. "On that note, I'll excuse myself for the night. We've had no problems since we've been here, so you can rest soundly."

"Thanks," I said.

Clutch waved as he walked away. The remaining

Marshall survivors followed soon after.

"So…" Jase drawled out. "Are we taking them back to New Eden with us?"

Clutch spoke. "We haven't mentioned it to them, but so far I don't see why not."

"I'm cool with it," I said. "But, I want to find out why the prof is so protective of the priest's quarters."

"What do you mean?" Clutch asked quickly.

"He made it clear he didn't want anybody in the priest's crib," Jase said. "I figured he's keeping the good booze back there."

Clutch motioned to Griz, who nodded and came right over.

"You have your weapon ready?" Clutch asked.

Griz patted his back, where his machete was strapped. "Always. We got a date?"

"We need to find out why Caler doesn't want us anywhere outside this area."

Clutch and Griz quickly filled in the rest of the squadron, leaving them behind but ready to jump into action in an instant. I grabbed a candle. The four of us crossed the altar and walked past the confessional booths and down the narrow hallway lined with robes. As the hallway continued, we passed doors, each with a sign conveying what lay behind. When we reached the sign that read *Private Residence*, we stopped.

Clutch eyed each of us with his "you ready" look. I nodded.

He opened the door. The room to the left was dark,

but a candle glow filtered out from the room on the right. Clutch and Griz took lead, and Jase and I followed. I held the candle in my left hand and my machete in my right.

Clutch stopped cold inside the doorway. He glanced to me and back to the room, his sword frozen in the air. I entered and became a statue.

In the bed lay two kids — their faces all too familiar to Clutch and me. We'd seen them once before. Many months ago. I'd never forget their faces, and neither would Clutch.

"What the hell?" Griz whispered.

"It's impossible," I said breathlessly, and I felt Jase hold me up.

The kids opened their jaundiced eyes and sat up, removing any doubt that these were the kids...the two zed kids from the convenience store.

CHAPTER XIII

"**S**top," A man jumped from the darkened corner and stood between Clutch and the two zeds. "They won't harm you."

I frowned, my gaze flitting between the man and the pair sitting on the bed.

"They're not violent," The man continued before turning back to the two and stroking their hair. "But, they are special. Very, very special."

The zeds watched us with droll stares. The younger girl cocked her head, but no sign of emotion flickered on her face. They weren't like us, but they also weren't like the other zeds. They were something different.

"They're like Henry," I said softly. "Zen zeds."

The man frowned and eyed me. "You've found another survivor of the infection?"

I watched him for a moment. A sense of familiarity

niggled the back of my mind. I raised the candle to illuminate his features. "Dr. Gidar?"

He blinked. "You know me?"

I nodded. "You were in Doctors Without Borders with my father, Dr. Ryan. I met you in Nigeria."

His mouth slowly parted before a smile crossed his face. "Mia? My girl, you're all grown up now. I didn't even recognize you."

"I was twelve during that trip," I replied drily. It had been the best summer vacation I'd ever had.

"Your name is Mia? Seriously?" Griz asked with a smirk. "Like Mama Mia?"

I smacked his arm. "No, like Mia Farrow. My mom loved scary movies."

"We can swap stories later," Clutch growled. "Right now, I want to know why this guy has two zeds in a building with the rest of us with no security to keep them from us."

"I told you," Dr. Gidar said. "These children aren't zeds. The virus didn't take over completely. I'd thought it was something miraculous about their genes since they are siblings, but you said you found another. Tell me about him."

"Later." Clutch pointed to the kids. "Once you secure those two, you're going to come out and tell us what you've been hiding in here."

Without waiting for an answer, Clutch motioned for us to leave, and I found my feet hustling from the room. Too many months of being chased by zeds made me skittish around them. And those two zed kids had haunted too many of my dreams already.

They were the first zeds we'd come across that had a spark of intelligence in their eyes. They were also the first that hadn't tried to eat us when they'd seen us. Instead, they'd stood there, holding hands, and watched us.

That happened before summer hit. Later, Clutch and I had racked our brains trying to figure them out, until we finally gave up. I'd done a decent job at not thinking about them again since we hadn't come across any other zeds like them. Until we'd come across Henry.

Once we reached the hallway, Jase blew out a breath. "Man, Cash. Those kids threw me. They remind me of the pair you and Clutch talked about."

"That's because they *are* the same kids," I said.

Jase frowned. "But you said you saw those two back near Fox Park. How'd they get all the way out here?"

"I have no idea."

When we emerged from the hallway, the rest of the squadron was waiting for us, armed and spread out across the open area.

"What'd you find?" Marco asked, nodding toward the hallway.

"They've got two Henrys back there," Griz said.

Marco frowned briefly before his eyes grew wide. "No shit?"

"What's a Henry?" Tom asked.

"They're zeds but they're different," Griz replied.

"Not openly aggressive, but I still don't trust 'em."

"They have them in the open, with no restraints," Clutch said. "I don't know if they're dangerous, but it would only take one bite to ruin a perfectly good day."

"They won't bite you," The professor said as he entered with Dr. Gidar and Nathan at his side. Nathan carried his baseball bat, and I believed he would defend Caler to the death if he had to.

"They are the key to a vaccine," Dr. Gidar said before taking a seat near the altar. "They are the first subjects we've found who were infected but didn't fully succumb to the zonbistis virus or die, which means they carry the antigen in their blood. They suffered some level of neurological damage, but that their hearts still beat is a miracle in itself."

My jaw dropped. "A vaccine is possible?"

"Yes, I'm sure of it," the doctor replied. "I'm making progress on isolating the antigen, but it's been slow. At the university, I had the resources available, but we didn't have the children. I had hypothesized there would be survivors of the virus, but I had no proof until we found these children while we ran from the herds. The hospitals we've come across have either been bombed, are full of the infected, or have no generators to power the equipment I need to isolate the antigen from the virus and strengthen it to be replicable as a vaccine."

"We have power at New Eden," Tom offered. "And we have a medical staff. If you gave us a list of instruments you needed, we could search for them."

Dr. Gidar lightened up. "You must take us with you. This can change everything."

I glared at Tom for sharing information that no one outside New Eden needed to know.

"Tom," Clutch cautioned.

Tom looked at Clutch and frowned. "Well, it's not like we'd leave these folks behind. New Eden takes in all survivors who don't pose a threat."

"And, we haven't determined these guys don't pose a threat," Clutch said.

"I can assure you that we pose no threat. Additionally, you don't have to take all of us. At least take Richard and the two children," Professor Caler said. "But, Richard's work is far too important. Until we have a vaccine, we'll always be a step behind this virus."

"But, the government nuked the south," Jase said. "The herds are gone. All that's left are the stragglers."

"There's still a government?" the professor asked.

"They dropped warheads on the infected?" Dr. Gidar asked quickly. "That would've killed innocent infected as much as the violent infected."

"Like Caler said," Clutch chimed in. "We were always a step behind. We had to lower their numbers."

"But, that's not...well, I can't condone what they've done," Gidar said. "The south would now be a highly contagious zone."

"What do you mean?" I asked.

"Consider the case of the fungi found in the tropical forests. You see, there are several species of fungus lumped together and called the zombie fungus in layman's terms. They control the behavior of their host body — ants in this case — until the host body can no longer continue. The fungus then creates spores so that it can spread."

"But this is a virus, not a fungus," I said. "I remember seeing the news."

"Correct," he said. "But this particular virus is operating in a consistently similar fashion, but it is far more potent. *Zonbistis* controls the behaviors of its host body until the host body can no longer continue, but the virus can be contracted long after its host body's final death. You see, at the university, I tested the *zonbistis* life cycle in great detail. Not only did the virus survive in the host body nearly four days following death, it became tremendously more virulent until it finally burned itself out."

I frowned. "I don't understand. The virus spreads through bites and cuts. It needs contact with our blood."

The doctor shook his head. "Bites from the infected are contagious, but *zonbistis* is far more devious than that. When the virus loses its host, it puts all of its energy into spreading itself. I call this component the 'eleventh hour virulence,' and this is the reason why the virus spread so quickly at the outset."

"That's why the blood-coated bullets took down our guys so fast," Clutch mused.

"Bullets were coated with infected blood?" the doctor asked.

Clutch nodded.

"Well, that would certainly pose a high risk," Gidar said. "It wouldn't take someone long to succumb to the virus if it was outside its host body and within the four-day window."

"Holy shit," I said as the pieces began to click. We'd always been careful to avoid coming into contact with zed blood, but we'd all gotten it on us before. Plenty of times. I blew out a breath. "They said the virus started in a bad batch of lettuce and vegetables from the same processing plant. Something must've happened at the plant, and the virus tainted all the lettuce."

"Yes," Dr. Gidar said. "Produce was shipped across the country in under a day. The virus would've been at its highest potency at that point. It explains why people succumbed so quickly."

I swallowed. "We've been lucky."

"Very lucky," Clutch added.

Dr. Gidar continued. "The 'eleventh hour virulence' of *zonbistis* is precisely why the virus will never be defeated until we become immune to it. Think of measles. We've eradicated it from the U.S. before, but outbreaks continue to occur as long as the virus exists somewhere in the world. We will never completely destroy the virus—that's impossible, but we can better defend against it. There will continue to be outbreaks until we build immunity to the virus. Viruses can lay dormant for weeks, months, even years, and then erupt. We can't be myopic and focus only on the risk of infection today. We have to make the world safe for tomorrow."

I narrowed my gaze upon the doctor. "So, Dr. Gidar, you're saying you can produce a vaccine, which will keep any of us from getting infected?"

"I believe so, yes. But, I need resources, including this Henry fellow you mentioned. He, too, would carry the antigen."

"Give us tonight to talk about it," Clutch said. "If what you're saying is true, it can help end the zed threat. But, you're also talking about bringing zeds into a town filled with innocent people."

"I assure you, they pose little risk," the doctor said. "And, I'm sure we can work out an arrangement where they are secured from the general population."

"We'll be back up here in the morning," Professor Caler said. "To give you time to make your decision. I hope you understand that what you decide can change the entire world."

They came to their feet and headed toward the hallway.

"Wait." Tom jumped up. "You're a doctor, right?"

Dr. Gidar nodded. "I am."

"You need to help Jack. He was bit."

His lips tightened. "I'm sorry. I can't do anything for your friend."

"You don't understand. He was bit by a dog, not by a

zed."

"Did the dog look ill?"

"Yeah. It might have had rabies."

He held out his hands, palms facing us. "I can't help him. There's no vaccine."

"He's got zabies," Nathan said. "We lost two of ours to dog bites."

"What Nathan calls zabies is a mutated form of the zonbistis virus," Dr. Gidar said. "It's a less severe strain, where the virus functions much like rabies."

"Are you saying the virus mutated?" I asked.

"Viruses constantly mutate," the doctor replied. "It's their nature. At least this strain only makes the infected sick and doesn't turn them into what we call zeds. In the case of animal bites, the virus runs its course in roughly forty-eight hours for humans. I don't have a lab with the security and equipment to determine a timeline for infected animals."

I swallowed. "What happens after forty-eight hours?"

He watched me for a moment before he understood the repercussion of my question. "At least your friend will not become a zed. Like rabies, this virus has a high mortality rate. He will succumb to the virus and die."

By the tone of his words, it was clear he believed death wasn't a bad alternative. By the raised voices in the room, everyone believed differently.

"There has to be something you can do," Tom demanded.

"I can offer some painkillers. It will ease the pain."

"That's not good enough," someone else said.

"You can't just let him die," another said.

"I am sorry, but I don't have anything to combat the virus," Dr. Gidar said. "Without equipment, power, and support staff, there's nothing I can do."

"Are you saying if we can get you those things, you can help?" I asked.

"No, I'm afraid even with unlimited resources, it could take weeks, or even months, before I make any kind of breakthrough in terms of a vaccine, and that's assuming a breakthrough is even possible. However, a vaccine is a prevention, not a treatment. As I said already, as is the case for rabies, there is no cure."

"What you will do is check on Jack every three hours and make sure he's doing okay," Clutch said after a long silence. "My guys and I are heading out at sunrise. We'll let you know if you're coming thirty minutes before we leave."

"We'll be ready," the professor said before adding with a smile, "In case you say we can accompany you."

Once they left, Clutch walked over to the pew he'd claimed earlier and shrugged off his backpack.

"Dr. Gidar is brilliant," I started. "My father admired him, which says a lot. If anyone can find a vaccine, I bet he could. I don't see how we can leave them behind."

"We'll take them to New Eden and hold them in quarantine until we talk with Justin," Clutch said. "That way, we can ensure they're safe without putting the town at risk. Now, if you're not on watch, get some rest. We head home tomorrow." He laid down on the bench seat and closed his eyes.

I glanced at Jase and smirked. He nodded. Clutch had never been one for long discussions. That I hadn't disagreed with him tonight was a relief. I was too tired to argue with him. Clutch was a lousy debater — he never gave up, no matter how lost his cause was.

Jase and I laid down near Clutch, and my world slipped away within seconds of closing my eyes. Somehow, I managed to sleep until my early morning shift, when Marco woke Jase and me. I was glad to be awake. I had been deep into a vivid dream where the two zed kids were chasing me, and I was trying to run through a deep stream. No matter how hard I pushed myself, I wasn't getting anywhere, while the kids kept walking toward me, holding hands.

I was still breathing heavily when I sat up, grabbed my gear and walked softly around Clutch to not wake him. Jase caught up to me, and we started to walk our first round, stopping to look out every window. He looked grumbly, like he did anytime he woke up, but he never complained when he was on duty.

At the third window, I looked out onto a world bathed in moonlight. As I tried to figure out the constellations, Jase fogged up the glass with his breath and used his fist and fingers to make little footprints on the glass.

"Cute," I said softly and started walking. "I should

pick you up some finger paints."

"Watch out. I'd be the Michelangelo of the new world. All the girls would be chasing me," he whispered.

"And Hali will kick their collective ass."

He chuckled and then faked a straight face. "I have no idea what you're talking about."

I rolled my eyes. "Whatever you say, King of Denial."

We continued making our rounds for the next hour until it was time to wake everyone up. Professor Caler and the rest of his group came upstairs soon after. Dr. Gidar stood with the two kids before him, a hand on their shoulders. Everyone had bags, and several carried plastic totes.

"Have you reached a decision?" the professor asked when Clutch had his gear and strolled over to meet them.

"You can come to New Eden. You'll need to go straight into quarantine until you're deemed safe. That's non-negotiable. Can you live with that?"

Professor Caler scanned his people's faces before beaming a wide grin back at Clutch. "Your terms are acceptable. Thank you."

Clutch nodded. "We'll head out when the sun comes up."

"We're ready to go whenever you are ready," the professor said.

As moonlight gave way to twilight, we realized leaving the church would be more challenging than we'd planned.

"Aw, hell," Clutch said at my side.

I closed my eyes and rested my forehead against the glass door. When I opened my eyes, nothing had changed. Dogs—hundreds of them—weaved around the trucks, watching us.

"How'd they find us?" Tom asked.

"Dogs have an incredible sense of smell," Jase said. "And, the food supply is slim around here. They've probably been following us since yesterday and finally caught up."

"We'll have to sacrifice some of our food to distract them," I said.

Clutch scowled and motioned everyone to the center of the church. "We'll send a team at a time. One team per vehicle, except we'll leave the car behind in case we need it later. That's six teams. Carry only what you can run with. Leave everything else behind. We may be able to come back for it."

"The children can't run," Dr. Gidar said.

"Then carry them," Clutch retorted. "Team leads are Griz, Marco, Tom, Nick, Randy, and me. Leads, you have five minutes to pick your vehicle and teams. Let's move fast before those packs out there multiply. Trust me, they will get bigger."

"Why don't we wait them out?" someone asked. "You know, like we did at the store?"

"Because once the dogs knew we were in the store, they stuck around. The packs didn't start to thin until we'd stayed hidden for a couple days, and even then, there were too many. It could take a week or longer, and we can't wait."

"Why not?" the professor asked.

"Two reasons." Clutch held up a finger. "One, Jack doesn't have that long. And two," he held up a second finger. "I don't want to get snowed into this church for the winter."

"Snow? What are you talking —"

Clutch cut off the professor's words by pointing outside.

I moaned. "You've got to be kidding me." Sure enough, large snowflakes were beginning to dot the dogs' darker fur and the trucks' windshields. Without a weather forecast, we had no idea if we'd get a dusting or two feet. We hadn't found anyone with a knack at reading weather patterns yet, so we always had to play it conservatively. Without snowplows, it wouldn't take much to leave us stranded.

"But, we cannot leave my equipment behind," Dr. Gidar said. "I can't continue my research without it."

"We'll come back for it later," Clutch said, before adding, "We're heading out. Any more questions?"

No one spoke, and Clutch joined Jase and me in organizing everything we needed to evacuate. I wasn't the least bit surprised that Clutch hadn't named Jase or me as a lead. I didn't take it personally. I would've done the same thing. After all, we were family. We stayed together. Griz should've been with us, too, but Clutch and Griz had a different kind of relationship. I figured it was because they were both Army Rangers and that shared history meant something to them. They were brothers, and both treated Jase and me as though we were theirs to protect.

They had it wrong. We were each other's to protect.

Clutch took Jack onto his team. Since we had Jase's truck, four was plenty. Even at four, Clutch was going to take the back of the truck, which would make for a freezing ride back to New Eden. But, when I pointed that out, he didn't seem to mind one bit.

Each team had a crate of food they would toss out before they ran to their truck. They'd then use their truck to help create a blockade between the next team and the dogs. Griz volunteered his team to go first. Clutch's team would go last. We were the only ones with any ammo, and it was our job to take out dogs that got too close to any of the teams.

Griz's team waited at the door. Clutch and Jase stood at each door, ready to fling them open for the team and yank them closed the moment the team was through. Griz's team consisted of four able-bodied men. Clutch and Griz wanted a team outside to help fight off dogs if things went downhill.

"Ready?" Clutch asked.

"Let's rock and roll," Griz answered.

Clutch and Jase threw the doors open, and Griz's team lobbed out open cans of chicken. Dogs skidded around and dove after the food. Griz led his team as they sprinted out the door, which was closed as soon as they were outside. One dog turned and snapped at Griz, and he hacked at it with his machete. It cried out and fell, but other dogs that couldn't reach the food switched direction to go after the team. Griz had already made it to his truck—one of New Eden's supply trucks. He had the door open, and his men jumped in one at a time while Griz and they hacked at dogs.

Animals yelped and growled but kept coming.

I didn't let out the breath I'd been holding until Griz was in the truck and his door slammed shut. "Thank God," I said breathlessly. "One down, five to go."

Randy's team went next. Then, Nick's. Each time, the food worked, but more and more dogs showed up. Nick's squad spent as much time hacking as they did running. Clutch cracked the door open, and I took shots at the dogs coming up behind the team. One of their team may have been bitten, but at least they all made it into their truck.

Marco's team had the little girl and Tom's team had the boy since everyone thought having both kids on one team could slow down that team too much. Nathan carried the girl, but he moved clumsily with her. Before Clutch and Jase opened the doors, Marco cussed. "Jesus Christ, give her to me." He grabbed the girl, slung her over his shoulder as if she were a rag doll.

"Be careful with her," Dr. Gidar called out, but Marco was already outside.

The other two members of Marco's team were behind

him. They threw food, but the dogs didn't go for it. Instead, they lunged at Marco's team. I opened fire at the mobs forming around Marco and his team. I prayed no shots ricocheted off the pavement and hit one of our people. They had nearly reached the truck when my rifle clicked.

"I'm empty!"

Clutch shut the door, but I noticed him gripping his sword. He moved from one foot to the other. A large dog leapt at one of Marco's men, and the man went down.

Marco tossed the girl inside the truck and shoved Nathan inside. Marco then turned for his other man, his features strained when he saw the dogs tearing into the man who had not once screamed during the attack. Though, that likely just meant a dog had torn out his throat.

Marco climbed inside the truck and started it up. Like the others, he pulled around to create a path for us to reach our truck and Tom's team to reach the minivan. Dogs ran under and around the trucks to come at us. The sickest of the animals didn't seem to remember what glass was and ran headfirst into it. Snow flew from their fur with each collision.

"We can't go," Tom said in a rush. "The dogs have learned. They prefer us to the canned food. We'll never make it."

"It must be something about the virus that even this strain makes them crave blood over food," Professor

Caler said.

"I believe these dogs suffer from an iron deficiency in the same way those infected with zonbistis suffer," Dr. Gidar replied.

"Write your thesis later," Clutch said. "We've got forty feet between point A and point B with a shit-ton of rabid, pissed off mutts covering every inch. I could use some ideas right about now."

"I say we wait," Tom said.

"Then Jack dies," Clutch said.

"But, he —" Dr. Gidar started, but Clutch's hard glare stopped him.

"And we could get stuck here," Clutch added.

"What if we hide and the squadron heads out slowly and draws the packs away?" Jase offered.

Clutch turned. "Now *that* is an idea." He picked up his radio and relayed Jase's plan. After locking the door, we followed Tom down the hallway. Dr. Gidar led the boy. Jase had stuck Boy, their small dog, into his backpack. Clutch and Jase carried an unconscious Jack. Behind us, dogs howled. Trying to ignore the sounds, we headed down to the basement because Gidar thought it would provide us the best chance to not be heard or scented by the dogs outside.

Clutch spoke into his radio. "Church is secure. Bug out."

"*Affirm*," Griz's voice came through the radio. "*Squadron is bugging out. Will report in sixty.*"

The boy tried to walk back upstairs, but Gidar

directed him back toward us. The boy then let out a howl, the first sound I'd ever heard him make. And it gave me the shivers.

The sounds of dogs outside grew louder.

Clutch scowled. "Christ, Doc. Shut that kid up or else the dogs will never follow the squadron."

Dr. Gidar bore an agitated expression. "There's nothing I can do. He gets uncomfortable without his sister. She will be even worse. They are quite dependent on each other."

"Can you give him something to settle him down?" Professor Caler asked.

Dr. Gidar shook his head. "He has a compromised system. He hasn't responded well to drugs in the past. I'm afraid it could make things worse."

"We need to give the squadron sixty minutes to draw the packs away," Clutch said.

Jack moaned and moved restlessly. I pulled out a tissue and wiped his sweaty brow. "Sh," I murmured. "Everything will be fine."

Dr. Gidar held the boy, who slowly returned to his vegetative state.

As we sat and waited, I watched the boy. "What's his name?" I asked quietly.

Dr. Gidar looked up. "I don't know. Neither child speaks."

I frowned. "What do you call him then?"

"I call them 'child,'" he replied.

"We decided it was impersonal to give them names

that weren't theirs," Professor Caler said.

My brow rose. "More impersonal than calling them 'child?'" I thought for a moment. "I think I'd want a name, even if it wasn't my real one."

"Forty minutes to go," Jase whispered.

"I still hear the dogs out there. It doesn't sound like they've left," Tom said.

"Give the squadron a chance," Clutch said the instant before the sound of an engine and horn broke through the sounds of animals. "See? My guys know how to make a sales pitch."

For the next forty minutes, we sat there, the only sounds coming randomly from Jack and the boy. The boy grew more and more agitated, his jaundiced eyes flitting around the room, as though he was searching for something. The time passed interminably slow. I could hear fewer and fewer dogs. The engines disappeared.

When Griz finally called in, the radio startled me.

"We've led away what we could," Griz said. *"But, some refused to follow. There are some hardheaded ones out there. I hate to say it, but the snow is really coming down. These trucks don't have tires for snow."*

Clutch spoke into the radio. "We'll take it from here. Head to New Eden before you get stranded."

A pause. *"We'll come back for you."*

"Don't worry about us. Now, head on home." Clutch lowered the radio and came to his feet. "We have two options. We wait out these animals and run the risk of being stranded here, potentially for a month or longer.

Or, we head out of here before the snow gets deeper and face the dogs that are still out there."

"I say we wait," Tom said.

Dr. Gidar shook his head. "No, I need to work on the vaccine. We can't afford to wait."

Professor Caler stood and walked toward the stairs. "There is another way. You're heading home today. The vaccine must be made and distributed."

"What's your plan?" Clutch asked, but the professor had already disappeared up the stairs.

Clutch and Jase hurriedly grabbed Jack and we followed the professor. I glanced back to see Tom waiting for Dr. Gidar who was coaxing the boy into his arms.

Professor Caler stood at the front door. When I reached him, I counted over three dozen dogs on the other side of the glass, watching us with glazed eyes. Caler seemed to stare off into nowhere. "Are you ready?"

"What are you planning to do?" I asked.

He kept staring out through the door. "I'll draw their attention and buy you the time you need."

"You can't do this, John," Dr. Gidar said. "You can't sacrifice yourself."

The professor sighed. "The day of the outbreak, I was receiving my first chemo treatment. My doctor had said that even with the treatments, my chances were only twenty percent I'd make it a year." He turned and faced us. His gaze was tired, showing the type of exhaustion that sleep couldn't fix. "I've had enough of this world. If there's one thing I can do that helps others one last time, then by God, let me do it."

I couldn't speak. Instead, I could only stare at the hard conviction in his eyes.

"We'll find another way," Tom said.

"Every minute you spend trying to find an alternative," the professor started. "More snow and more dogs arrive. Now, I'm stepping out this door in ten seconds. It's up to you if you let my last moments be in vain."

"Thank you, sir," Clutch said.

Professor Caler gave a slight nod and then unzipped his coat.

I pulled out my pistol. It had only one round left in it. I'd always refused to give up that single round in case I needed it for myself, but it felt selfish to hold onto it. I handed it to Clutch. He checked the mag, frowned, and then shoved it into his belt.

Professor Caler pushed open the door and ran with more energy than I'd thought possible. The dogs went after him. I couldn't watch. I burst out the door and swung my machete like a pendulum as I ran toward the truck. Already at least a couple inches of snow covered the ground, slowing my pace. I knew the others were behind me, and I kept running.

The professor screamed in agony as I opened the truck door. I found myself shoved inside with Jack thrown on me. Jase crawled in behind the wheel, and

Clutch jumped into the back. Jase revved the engine and threw the truck into gear. The van moved, and I knew Caler's sacrifice had saved all our lives.

After I situated Jack in between Jase and me, I looked out the window to see the professor tangled in a rose bush. He writhed and screamed. A shot rang out in the frozen air. The man's head fell back, and he moved no more.

I looked back to make sure Clutch was safe. He held up a thumb. I leaned back and closed my eyes as Jase slipped and slid out of the parking lot. Jase drove, with the minivan behind us, for about thirty minutes before he stopped, and Clutch squeezed up front with us. It was tight, but he was in no mood to sit in the minivan. I pulled Jack onto Clutch and my laps and checked his temperature every few minutes. "I think his fever may be breaking," I said after the third or fourth check.

The snow kept coming down, and the winds picked up. We drove at a snail's pace. Jase recommended we stay at the place where he'd found his truck, but when I mentioned the people we'd seen on horseback, Clutch decided to brave the roads.

I don't know how many hours passed before Jase pointed. "Home sweet home."

I smiled at seeing the other trucks parked inside the gates. "We made it," I said and patted Jack's chest, only to find it wasn't moving.

Jack had already died.

FORTITUDE

CHAPTER XIV

Twenty-four hours later

"It's perfect," Deb said as she looked over the baby seat Marco had brought back from the store. Marco beamed with pride as he knelt near her, helping her figure out the new baby seat. "Thank you," she added as she bent down and gave him a tender kiss. "Did you tell them?"

"No," Marco replied. "I thought you'd want to be the one to tell them the news."

Deb looked up at us, her face beaming, and grabbed his hand. "We're getting married!"

Surprise was quickly washed over with joy. Everyone in the living room cheered.

"'Bout time you manned up the nerve to ask her," Griz said, grinning.

I hustled over to the couple, and hugged them both.

"Congratulations!"

"Way to go. Will you have white cake? It's my favorite," Benji said, evidently knowing what weddings were all about. He broke out into the chicken dance, while Diesel and Boy danced around him in mutual excitement.

"We'll have cake, Benji," Vicki said, wearing a rare smile.

Deb motioned for the older woman. "Vicki is going to be my maid of honor," Deb said.

Vicki laughed. "I'm long past being a maid. But I'll gladly be your matron of honor."

"Griz is standing in as my best man," Marco said.

"As long as I don't have to wear a tux," Griz said. "Although I would be the finest looking man around here."

"Justin is going to make it a town event next week. We hope you all can be there," Deb said.

"We wouldn't miss it for the world," I said.

After the celebration simmered down, I headed out to tell Clutch the good news. He'd been with Justin, debriefing him on the last several days' events while the rest of us had returned to the house as soon as our night in quarantine was over. The Marshall survivors were still in "quarantine," but really, Justin was keeping them in a separate building until he figured out how to handle them—and the two kids. He hadn't mentioned the kids to the rest of New Eden yet, and we weren't talking, though I had no doubt the rumors would quickly spread.

Marco had said the girl yelled until she passed out on the drive back to New Eden. I could only imagine how the two kids must've latched onto each other when they were brought back together. I suspected no one would be able to separate them as easily again.

I tromped through the six inches of snow that covered everything in a pristine white. My smile stayed glued on my face, despite the cold and despite having seen two men die only a day ago. Marco and Deb proved that good things could still happen in this new world.

Even though the baby wasn't Marco's, for all intents and purposes, he acted as though he was the father. Whenever Deb needed to go to the clinic or was too sick to pick up her rations, Marco was there, as though they'd been married for years. That was only one example of how things had changed since the outbreak. There were no longer things such as dating or drawn-out engagements. Life had no guarantees, especially now, and everyone knew it.

Their wedding would remind us that happiness wasn't extinct, a reminder each one of us desperately needed. Benji, with his innocent child resilience, had always been our poster child for a future that was worth protecting. Marco and Deb also belonged on that poster.

By the time I reached Justin's house, the cold had seeped through my skin, and I shivered. I jogged up the steps and walked inside. Justin was in his dining room—where he always was—with his two assistants, Clutch, Zach, Dr. Edmund, and Dr. Gidar. It was a full room.

Clutch glanced up while the others were deeply engaged by the papers on the table. "That should work nicely," Dr. Gidar said as he ran his finger down a list of handwritten items.

"We're working out a setup for Dr. Gidar to do his research," Clutch said. "I think we can make it happen without putting New Eden at any risk."

"That's nice," I replied before my smile grew.

"What is it?" he asked.

"Deb and Marco are getting married."

His brows rose before he nodded and grinned. "Good for them."

"So, it's official then," Justin said. "That's a relief. I wasn't going to be able to keep it a secret much longer. This will be the biggest event New Eden's ever had." He sobered. "We could use the good news. Folks can cope with not having a Thanksgiving feast. Losing Jack will be harder. He's been with us since the beginning. Hopefully, Dr. Gidar here can make it so we don't lose anyone else to this godforsaken virus."

"Well, there are no guarantees," Dr. Gidar started, but he didn't continue, because the door burst open and about a dozen residents hurried inside and fanned around the room.

"There are zeds inside New Eden?" a woman asked in a shrill voice.

"You're going to get us all killed," a man from the back called out.

"Calm down so we can discuss this," Justin said.

"Not until you get the zeds out of New Eden."

Yelling erupted.

Clutch came to his feet, pulled out his sword and slammed it against the table. The sound of metal on wood reverberated through the house. "Enough!"

The newcomers silenced.

Clutch continued. "I would never allow anyone through those gates who I felt was a risk to New Eden. Those two kids may be different, but whatever they are, they sure as hell aren't zeds. At least not zeds like we know them to be. Dr. Gidar here believes they are the key to creating a vaccine for the zed virus. I don't know about you, but I for one would like to see that happen. These guys have been working all morning on a plan, which I'm sure they'd be happy to share with you."

He sheathed his sword and pushed through the crowd. I followed. Once we were outside, I kept pace with him. "Wow, I didn't realize you were a diplomat."

"Irrational people drive me crazy," he said. "I've never gotten why some fly off the handle without thinking."

"Because they're being irrational," I joked. "It's a curse of being human. We're all doomed to act irrationally every now and then."

He smirked. "Speak for yourself."

I bent down, grabbed a handful of snow, and threw it

at him.

"Hey!"

I jumped back, laughing. Clutch started making a snowball, and I did the same. We threw about the same time; mine hit his chest, while his hit me right in the head. "Oh! That's mean."

He laughed.

The ground rumbled, and I girded myself as though an earthquake was coming. But, this was Nebraska. Earthquakes didn't happen.

Clutch looked around. "What was—"

A house at the edge of town exploded into a ball of fire.

I gasped and brought my hand over my mouth.

"Fire!" Clutch shouted. He looked back at me, his eyes wide.

I knew mine were just as wide, because I was thinking the exact same thing.

We had no working fire truck.

We burst into action at the same instant, and we took off toward the fire. I had no idea what caused it. Had someone bombed us? What else could cause an explosion like that?

Justin came running up by us. "It's the gas lines! I heard about this happening at another town. We have to shut all the lines off. This fire will keep going wherever the gas goes."

"How do we turn off the gas?" I asked as we ran.

"There are shut-off valves outside every house," he

replied. "Wrenches should work. Spread the word, starting with the houses near the fire."

"Do the gas lines go to the silo?" Clutch asked.

"No, the silo is on its own grid. Generators and propane tanks only," Justin said.

"Good," Clutch said. "I'm familiar with gas shutoff valves. I'll start turning them off. Cash, you tell everyone you can to get their valves shut off and fast. And then tell them to head to the silo. They'll be safe there."

"Okay!" I yelled and slowed down. I looked from side to side and had no fucking idea where to go first. When I saw Zach headed our way, I ran up to him and passed along the info. He headed west, and I headed east. I ran to each house. Most people were already standing on their porches, making my job easier. But, many were like me and had no idea where their shutoff valves were located. "Just find it already!" I yelled and moved on.

I kept running, even though the snow slowed me down, and I had no real plan of who to tell first, so I set up a path that would bring me to house Twenty-Six. When I reached it, everyone was already standing outside. "Turn off the gas shutoff valve!" I yelled, my voice coarse from the smoke tainting the air.

Frost nodded. "I was suspecting that was the case, so I already turned off our valve and told our neighbors to do the same."

"What do we do now?" Vicki asked.

A second explosion rocked the town. This one was in the center of town, nowhere near the first explosion, and I prayed Clutch was far from the deadly blast. The fires were spreading from both explosions, and smoke had blocked out the sun.

I looked back to Frost and the others. "Get to the silo!"

I jogged down to warn the next houses, but a third house exploded less than a block away, and I found myself trying to run faster, only to stumble and fall onto my knees. I climbed to my feet and stared at people running in the street. Clutch came running at me, a wall of smoke and fire behind him, and I blinked to make sure it was really him.

He didn't stop until he reached me. Even then, he pretty much plowed into me and pulled me to him. "Are you hurt?"

I shook my head. "I'm fine."

"We need to get to the silo," he said and grabbed my hand. "There's no stopping this."

We quickly caught up to the others. Jase and Hali were in lead, both of them like gazelles in the snow. Frost held Benji's hand, and Vicki hustled alongside them. Marco and Griz were helping Deb walk as quickly as she could, which wasn't nearly fast enough. The silo was on the other side of town, with fire and likely more explosions between us and it.

We made it about two blocks before Marco stopped and turned around. He pointed and said something, but

Deb shook her head. "I can keep going."

Marco sprinted toward a wheelbarrow on the front porch of the house. "Hold on a second. I'm grabbing this for Deb!"

Everyone slowed and then stopped.

Marco grabbed the wheelbarrow, looked up and grinned while he stood on the front porch. "Got it!"

The house exploded outward, engulfing Marco in its flames. Glass shards shot from the windows. Heat blasted my face and burned my eyes. Debris pebbled my skin.

"Marco!" Deb screamed. She lunged toward the fire, but Griz held her back.

"God," Clutch muttered, and he tried to take steps toward the house, his arm covering his face, but the heat forced him back.

The flames licked out from the house. Still, I faced the house and tried to find Marco. I swear my mind still saw him standing on the porch, holding the wheelbarrow, but I knew it was an illusion. There was no sign of Marco. The explosion hadn't thrown him from the house. He had to be still up there, enveloped within flames that I could feel the heat of from sixty feet away.

Clutch returned and grabbed onto me as though I was his lifeline, and I sobbed, still watching the house.

"We have to go," Griz said softly to Deb.

"No, no, no," she said over and over again before she collapsed and Griz caught her.

The others had gathered around her, also searching for Marco. Jase had gotten closer to the house than Clutch had, but even he had to back off from the growing flames.

Griz carried Deb, his features clenched as though it was taking everything to hold back his pain. Like automatons, we left Marco behind. We weaved around streets and walked toward the silo. As we walked by the church, its cross burned radiantly, and its organ played an unholy tune of misshapen, dying notes.

We passed some people moving more slowly than us, while others hurried around us.

Clutch held onto me as we walked, and I held onto him. With every explosion, I cringed. When we finally reached the silo, before walking through the doorway, I turned around to see New Eden burning behind us. Numb, I blankly walked into the dark cavern where we would be safe. Most of us, anyway.

CHAPTER XV

The next two days went by interminably slowly. At first, a team went up every hour to check the status of the fires and to look for any of the twenty-six missing residents—though at least three were confirmed dead. Stragglers arrived within the first few hours, including Dr. Gidar and the two kids. A riot ensued to keep the kids out of the silo, but Justin allowed them inside, assuring everyone that they would be secured in a locked room along with the doctor.

The fires continued to burn but had not come closer to the silo. From the higher floors, I could hear explosions and crashes as more and more houses succumbed to the fires. Once it was clear we were safe in here from the fires, Justin had teams go up only every four hours.

The lower levels still had standing water in them,

giving the silo's air a cold dampness. Our clothes were saturated with smoke. Coupled with the heavy air, the smell of smoke hung everywhere. People coughed in the dimly lit corridors. Deb — and others — cried softly. It was dark enough that no one saw me cry.

Even after working every day, crews had only managed to repair the silo's flooring, lights, and vents. No rooms were ready in the silo yet, so everyone had to camp out on the metal grid floors, with only blankets for cushioning. Buckets were lined up in cordoned-off room, which served as toilets. Diesel, Boy, and the other dogs in the town had nowhere to go. Thankfully, most of New Eden's supplies were stored in the silo. Plastic bags quickly became the most useful resource.

At mealtime, each person was given an open can of beans. No one complained. We'd all been through tougher times and were thankful to be safely tucked inside a building when we could be out in the middle of a Nebraska winter with no shelter. Few spoke. After all, what could be said that didn't make matters even worse?

Unlike Clutch, Griz, Jase, Hali, and me who wore our backpacks everywhere, most had nothing with them — anything they'd owned was burning to ash outside. We still had our weapons, a change of clothes, and some basic survival supplies. I spent a lot of time curled into Clutch, and it wasn't just to stay warm. He grounded me. Griz sat with us, but he spent as much time doing sit-ups and push-ups as he did sleeping. Hali and Jase were inseparable, and our small group stayed within ten feet of one another. I guess we all felt the same. We'd been through homes before. When we had nothing else, we still had each other.

Frost had found a nice corner for Benji and his dogs. The boy was resilient, but he needed routines, and he exhausted easily. Deb hadn't fared as well. Contractions started during the first night, and Dr. Edmund was at her side every moment he wasn't helping the injured. Vicki stayed with her constantly. I made the mistake and mentioned that Dr. Gidar could help, but with the backlash I received from the New Eden residents, it was clear they weren't ready for "that man" to be out among them yet.

I didn't offer any ideas after that and rode out the time. I tried not to make eye contact with anyone while we took our hourly walks through the silo for exercise. When I failed, I'd see the exhaustion and despair in their soot-covered gazes. Hell, I probably had the same look.

I watched Clutch. We could carry on an entire conversation without speaking, and I know I gave him strength like he gave me.

New Eden's citizens stayed days in the silo before Zach returned to say the fires were just smoldering embers now. After Justin saw for himself, he gave the green light for everyone to venture out.

"Watch out for dogs and zeds," he'd said. "Everyone, analyze what needs done today to secure New Eden. But, be back to the silo before sunset."

Some rushed outside. Others dragged their feet. I was somewhere in between. Shit, I was beyond stir-crazy, but I dreaded seeing what awaited us outside.

And, I had good reason to dread.

Armageddon had come to New Eden. I could see all the way across town. No buildings obstructed my view. Sure, the skeletal remains of houses stood like splinters, but the fire had been thorough. Not a single house came through unscathed, but at least five houses were still usable. Surprisingly, much of the fence still stood. It had been built far enough out the fire hadn't consumed it. Sections were charred, and boards pressed against the wire, but it was better than standing out here naked to the world. There were clearly still some holes in the fences, because animal tracks dotted the snow.

When Clutch and I came across Romeo's body — New Eden's vagrant — all that was left was his coat and boots. Wild animals had eaten everything else. Most of the bodies of the missing residents were never found, like that of Jase's partner, Dick. Or the woman who always smiled when I met her on the streets.

Or Marco.

It was like he'd vanished, leaving no trace behind. Maybe it was better that way; then we could all pretend that he hadn't suffered.

The fires had raged in the area for days, and they weren't completely gone. Smoke rose in the distance, and an explosion was heard that had to come from fifty miles away. Evidently, the gas line was still seeking out new victims.

We walked the fence line and made notes of needed repairs, though Clutch and Griz thought it would be better to focus on reinforcing the fence that encircled the silo to make a smaller area more defensible. Besides, there wasn't much out here left to protect.

Everyone congregated around the few buildings that still stood. Justin had a table set up, and his assistants were taking down notes as people spoke of what they needed. Dr. Gidar, sans kids, had his hand raised. "I need assistants. I need to continue my work. That is more important than anything."

Someone punched him — I couldn't remember the resident's name — and people cheered.

Dr. Gidar held his bloody nose. "Fool," he said, his voice muffled as though he had a cold. "If I can't find a vaccine, we're all only one bite away from death."

People quieted down, but their gazes were murderous. Dr. Gidar needed to learn that empathy was still a valued trait. People weren't being naïve. They simply couldn't fathom looking ahead to tomorrow when they were struggling to get through today.

We didn't stick around. We headed back to our house to find it about halfway burned. Some of the windows were, amazingly, intact. Still, Frost wouldn't let us sift through the debris for fear the floor would collapse. So, we stood there and stared through the broken living room window. Still sitting on the coffee table was a melted and charred baby seat.

CHAPTER XVI

For the next several days after the gas lines blew, new fires popped up from old embers. After we buried the dead—those we could find—in the frozen ground, we worked frantically to repair fences and turn the silo into New Eden. With over three hundred people working in the silo, we had indoor plumbing in three days, and had the water drained from the lower levels in ten days.

Within two weeks, we had the fences repaired so the wild dogs couldn't get through. But, they didn't give up. Once the smoke dissipated, the numbers of wild animals trolling outside the fences grew. One of the best parts about the silo was that we didn't have to hear the animals' howls at night.

The silo was huge, but much of the space was open air and not set up in any kind of livable configuration, at least not yet. There were nowhere near enough rooms for any semblance of personal space. At least the dormitory rooms had been completed, and we had enough beds to require only two sleeping shifts. Three weeks after the gas line explosions, we fell into a comfortable routine of living in the silo.

Everyone stayed in the silo with the exception of Dr. Gidar, his assistants, and the two zed kids. They were set up in one of the few remaining buildings — a tiny, old house — using a generator to power their medical equipment and lights. The only heat in the house was from a wood fireplace. No one liked taking fuel from the silo generators for Dr. Gidar's house, but New Eden's residents liked the idea of the zed kids in the silo even less.

The busyness of working in and around the silo helped take our minds off what we'd lost, but it wasn't nearly enough to make us forget. If Clutch wasn't barking out orders, he didn't speak. Losing Marco threw Clutch back into that dark place where he'd close himself off from everyone. He developed a knack at not coming to bed until after I'd fallen asleep and getting up before I woke.

Deb acted much the same as when she lost Tack, the father of her unborn child: she buried her emotions and went on. She had contractions nearly every day, and Dr. Edmund told her she needed to lower her stress levels. I imagined that was tough for Deb to do when she watched her fiancé burn alive a few weeks ago. Her gaze revealed the losses she'd suffered, and I prayed she'd be able to keep it together long enough to carry the baby full-term.

"Here." Zach handed me a box of toilet paper before grabbing one for himself.

We were on duty, but things had changed because New Eden had shrunk from a town sitting on three square miles to a town of two city blocks, with each block — the silo and the buildings — sitting nearly a quarter mile from each other. The squadron and security forces had been merged, and our shifts were as much working on the silo as keeping the peace.

Zach and I carried our loads up a flight of stairs, I dropped off a half dozen rolls of toilet paper at the first bathroom, and we continued up the next two floors.

"We're lucky Justin thought to store everything in the silo," I said while Zach placed rolls by the next bathroom.

He chuckled. "Yeah. Good thing he didn't listen to me. I told him he should've stored everything in a building. I kept telling him that, with our luck, this silo would probably flood in the spring and ruin everything."

"Unfortunately, we didn't keep enough in the silo," Justin said as he walked up the stairs and overheard us talking. "We had only one radio with the range to reach the capital, and it's a melted mess of wires and metal. Being separated from everyone else is a bit unsettling." He sighed. "I know, I have to be patient. I'm sure they'll send someone down here to check on us and get us hooked back up." He looked at the boxes we carried and then looked back up at us. "Are you heading topside?"

"Yeah," I replied.

He smiled. "Can you bring this to the lab? Dr. Gidar said he needed more Q-tips."

I took the blue and white package of cotton swabs, and Justin tipped his hat before heading up the next flight of steel stairs and disappearing. We continued restocking our toilet paper until only a few rolls remained. I stuffed them into my backpack, zipped my coat, and pulled on my stocking hat and gloves. "Hopefully, it's warmed up a bit," I said. "It was frigid out there this morning."

"I haven't been out yet today," Zach said. "Fresh air sounds nice right now. Even if it is freezing."

I pushed open the door, and a cold wind blasted my face. I pulled my neck gaiter up over my mouth and nose.

"Good afternoon."

I looked to my left to see Frost leaning against the downwind side of the silo's concrete entryway. His arms were crossed tightly over his chest. "Dog duty?" I asked.

"Yep," he replied before glancing at three dogs hopping around the snow. A smaller black and white dog bounded under the bigger dog's legs.

"So you've adopted Boy and Buddy now, too?"

Frost grunted. "Buddy comes and goes. But, poor

Boy was forgotten after the fires. Benji found him hiding under a burnt porch and decided we needed another dog."

I could only imagine the evil looks Frost would get now. First, one dog eating precious food. Now, two? Though, I suspected all the animosity of New Eden was far easier for Frost to stomach compared to the displeasure of his grandson letting a dog go without a home. Not that he was the only dog without a home. But, those still alive outside the fence were either sick, feral, or both.

I looked at the fences surrounding the silo. Only a few feral animals hung around today; evidently the weather was too cold for even them to stalk us.

I turned back to Frost. "See you later."

Zach and I headed to the small wood enclosure, which served as the guard station at the gate. The fence, connected to the gate, encircled the silo with a narrow, fenced path wide enough for a truck drive through. At the end of the path was a second gate that opened to the old New Eden. There, the fences had been somewhat repaired, enough to close gaps against animals but not strong enough to hold off a vehicle ramming it or a sudden crush of zeds.

Jase and Hali were at the guard station, cuddling in the cold. When they saw us walking toward them, they awkwardly separated. Hali waved, and Jase opened the gate. "Have a nice walk," he said as Zach and I passed through. "Bring me back something from Burger King."

"I'll get right on that," I said sarcastically, and started to jog down the path.

When Hali found out Jase and I left to go after the squadron, she'd made up her mind then and there that she wouldn't be left behind again. She was still learning how to use a machete and had never fired a gun before, but she had spunk. And she'd been relentless in asking Justin for the transfer to the security team, so he'd finally relented.

Now that the squadron and security forces were merged, Zach had stepped down to have Clutch be leader of the new, combined force. Zach and Griz were Clutch's seconds. Everyone had partners except for Clutch, who worked much of both shifts to drive things. He was working too hard and not sleeping enough, and it showed in his face. But, I knew it was his way of coping — of avoiding having to think of those he'd lost and blamed himself for. There was nothing Clutch could've done to prevent Marco's death, but I knew Clutch. That fact wouldn't have stopped Clutch from blaming himself, anyway.

I did the only thing I knew that seemed to work with Clutch. I gave him space and made it clear I was there when he was ready to come back.

I counted the fence posts in the quarter mile connector between the silo and the burnt-out city as Zach and I jogged. We jogged for exercise and for warmth. We didn't stop until we reached the next gate. Here, one guard watched while the other opened the gate for us, and we hustled through.

The gate closed behind us. I pulled out my machete. Before us stood the ruins of New Eden. Even though the fences remained, the town now had a forbidding presence. It could've been the lives lost here, or the hopes crushed. Either way, I no longer enjoyed walking these streets. Zach felt the same. Both of us were on edge, and neither of us spoke while we patrolled the "old" New Eden.

Justin believed we could rebuild the town in the spring. I offered up the idea of relocating the town to Fox Park, but many New Eden residents clung to the silo's safety. The majority of the town wanted to convert the silo into a permanent home, but some contemplated relocating to Moose Jaw to be a part of the new capital. I suspected that, come spring, some groups would leave the silo. I was planning to be in one of those groups.

Hiding underground was no way to survive.

The walk to Dr. Gidar's lab was short. The small cluster of surviving houses sat on the western end of the town, near the silo. The snow had been trampled down and was now as hard as the street below it. We didn't jog, because there were too many icy patches, but we still walked briskly.

I hurried up the two steps to the front door and stepped inside. The kitchen had been turned into the lab, while the zed kids had been set up in a baby pen in the living room.

Like Zach did every time we came here, he walked

over and watched the boy sitting in the pen. The kid was watching a cartoon on a tablet computer they'd evidently charged off the generator. Zach seemed as captivated with the boy as the boy was with the show.

Currently, the little girl was in the kitchen, and Dr. Gidar had his stethoscope on her chest. The girl kept reaching for the instrument, and the doctor kept brushing her hand away. Hugh stood by and watched, slowly shaking his head. Bonnie was sitting at the kitchen countertop, placing droplets of a clear liquid on slides.

"Child B's heart rhythm is normal," Dr. Gidar said while Hugh jotted down notes. The doctor handed the stethoscope to the girl, who took it and examined it, making the metal reflect the light.

I set the box of cotton swabs and a few rolls of toilet paper on a table. "You still haven't named them?"

"They have names already," Dr. Gidar replied. "If they can learn to speak again, they'll tell us those names."

I shrugged. "Whatever you say. I still think they'd like to be called something else besides 'child.'"

"Do they look like they care?" Hugh said. "They're infected. They're a few fries short of a Happy Meal."

"Now, Hugh," the doctor said, "we don't know the extent of their brain damage yet. That they understand language and don't require diapers signifies some level of advanced cognitive function. Even more so, the boy had opened tin cans of food and kept both him and his sister alive for six months. That is not a sign of severely limited brain function. I suspect the virus targets the prefrontal cortex, but I don't have the equipment to run the tests I need."

"What do you need?" I asked.

"An MRI scanner, to start with," the doctor replied.

I smirked. "Good luck getting one of those."

"I know, I know. We're trying to continue modern medicine in a Dark Ages world. I'll make do. It will take longer, but I'll make do."

I watched while he prepared a syringe. "What's that?" I asked.

He looked up. "Prednisone. It's the only drug we have that helps her asthma."

As he injected the young girl, she snarled and snapped at him, and he jumped back. I lunged forward with my machete raised, but Dr. Gidar jumped in between us. "Don't harm her."

I slowly raised my weapon. "You do realize that if she bites you, you'd very likely become infected?"

"Possibly, not likely," he said. "My tests have shown these two children have fought the virus into remission. If she bit me, yes, she would transmit the virus, but she also may transmit the antigen her body has created to fight the virus."

"Then, you'd be like her?" I asked.

He scowled. "That is undetermined." He turned back to the girl and took her new toy. "Well, aren't you peckish today." He shook his finger at her. "No biting."

Once she settled back down, Dr. Gidar motioned to Hugh. "We're finished for now."

Hugh gingerly picked up the small girl as though she were a baby with soiled diapers. He carried her over to the pen and warily set her down. She moved to her brother and became instantly entranced by the show. Hugh took a step back with haste. Distaste wrinkled his features as he looked at his hands, and he disappeared around the corner. I heard the splashing of water seconds later.

I watched the children. Except for their jaundiced eyes and skin, they looked like any other kids slouching in front of a television, watching their favorite show. What went on in their heads? Did they feel fear or hunger or sadness and couldn't convey their needs? Or, were they vegetables, going through the motions of a child but truly a zombie inside?

"Are the kids showing any improvement?" I asked. "Do you think they can recover?"

"It's too early to tell," Dr. Gidar said. "Their health has improved, but for their ages, I'm amazed the children survived for six months out there alone. They were fortunate to have been left inside a restaurant stocked with plenty of food and safely out of harm's way. In fact, I suspect the children locked themselves inside there during the outbreak. They clearly show signs of intelligence."

"I'll take your word for it," I said. "I've never seen a zed with a fraction of those kinds of smarts before." I looked down at my watch. "Well, Zach and I need to get back on patrol. If you need anything else from the silo, make a list for someone to pick up tomorrow."

"I do have one thing I need," Dr. Gidar said as Zach and I walked toward the door.

I paused and slowly turned. I already knew what he'd ask for. He asked for the same thing for every day. "Listen. We can't go pick up Henry until the snow melts off the roads a bit."

"But, I saw the snowmobiles in the garage," he countered.

"No one wants a zed—or whatever Henry is—riding along behind them. The risk is too high."

"I've isolated the antigen," he said. "Only if I have different blood to test—blood that is unrelated to these children—will I know that the antigen is universal."

"I give you my word," I said. "As soon as the snow gets below three inches, I'll take a truck out to find Henry."

"Trucks can handle deeper snow than that," the doctor grumbled and then stepped over to Bonnie.

He said something I couldn't hear, and she looked up, aghast. "No, doctor. You can't."

"This is not up for discussion," he scolded.

She took a syringe, dipped the tip into the liquid she was working with, and pulled back the plunger. Dr. Gidar rolled up his sleeve.

A foreboding feeling built in my gut. "What are you doing, Doctor?"

When Bonnie held up the syringe, he snatched it from her hands and held it in the air. "You know me. I am not a foolish or impetuous man. But, developing a vaccine is more important than anything else we do. Yet, my team has been ostracized, and my work has been shoved into a freezing corner of a dead town. I do not want to do this, but I must. I will not put my team at risk, so there is no other choice."

"You always have a choice," I said.

"This," he held up the syringe, "is the antigen I've created off these children's blood. I have 94.5% confidence that this antigen will equip our bodies with the antibodies we need to fight off the zonbistis virus without loss of cognitive function. I could raise the level of confidence by at least one percentage point with a third test subject. But, I know when I'm being stonewalled."

"You're not being stonewalled," Zach said.

"We have to play things safe," I added. "When the roads are covered in snow, we could drive over a chunk of metal and shred our tires. Be patient a little longer."

"Patience I have, but not when it comes to delay tactics, one after the other. My work will never be taken seriously until after it's too late. People need vaccinated against this virus *before* they are bitten."

He took a deep breath. "I had a good life. I was giving a speech at Marshall on the day of the outbreak, and it was by a series of miracles that we survived. We did survive, and we had all the facilities we needed to work on a vaccine. We made leaps and bounds during the months we spent at Marshall, but were never able to isolate an antigen. Then, the herds came, and we were forced to leave everything behind except for my journals. For weeks we ran, until we stopped at a gas station for the night and found these two children—clearly infected yet non-violent—hiding in a small café. Within a week after studying their blood, I had reached a major breakthrough. These children gave me more than their blood. They gave us all hope there could be a world where the virus didn't dominate. Entire families have been wiped off the face of this planet for eternity, but the world will continue."

He smiled. It was a sad smile, devoid of anything. "Hope demands sacrifice. And, every vaccine needs its first live trial."

"Don't do this," I said.

"No, doctor!" Bonnie yelled, and the kids started to grunt in response.

Features tight, he injected the syringe into his arm. He pulled the plunger slightly and a tiny burst of red entered the syringe like a red lily in a clear field. Swallowing, he pressed the plunger down, and the liquid disappeared into his vein.

I stared as he pulled out the needle. "What have you done?"

He looked at the syringe before looking up. "I did what had to be done. Now, we'll see if my research is correct or if I'll become a test subject."

CHAPTER XVII

It took only twelve hours for Dr. Gidar to develop a fever. He said it was normal, but as his fever worsened, he couldn't hide the doubt in his eyes.

Justin and Clutch had both agreed Dr. Gidar needed to be quarantined until we could prove he was safe. Zach and I were assigned to watch him twenty-four/seven. We rotated shifts, and our days became alternating six-hour shifts. Hugh and Bonnie were allowed to return to the silo, but both had chosen to stay in the lab with Gidar and the kids.

The only people allowed to enter or leave the lab were Justin and Clutch. Even then, Justin had stopped in only once, on the first day. Griz had taken on much of Clutch's duties, so Clutch could be at the lab for much of each day. I could tell he hated that I was caught up in this mess, but he never voiced it. Instead, he hung out and kept a close eye on both Dr. Gidar and the kids.

Jase and Hali stopped by our porch at the beginning and end of their shifts, staying to chat through the window as long as they could. The others stayed in the silo, and I couldn't blame them. It wasn't exactly fun hanging out in an 800-square-foot house in the middle of a town graveyard and listening to the howls every night.

"Water," Dr. Gidar said weakly, and Bonnie rushed over with a glass.

Dr. Gidar worked until the third day, when he was too sick to continue. He still directed Bonnie and Hugh to run tests, this time on his blood, but neither had any kind of background or expertise.

The doctor now lay on the couch, while the kids watched the same cartoon they had one hundred times before. When Bonnie took the glass away, he struggled to sit up, and I rushed over to help. Clutch came to his feet and stepped closer.

"You must promise me something," he said.

"I know, I know. I need to bring Henry here," I replied.

He shook his head. "It's too late for that now. You need to bring my research to someone who can continue it."

I frowned. "Um. I would if I could, Doctor, but I don't know any hematologists around here."

"I know, but the government would have teams working on a vaccine."

I nodded, but we hadn't heard from the capital since the fires. "I'll try."

"No." He shook his head harder and pulled out a slip of paper. He held it out, and I grabbed it. He continued. "You must promise me that you'll deliver these items to the capital. You must do it soon, before the samples start to break down. Bonnie can direct you on the temperatures they need to be maintained at."

I read the list. His journals, blood samples from the kids, him, and Henry, and the antigen samples. I handed the note to Clutch and watched him as he read it.

"I'm dying," Dr. Gidar said. "But my research will save countless lives. That's why I need you to bring it to the capital. I know you'll have to leave the safety of New Eden. It's dangerous out there, but I remember your father telling me you had become a pilot." He smiled. "He was so proud of you. He spoke of how you succeeded at anything you set your mind to. You'll make it through."

He coughed and winced. Blood speckled his lips. "Your father was a man of his word, so I'm counting on the same from you. I need your word that you'll deliver these items to the capital as soon as you can."

I looked at Clutch, pleading for I don't know what in my gaze. He watched me, his jaw hard but his gaze soft. "If you do this, I'm going with you."

I gave a tight nod and inhaled deeply. "You have my word, Dr. Gidar. I'll deliver your research and samples to the capital."

"Good," he said, and he sank down into the couch.

He died several minutes later. Clutch and I stood there, Clutch with his sword, and I with my machete, ready for Dr. Gidar to awaken.

Thank God he never did.

We waited an hour before we let Bonnie check his pulse and take several blood samples. We carried him out the back and placed him in the wood coffin Hugh had built. The two of us stood outside, and I went to close the coffin, when Clutch put a hand on my arm. He pulled out his knife. "We need to play it safe."

I nodded and took a step back as Clutch stood by Gidar's head. I watched Clutch lift the blade and bring it down. No blood splattered, but I knew Clutch hadn't missed. He shut the coffin and we headed back inside.

Bonnie came running out. "Wait! Bring him back inside."

"But he's dead," I said.

"His heart rate had slowed too much for me to get a pulse. But, his cells were still alive when I checked them. He'll be like the kids, but he'll live."

I swallowed the bile rising in my throat. Bonnie must've seen something in our gazes because she shoved past us and to the coffin. She raised the cover and gasped. "What have you done?"

"We thought he was dead," I said weakly.

"I take full responsibility," Clutch added.

"You killed him." Her words dripped with venom.

"We couldn't risk him turning," Clutch said.

She watched us, her jaw lax, for a long moment. Finally, her eyes narrowed and her jaw clenched. "Don't let his death be in vain. Make sure you do what you promised him."

I lifted my chin. "We will."

I spun around and cut through the house and out the front door. Clutch caught up and kept pace alongside me. I reached out my hand, and he took it. He didn't let go, not even after we reached the silo.

Inside, we went straight to Justin's room. "Dr. Gidar is dead," I said. Not waiting for a response, we left and headed to the dorm where the remaining Fox survivors were eating. Clutch and I took turns in telling the events that had transpired and our mission.

"I'm in," Griz said.

"You're not going anywhere without me," Jase added.

"Without *us*," Hali said, giving Jase a look. "We're a team."

"You know I'll go," Vicki said.

"I would go, too," Deb started. "But..."

"I know," I said. "And, I understand."

"Are we going to fly?" Benji asked, his eyes wide. "I've never flown before."

I smiled. "You'll go on the next trip. We don't have much room this time. Actually," I said sheepishly. "I've never flown anything bigger than a four-seater."

"We can't all go," Clutch said. "We'll scout airports

tomorrow. There are two within twenty miles of here."

Jase raised his hand. "Uh, we know the capital is in Saskatchewan, but that's a pretty big area. Any idea exactly where we're going?"

"A place called Moose Jaw."

JUSTICE

CHAPTER XVIII

Christmas lights draped from the guardrails of the walkways, giving the silo a festive ambience. Except for the Marshall survivors, no one seemed to notice that a brilliant man had died yesterday. Justin had given everyone the day off. The excitement was palpable as residents prepared for tonight's Christmas Eve celebration. Nearly everyone—even the non-Christians—was helping decorate and plan skits. People were smiling. Benji was in a wild group of seven kids running down the walkways.

Clutch, Griz, and I were included in the few exceptions. We were fully geared up and on our way topside when we ran into Justin. "Good morning," he said with more enthusiasm than usual. "You'll be back before dark, won't you? Everyone's been looking forward to the banquet for some time."

"That's the plan," Clutch said.

"One, maybe two airports, and then invite Sister Donaldson and Connie to tonight's banquet," I said, neglecting to mention Henry's name. "It's a full day."

Justin nodded. "If they happen to bring Connie's husband, we'll have him stay in the lab with the others."

"Understood," Clutch said. "We'd better head out."

Justin stood off to the side. "It looks to be another sunny day. Be careful out there."

"We always are," Griz said as we walked past Justin and outside.

New Eden's vehicles were all parked outside the silo by a new gate installed after the fires.

Dozens, if not hundreds, of starlings flew over the ruins of New Eden. Birds were one of the few species that multiplied after the outbreak. Like mice and cats, they were everywhere now, and I had nightmares where the birds became sick like the dogs and wolves and would dive-bomb us. It wasn't as bad a nightmare as some.

Luckily, these starlings seemed to have no interest in us, to dive-bomb or otherwise, as we headed toward our vehicle. Clutch and Griz chose our Humvee since a few inches of snow still blanketed everything. It was full of gas, along with six five-gallon containers full—we always kept everything ready in case we had to make a sudden evacuation.

As we approached the vehicle, I glanced at Griz. "Shotgun, sucker."

Griz held up the key, a shit-ass grin on his face.

My eyes widened, and I made eye contact with Clutch. He took off running, and I leapt forward. He had a head start and reached the passenger side first. When he reached for the door, I tackled him from behind. He went down on a knee before catching himself and somehow managing to grab me and flip me over him. I landed on my back with a thud, and the air was knocked from my lungs.

I looked up to see Clutch standing over me. He tried to give me his mean look but failed, and he held out a hand. I grabbed it, and he pulled me to my feet. I pouted. "Bully."

"It was self-defense," he countered before he brushed snow from my hat. When he looked at me, I could see warm love in his brown eyes, and it melted me. I smiled and leaned into him, and he wrapped his arms around me.

The Humvee's engine roared to life, and we broke apart. Clutch opened the front passenger door, but instead of climbing in, he held the door open for me. I grinned and jumped in. "Thank you."

He climbed in the backseat, "Remember, paybacks are hell."

Griz drove through the gate, which the guards closed as soon as we'd left the safety of New Eden. The roads weren't as bad as I'd expected. Other than a few high drifts, which Griz seemed to take pleasure in plowing through, we made pretty decent time to the first airport, where we were able to fill up over fifty gallons of avgas into plastic containers and stack them in the Humvee. It was a small airport with fourteen hangars and without a zed in the vicinity. After we scared off the lone dog, we checked out each hangar. Unfortunately, not a single plane would start. We could jump start a couple, but I was hoping to find a plane that started without any issues the first time. Call me superstitious, but I felt more comfortable in a plane that didn't need encouragement to run.

After burning two hours there, we moved on to the second airport, which was only twelve miles away. The drive was peaceful, and I found it odd how not a single zed shambled around. No animals roamed the fields — the packs of dogs seemed to stay near towns. Every field we passed could've come straight out of a Bob Ross painting.

The second airport was larger than the first, with both a paved and a grass runway. I didn't like the row of trees off the end of the paved runway. Too many things — both two-legged and four-legged — could be hiding in there. The airport had twice as many hangars, with a large corporate hangar close to the airport office. Three zeds watched us from inside the office, and we quickly dispatched them.

This time, we only had to go through three hangars to find a plane that started. A big Cessna 210. It was more complex than anything I'd flown before, but it had four seats and could be loaded down with anything we could stuff into it. Like enough fuel to get us to the capital and back home again.

I gave one final look at the plane and put my hands on my hips. "Project Moose Jaw is a go."

"You're so adorable when you try to talk Army," Griz said as he and Clutch pulled the hangar door closed.

An eagle soared overhead, and I watched it ride a thermal. My soul lifted. Soon, I'd be up there again, like that eagle.

Our last stop of the day was Picadilly and Connie's house. The only other time we'd been there before, we'd left in a hurry. Since that visit two months ago, the squadron dropped off a box of food every other week...up until the snowstorm, when all travel had been halted.

We drove past the small store that served as a New Eden outpost and pulled up outside the two-story house. We cautiously stepped through undisturbed snow and up porch steps. I looked through the window. A wilted peace lily sat in the center of the kitchen table. "Looks like nobody's been here for a while."

After throwing a quick glance at Griz and me, Clutch knocked on the front door. "Sister Picadilly? Connie? We're from New Eden. Anyone home?" He waited for a minute before knocking again. "We're coming in."

He turned the handle and then shoved his shoulder into the door. It burst open, and we stepped inside. No fire burned in the fireplace, and I could see my breath.

The boxes the squadron delivered sat in the kitchen, filled with empty cans and garbage.

"Hello?" Clutch called out.

I looked around. "Maybe they're out."

"Yeah, maybe they went to the mall," Griz said.

I flipped him off and followed Clutch up the stairs.

As soon as the smell hit me, I reached for my machete. *Death.*

Zeds smelled like death.

Two doors were open. The only closed door was to the same room Henry had been in when we were here last time. Griz moved from behind me and checked the first of the open bedrooms while Clutch checked the other. I stood in the hallway and watched the closed door, while glancing down the stairs every few seconds.

When Clutch and Griz returned, they moved to the closed door. I stayed behind them. Clutch rapped his knuckles on the door. Nothing. He looked back to Griz who nodded, and Clutch opened the door.

No zed jumped out, and Clutch stepped inside. Griz followed.

"What the hell?" Griz said.

"What is it?" I asked, still keeping an eye on the hallway.

Neither answered, and both emerged from the room and closed the door.

I looked at both of them. "What's in there?"

"They're dead," Clutch said. "All three of them."

I frowned while I tried to make sense of his words.

"They'd survived so long. Why would they give up now?"

"Oh, they didn't give up," Griz said and brushed past me.

"What? What do you mean?"

"They were killed," Clutch replied.

"Are you sure?" I asked. "There weren't any signs of violence downstairs."

"Trust me," he said. "They didn't die by their own hands. Whoever killed them was thorough."

"Oh." Thankful I wouldn't have the images of the corpses of Picadilly, Connie, and Henry seared into my brain, I followed Clutch downstairs. "They were good people. Who would do such a thing?"

Downstairs, Griz stood by the back door and held up a hand. He made a gesture to Clutch, who nodded and moved closer to him. Clutch looked at me, held up his hand, and then pointed at the ground. *Stay here.* I frowned but nodded, not moving. What had Griz seen or heard?

Griz opened the door, and the two took silent steps outside. I moved to the door but didn't go outside. Clutch and Griz were at the small detached garage. They slammed open the door and rushed inside. A racket ensued as though an entire shelf of paint cans fell at once. Someone shouted and then there was eerie silence.

After an interminably long minute, Clutch and Griz emerged, dragging an unconscious man with greasy brown hair between them. I ran outside and stopped cold when I recognized who they'd found. He had three fingers missing from his left hand.

I felt myself grow faint.

Hodge.

CHAPTER XIX

Christmas day

Hodge wasn't dead. The leader of the Black Sheep — Camp Fox's captor — was alive. He bore a scar from where my bullet had skimmed his neck. If my shot had been one inch more accurate, the murderer would've been dead.

I stood outside the silo, my shirt doing nothing to block the cold air. "They'd be alive if I'd killed him when I'd had the chance."

"It's not your fault, so get that thought out of your head," Jase said while he rolled snow into a ball. "There aren't any guarantees in this life. Picadilly and the others could've just as easily been killed by zeds or animals than by Hodge. That you clipped him while he was speeding away with his tail between his legs is amazing enough."

I sighed and rested my head against the concrete wall. "I can't believe that he's been near New Eden for months. We've been feeding him. For all we know, we led him to the house, and he killed them."

"You can spend all day wondering what happened, but unless he talks, we'll never know. So, quit beating yourself up over it."

"But, Camp Fox is gone because of him. He killed so many people...Tyler—"

"I know," Jase said softly before scowling and tossing the snowball at a tree. "But, he's not going to hurt anyone else ever again."

I sighed. "Yeah, I guess you're right."

He stuck out his chest. "Of course I'm right. Now, let's get inside before we freeze to death out here."

We entered the silo to find a flurry of activity. I stopped the first person we came to. "What's going on? I didn't think the Christmas stuff was starting for a couple hours yet."

"Justin decided to get Hodge's trial out of the way. They're bringing him up now."

Jase and I glanced at each other, and we both hustled toward the control room, which served as town hall. Justin stood there, with Dr. Edmund at his side. Clutch and Griz, surrounded by a dozen other guards, led a bound Hodge up the steps and before Justin.

Hodge was clean now, a stark difference from how he'd been a few hours earlier. My brain would be forever scarred with seeing his naked body after we brought him to New Eden. I'd stood guard while Clutch and Griz had stripped him out of his flea- and lice-infested clothes before bringing him into the silo. The man hadn't bathed in months and reeked of sweat and shit. He'd even had the gall to wag his tongue at me when he stood naked in the snow.

"Like what you see, don't ya," he'd said.

"Not impressed," I'd said drily.

Clutch had also replied for me with a punch to Hodge's stomach. I'd smiled when the man was bent over, dry heaving his guts out. It was then I'd seen the scar across the side of his throat — the one I gave him.

He should've been dead.

Instead, he stood in New Eden, healthy and fed.

"Hodge, you have been judged and found guilty by a jury of New Eden citizens. You are here today to receive sentencing for your crimes in leading a group of bandits into ruthlessly attacking, without provocation, the peaceful citizens of New Eden, Camp Fox, and other groups of survivors. Your Black Sheep are responsible for over one hundred murders of innocent people, including children. You have been a festering sore on the communities working hard to rebuild after the outbreak. What do you have to say for yourself?"

Hodge spat on the floor. "Fuck you."

"So be it," Justin said. "Whether you live or die will be in the hands of fate."

Hodge laughed. "You think you can live like you could before? That you can have laws and jails? That's bullshit. The zeds have already won the war. To survive, you have to be like the zeds. You have to take what you need, or else you'll die. Hell, you're dead already. You just don't know it yet."

"It's ironic you say you must be like the zeds," Justin said. "Because, in a way, that's your punishment."

Hodge cocked his head.

Justin continued. "Our people are working on a vaccine against the virus. We lost our lead researcher two days ago, but our research team, with the guidance of Dr. Edmund, has isolated an antigen. You will serve as its test subject. If you survive, you will serve out the rest of your life, however long it may be, in a tiny prison cell."

"Ha," Hodge called out. "Give me what you got. I'll outlive you all."

"We shall see." Justin motioned to Dr. Edmund.

The doctor stepped forward with a syringe. We all watched in silence as Dr. Edmund injected Hodge with the antigen.

"It's done," the doctor said and took a step back.

I prayed Hodge survived, because I wanted to be the one who killed him.

CHAPTER XX

Six days later

The fucker survived. He hadn't even caught a serious fever.

I was one of the four guards on duty at the lab, and tried not to look at him while he ate New Eden food. Hodge was still imprisoned in the small house's dank cellar. One of his ankles was handcuffed to a chain that looped around the stairs. Each wrist was handcuffed to a chain looped through a cinderblock. No one was taking any chances at him escaping, though he seemed quite content to be in captivity.

No surprise there. He was safe, well fed, and didn't have to do shit for any of it.

He scooped up rice with his fingers (we refused to give him a spoon) and examined it. "This could use some salt," he said and popped it into his mouth.

We ignored him. Zach and I were stuck in the basement with him, while Jase and Hali were upstairs. We rotated with them every hour during our shift to keep Hodge from grinding too deeply on our nerves. Though, he tended to grind on my nerves within five minutes of every hour I spent in that basement.

"You know, your timing at picking me up was perfect. I just finished the last can of food you guys so generously dropped off."

I started a mental count to ten, trying my best to ignore him. Zach walked slowly over to Hodge, lifted his foot, and shoved the prisoner onto his back. Then, he snatched the bowl of rice, dumped it in the pail that served as Hodge's latrine, and returned to his position.

I gave Zach a grin.

Hodge pulled himself back up. "That wasn't nice. I wasn't finished yet."

"Oh, sorry," I said, my words laced with sarcasm. "With the way you kept yammering on and on, we assumed you must've been full."

He watched me for a moment and cocked his head. "Have we met?"

When I didn't answer, he continued. "You seem awfully familiar. Every day, I try to remember where I've seen you before. Have we fucked?"

I shot him a quick glare and turned back away.

"Don't worry. I'll remember, eventually."

I turned to face him then. "I'm surprised you don't remember me. You could say I left a lasting impression." I said as I ran my finger along the side of my throat.

When the meaning of my words hit him, his face tightened in an expression of pure rage. "You. You were a part of the group that put a hurtin' on my Sheep. I got stranded after that little adventure and didn't make it back to my Sheep until they'd all been wiped out, no thanks to the dickless wonders at New Eden." He chuckled drily. "And, you guys say you're peaceful. How many people have you killed?"

"We kill only those who've attacked innocents," Zach said.

"Innocents? Bah. There are no innocents anymore. All the innocents are rotting away while they eat their own families."

"Too bad the vaccine worked on you," Zach said. "I was looking forward to seeing you turn into one of those things."

Hodge sneered. "Instead, I have free room and board, and my own personal security detail. I'd say things worked out pretty good."

Zach's brow rose. "Pretty good, huh? You think Justin is going to keep you here and feed you? You really think that? You don't know Justin very well then."

Hodge's lips thinned.

Zach continued. "I can guarantee that whatever Justin is planning for you involves pain. Lots and lots of pain."

"We'll see about that," Hodge said. "I heard the lab rat talking upstairs. My blood carries the cure now. I'm carrying precious cargo."

Zach spoke. "Didn't you hear? Bonnie's done with you. That last liter of blood she took was all they needed to finish their research. Now, you're baggage." With that, Zach sat on his chair and stared at Hodge.

The prisoner turned his attention back onto me. His features relaxed, and his lips curled upward. "I remember you. You're the whore of one of those men my Sheep caught. You begged so pretty. I was looking forward to seeing what else you'd beg for."

I'd cried out when Hodge held a gun to Clutch's held, and I didn't regret it. My plea had saved his life. "You never would've gotten me to beg for anything else," I said.

"Oh, you would've begged. They *always* begged."

I heard boots hitting each step. Jase, then Hali, came into view. Their shoulders slumped; they looked as excited to be in this basement as I felt. "Thank God," I muttered, and turned from Hodge without another glance.

"Oh, goody," Hodge said from behind. "My favorite girl is back."

"Fuck you," Jase and Hali said at the same time.

"Soon enough, that's a promise," Hodge replied.

Jase sighed and shook his head.

Hali glanced at me. "I'm so glad this is our last hour for the day."

I gave her a knowing glance. "I promise."

With that, I took the stairs two at a time. Hodge was still talking when I reached the first floor, and Zach soon followed.

"Some folks grow on you over time," Zach said. "But, he's not one of them."

I dramatically shook my head. "No, he's not."

In the living room, the two kids were watching their same cartoon, while Bonnie was putting labels on vials. She glanced up. "I'll have everything packed and ready to go by tonight. Dr. Edmund said to keep everything below forty degrees and above freezing if you can. The samples can save the capital thousands of hours of work so they don't have to start from scratch from only Dr. Gidar's research notes."

"That shouldn't be a problem," I said. "As long as the weather holds, we'll head out first thing in the morning."

"What a way to kick off the New Year," Zach said before taking a seat by the kids. The boy looked at him, and Zach raised his hand. The boy mimicked, and Zach slowly moved his hand around. Zach looked up, surprised. "Hey, he's improving."

"They have good days and bad days," Bonnie said. "Without Dr. Gidar, we can't do anything for them except keep them comfortable and hope for the best. He planned to focus on the children once he worked out a vaccine. He truly was a brilliant man."

"Yeah," I agreed. Not only did his research lead to a

possible vaccine, his blood had been the breakthrough he'd been looking for. His calculations and tests had gotten him as far as he could go. When he introduced the antigen to his own system, the antigen became stronger, but too much of the live virus had been included. It had taken Dr. Edmund—a general practitioner—only a few hours of testing Dr. Gidar's blood to verify the results and find Dr. Gidar's mistake. The doctor hadn't purified the antigen before injecting himself.

Fortunately, the hour passed quickly. Griz and three other guards arrived, and I pulled on my coat with gusto. "Have fun with him," I said. "He's a talker today."

A smile crept up Griz's face. "He can talk. But, he won't like what I do to him every time he opens that pie hole."

I grinned as Griz and his partner headed down to the basement. When Jase and Hali came upstairs, they joined Zach and me on the long walk back to the silo. On our walk, we met Vicki, who had her eyes narrowed in an intense stare focused on the lab in front of her.

"Hi Vicki," I said. "Heading to the lab?"

Startled, she looked at us. She lifted the bag slightly. "I thought I'd bring some treats to Bonnie and the kids."

"They'll like that," Jase said.

She nodded and then continued on her way.

"Wow, she was in the zone," Hali said. "I don't think she would've even noticed us if you hadn't said something."

"She's had a lot on her mind. Seeing Hodge again really upset her,"

"I'm surprised she'd go anywhere near the lab with him in it," Jase said.

"Yeah," I said.

Vicki had been Camp Fox's cook, and she had developed more than a little crush on Tyler. She'd been resilient. No matter what happened, she'd always been rational and strong. Then, she'd watched Hodge kill Tyler in front of her. After that, she was still strong, but she was quieter, more distant. When we brought Hodge into the silo, I saw the pain in her eyes. At that moment, it was as though she was watching Tyler die all over again.

The only other people we met on our walk were the guards at each gate. The dogs were building in numbers again. Once the weather warmed somewhat, they showed back up, with their numbers doubling every day. They were starving. The sunlight cast shadows under rib bones and hipbones. I wanted to feed them, but I knew that would only draw more to us. And they were sick. While Bonnie said Dr. Gidar had told her the vaccine might also have some effect on dog bites, he hadn't done any analysis to validate the possibility.

"Poor things," Hali said.

"Those poor things want to eat you," Zach said.

Hali didn't reply.

"It does suck, though," Jase said. "To think most of

those dogs were people's pets at one time, and now they're sick and breeding out here. I wonder if there's hope for any of them."

"Some will survive," I said optimistically. "I would think they're like us. Some of us are surviving the outbreak. Some of them will, too."

"I hope so." After that, Jase said nothing else until we reached the silo and headed to our bunks.

I spent the next few hours with Clutch, planning our trip to the capital. It would be the longest flight I'd taken without GPS, so I wanted to be accurate on my flight plan, with any possible landing sites marked along the way.

Justin didn't have any radio frequency, let alone address, so I decided to fly into the Canadian Air Force base at Moose Jaw. I figured if any airport in the area were operational, it'd be that one.

At some point, Justin stopped by. "You two have a minute?"

"Sure," I said, stretching my stiff neck.

Justin looked at each of us. "Hodge is dead."

"He was alive and annoyingly well earlier today," I said.

"I'm sure he was. But, a couple dozen stab wounds didn't help."

"Wow," was all I said.

"Either of you have anything to do with it?"

My eyes widened. I looked at Clutch, who looked just as surprised, and back at Justin. "No. Not at all."

"This is the first I've heard of it," Clutch said.

Justin nodded and looked around. "Well, I figured as much. Griz and Joachim said they'd stepped away for only a few minutes. They said Hodge must've gotten a hold of a knife and stabbed himself. I think death by dozens of stab wounds is an interesting way to commit suicide."

"I'll talk to my people," Clutch said. "We had him under twenty-four hour surveillance. And none of my people had the authority to harm him unless he attempted escape. Griz would never disobey an order."

Justin shrugged. "It's okay. Hodge's death isn't a loss to New Eden, especially now that we have the antigen Dr. Gidar was seeking. If anything, it saves us time and resources. There will be an investigation, but I suspect we won't find anything. You know how these things go."

Clutch tilted his head into an almost nod.

"Well," Justin continued. "No need to keep you. You have to fly out early tomorrow. Get some rest. Just think, once the capital can create and distribute the vaccine to everyone, there will never be another zed again. Imagine that."

Once he left, I looked at Clutch. "Did you order Hodge's death?"

"I had nothing to do with his death."

"Do you think Griz did?"

"Griz wouldn't have killed him, not without talking it over with me first."

"You think Justin ordered it?"

"If he did, why ask us about it?"

I sighed. "Well, then we have a vigilante around here."

TEMPERANCE

CHAPTER XXI

Clutch, Griz, Zach, and I had doused ourselves with no-scent spray made for hunters. We figured it couldn't hurt in case we came across any dogs at the airport. I'd never thought of using the stuff until we found some in the store at Des Moines. I mused if it would also work to mask our scent from zeds.

Jase was pissed that we were taking Zach instead of him, but Clutch had been obstinate. He refused to take Jase, because that meant Hali would come, and if things went to shit, Jase would be distracted if Hali got hurt. Jase denied there was anything between him and Hali, but Clutch refused nonetheless.

"Weren't you being a tad hypocritical back there?" I asked as we walked toward the Humvee, carrying a small cooler. "You're as bad as Jase."

Clutch shot a look at me. "What do you mean?"

"What if something happened to me? You'd be distracted, too."

"Nothing will happen," he said gruffly. "I'll make sure of it.

I shook my head and chuckled drily. "You're such a he-man."

"It's not that you can't take care of yourself," he said. "I know you're more than capable. It's that," he paused, "I want to take care of you."

I let his words linger for a minute before speaking. "I think that's the most romantic thing you've ever said to me."

He didn't smile. Instead, he reached out and pulled me to him. "I mean it," he said quietly.

"No one's getting lucky on this trip," Griz said as he walked around us. "Not unless I'm the one getting lucky."

"You think you'll find some sheep on this trip?" Clutch asked.

Griz flipped him off and didn't look back again as he headed to the Humvee.

I laughed. Griz was a hot catch for any woman. Even with men outnumbering women seven to one in New Eden, women flocked to him. It was likely because he was young, able-bodied, and easy to get along with. Jase and I, though, gave him crap about it. We picked on him that the ladies were intent on finding out if the "once you go black" urban legend was actually true. Griz denied it and said it was his sparkling personality.

Griz dropped his gear into the back of the vehicle before climbing into the driver's seat. Everyone else's gear was loaded into the remaining cargo space. We'd loaded the avgas for the plane yesterday. We had more gear than usual since we had no idea how long the thousand-mile trip could take. Before the outbreak, I could've flown to Moose Jaw in less than six hours flight time, not counting a fuel stop and immigration check.

In the middle of winter, we had about eight hours of sunlight each day. We were planning to make Moose Jaw tomorrow, stopping this afternoon to refuel and camp down for the night. Doing anything after dark was dangerous and a risk none of us were willing to take.

The sun hadn't yet peeked over the horizon; we had a good head start on the day. When we reached the airport, everything was still and silent. No new zeds appeared in the office window. No dogs sniffed around the hangar when Zach pushed the door open. The white Cessna with a yellow and orange stripe sat patiently inside. I smiled and tapped the engine cowl. "Soon, baby. You'll be dancing on the clouds soon."

We pulled the plane out of the hangar. Clutch and I topped off the fuel while Griz and Zach loaded as much fuel as they could fit into the baggage. The rest of our gear would have to sit on our laps. The plane was going to be weighted down. It'd need much of the runway, but I'd done my calculations. We'd get off the ground. On a hot, humid day, we might not be so lucky. But the cold air was a pilot's friend. Cold air was more dense, which meant it provided more lift. An airplane could lift off the ground easier and faster, and that was exactly what I needed for today.

"It's full." I handed Clutch the half-full fuel jug. Before sliding down, I sat on the top wing another minute and watched the tip of the sun break the horizon. It was going to be a beautiful sunrise, one of those fiery orange ones. Movement in the direction of the airport office caught the corner of my eye, and I squinted to make out the dark shapes emerging from the tree line in the distance.

I sucked in a breath.

Clutch held out a hand to help me down. "Ready?"

I glanced down at him, my eyes wide.

"What's wrong?"

"We're being stalked." I pointed in the direction of the animals.

Clutch moved away to see for himself. "Griz, Zach. We need to get a move on. We've got company coming for breakfast."

Griz and Zach were holding the last of our bags, and Griz closed the back of the Humvee. He looked in the direction of the dogs. "Sneaky little bastards."

"They couldn't have smelled us," Zach said.

"They could've heard us," I said as I slid down the windshield to stand on the engine cowl. "The Humvee isn't exactly a stealth vehicle."

"Shit." I glanced over to see Zach drop everything

and kick at something. "Get away!"

Clutch grabbed his sword and ran over the same time Griz slammed his machete down on something. Clutch swung and a yelp echoed through the morning air. They each kept swinging until I saw three furred shapes lay lifeless on the ground.

Zach lifted his pant leg and looked up at the other two men. "Did you see them? Were they sick?"

"Yeah," Clutch said.

"Yeah, you saw them, or yeah, they were sick?" Zach asked.

A pause, then, "Both."

Zach swung his fist through the air. "Shit."

"Come on," Clutch said. "We've got to go."

Zach didn't move. "I think I'll sit this one out."

"They'll have a hospital at the capital. They can help."

"The earliest we'll reach them is tomorrow. By then, I'll be dead weight. No, I think I'll stick around here, watch the sun rise, and then head back to New Eden."

After a long moment, Clutch nodded tightly.

Griz patted Zach on the shoulder. "Take care of yourself." He grabbed his bags and put them into the plane.

Zach picked up the bags and handed them to Clutch. "I'll try to get their attention, draw them away from the plane and runway."

Zach looked my way and faked a grin. "Be careful with these two losers."

I forced a smile as well, while tears blurred my vision. "See you when we get back," I lied.

Unable to look at Zach without losing it, I slid off the Cessna and climbed into the pilot's seat. I pulled out the airplane's checklist, which I had spent hours studying last night, and laid it on my lap.

Clutch and Griz climbed in while I quickly went through each of the steps. I engaged the starter, and the Cessna's engine roared to life. The noise spurred the animals into action. No longer stalking, they ran toward the plane, slowing as they approached.

Suddenly, the Humvee sped in front of us, scattering the dogs and wolves in all directions. I taxied forward, using the distance to warm up the engine enough for takeoff. Zach drove the Humvee like a mad man, zigzagging around the airport and throwing the animals off their game.

When we reached the runway, I did a fast run-up on the engine before throttling back. I looked at both Clutch and Griz. "You guys buckled in?"

Clutch held up his thumb, and Griz said, "Let's rock and roll."

I checked the prop and mixture one last time, pressed the throttle in, and the engine roared. The plane moved forward, slowly at first, then quickly picking up speed. Even without Zach, the plane was weighted down, and the wheels didn't pop off until we were two-thirds of the way down the paved runway.

Careful to keep our climb shallow, I looked down to

see the Humvee come to a stop, and animals gathered around it, as though waiting for treats. I shivered and fought to stay focused on flying. If I dwelled on the fact we'd lost a man before the mission even started, then I'd be tempted to return to the safety of New Eden.

But I'd made a promise. A promise worth keeping, even if it killed me.

HOPE

CHAPTER XXII

"Things sure look different from up here," Griz said. "I could get used to traveling first-class."

"I was beginning to think you were going to sleep the entire trip," I said.

"I wasn't sleeping," he countered.

"You were snoring," I said.

"You snore like a rhino with a head cold," Clutch added.

"You guys make this shit up," Griz said. "I'm too pretty to snore."

Smiling, I looked out at the endless earth beneath us. At this altitude, we couldn't see anything moving, which gave the world a serenity I hadn't felt in a long time. Unplowed roads hid under a blanket of pure white, with no tire tracks or road salt to taint the snow. Trees and quiet houses were all that broke the rolling landscape.

Clutch looked up from the map. "Adjust ten degrees west."

I did as he instructed and savored the feeling of flying. I knew my days of stick and rudders were limited. At some point, all fuel would break down enough that no plane would run.

Clutch pointed in the distance where the horizon loomed higher. "We'll fly right over the Black Hills. Should be quite the view."

Boy, was it ever. Tree-covered hills went on farther than we could see. It was nature's splendor, untouched by the virus. I sighed. "I want to find a cabin and retire here." I looked to Clutch. "How about it? Want to retire here?"

He smiled. "I'm all for that."

The Black Hills soon gave way to North Dakota's flatlands, whose simple landscape had its own flavor of surreal peace. Once we flew over the bombed ruins of Bismarck, we approached the point of our journey to refuel and stay overnight. I began our descent and watched the trees for signs of the wind's direction and strength. "We're lucky," I said. "Hardly a breeze today."

The airport came into view from nearly ten miles away. That was an advantage of flatter land. About twenty other buildings dotted the airport on a circular drive. I read through my checklist several times before handing it over to Clutch. "I'll fly over to make sure the runway is clear," I said. "Then we'll come back around and land."

Except for a snowdrift at one end of the runway, the rest of the pavement was relatively clear. "We got lucky," I said. "I was afraid we'd have to deal with snow, but they must've gotten some strong winds here."

Clutch read each step on the checklist to me as I flew the pattern and lined up on final. Adrenaline pumped through my veins and I clenched the yoke. "Guys, you better make sure you're buckled in tight. I've never landed anything as big as this plane before."

I was a few hundred feet off the ground when the stall alert sounded. "Shit," I muttered, realizing I was trying to land the 210 like my Cub instead of like the much-heavier airplane it was. I added in power to pick up speed and lowered the rest of the flaps.

The runway came up way too fast, and I clenched my teeth as I brought the plane down. I made the mistake and let it drop, and the plane jumped right off the ground. After porpoising through another bounce, the plane settled on the ground. But, the snowdrift at the end of the runway was quickly approaching, and I slammed on the brakes. Clutch grabbed the dash to keep from crashing into the instruments. Gear banged around, and something slammed against the back of my seat.

The plane came to a stop less than ten feet from the snowdrift. After a moment of stillness, I breathed. "Wow, that wasn't pretty."

Griz laughed. "Pretty? More like it was the damn

near scariest thing I've ever seen."

"I guess I should've done a go-around."

"We're alive," Clutch said. "And the plane will fly again. I hope."

"I'm a bit rusty," I said as I turned the plane around and taxied toward the buildings. "And, in my defense, this plane is three times the size of my Cub."

"You did fine," Clutch said. "You're the best pilot I know."

"I'm the *only* pilot you know."

He shrugged and looked outside.

"How about I park by the airport office?" I asked.

"Which one is that?" Griz asked.

I pointed at the first building we'd reach. "I think that's the one."

"Looks as good as any," Clutch said.

"It's closest to the runway in case we need to make a fast exit," Griz said.

I taxied toward the small building, which bore the sign, *Welcome to Garrison Municipal Airport*. Three planes were tied down on the ramp, with small patches of snow accumulated around their tires. I pulled up to the small building and looked at its windows and glass door. "How's it look?" I asked. "We have a little over a quarter tank if we need to find another place."

"And have to go through another one of those landings?" Griz said. "Nah, this is good."

"You can fly next time," I offered.

"That landing was great," Griz said. "No complaints

here."

I parked the plane and cut the engine, and Clutch climbed out first, following by Griz. With weapons drawn, they approached the small building. I stayed in the plane in case we had to make a hasty retreat. They checked the door, the windows, and walked around the building.

The nearest town had less than two thousand people, which was why I selected this airport. It was big enough to have a runway I could use, but small enough that there shouldn't be a great risk of zeds or wild animals. Bandits were another story. There never seemed to be any rhyme or reason as to where those assholes showed up.

A moment later, Clutch reappeared and gave the all-clear, and I climbed out. I reached into the backseat and grabbed my backpack, which was what had flown loose during landing. The cooler still sat, safe, on the floorboard. I opened the baggage and began unloading fuel containers while Clutch and Griz argued over how best to break into the locked office. Ignoring them, I found a ladder near the airport's fuel tanks and began to refuel the Cessna.

I sighed when I saw the pay-at-pump machine and missed the days of easy convenience. Now, however many hundreds of gallons were waiting in the airport's fuel tank would wait in there forever. Six plastic containers later, the Cessna was refueled and ready to go. I checked the oil and frowned.

"What's wrong?"

"Jesus." I dropped the dipstick. After I picked it up, I turned and scowled at Clutch. "Don't sneak up on me like that. Trying to give me a heart attack?"

"I didn't sneak up on you."

"You didn't mean to, but you did," I said. "It's that Ranger thing. Griz does it, too. You guys are just like sneaky little kittens right before they pounce."

Clutch straightened. "I am *not* a kitten."

"Kitten or not," I said. "Can you find me some oil? We're running a couple quarts low already."

"Only if you promise to never call me 'kitten' again."

I thought about it for an exaggerated moment. "Okay, I promise."

Clutch smiled. "I'll find you some oil. What kind do you need?"

I shrugged.

"Okay," he said. "I'll find you something."

"Luckily, tomorrow will be a shorter flight, so we shouldn't burn quite as much oil. Plus, we'll have plenty of fuel left."

"Let's hope we won't need it."

"I give up," Griz said from several feet away. He threw down the screwdriver.

"You were trying to pick a lock with a screwdriver?" I asked.

He rolled his eyes. "Aw, shucks. Why didn't I think of that? I left my lock picking kit at home."

He picked up the brick doorstop sitting by the door.

Clutch spoke. "Don't break —"

Griz smashed the brick into the door. Glass shattered and shards fell.

"What are we going to use for a door now?" Clutch asked.

Griz shrugged. "You're smart. Figure something out." He reached through, unlocked the door, and peered inside. "Hello? Anybody home?"

After a long moment, Griz turned back to us. "Smells fresh enough." He held the door open. "After you, my lady."

"Why, thank you," I said with a curtsy and stepped inside.

Griz must've been confident there were no dangers inside, or else he never would've let me go in first. Both Clutch and he were a lot alike. They always were the first ones to walk into danger.

Glass crunched under my books as I crossed the tiled floor and grabbed several sectional maps for areas I didn't yet have. "This place is brand new," I said. "Most small airport offices are falling apart."

"There's your oil," Clutch said, pointing at a box by a display case.

"Well, that was easy," I said. "I should've held back from making that promise."

"Promise or no promise, it's the right thing to do."

I shrugged before testing the couch. "Ooh. Dibs on the couch."

"Go ahead," Griz said from the hallway. "I'm taking

a recliner."

I followed him into the pilot's lounge where two leather recliners sat in addition to a workstation. After we checked the restrooms, we broke into the vending machines and stocked up on candy bars. I left the chips for someone else, as most chips tasted too stale anymore.

Ten minutes later, we'd each downed a soda and candy bars. No one had spoken for a while, and I had something to get off my chest. "Hey, Griz?"

"Yep?" he mumbled after tossing a handful of Reese's Pieces into his mouth.

"What really happened to Hodge?"

His chewing paused for a moment before continuing. "He died."

Clutch was carefully watching Griz.

"Did you kill him?" I asked.

"Nope."

"But, you did have something to do with it," Clutch said.

Griz shrugged. "There was someone who wanted him dead more than I did."

I leaned back when the pieces fell into place. The last time I saw her, she'd seemed like a weight had been lifted from her shoulders. It had been so obvious, yet I hadn't even thought of her. "Vicki."

Griz didn't respond, which was as much an affirmation as agreement.

After a while, Griz spoke. "We all wanted to do it.

The bastard deserved it. She shouldn't be punished for delivering justice."

"She won't," Clutch said. "Hodge killed himself. End of story."

"End of story," I echoed.

"He begged," Griz said. "When we let her at him, he begged like the pansy he was."

"Good," Clutch said.

I inhaled deeply. I wanted to find pleasure in Hodge's death, but I only found retribution. It was good enough, and I took another bite.

Once we were full of food, we lounged around the office. It was cold in there and would be uncomfortable tonight, even with the small camp stove Clutch had brought along. But, it was better than flying at night and arriving at Moose Jaw in the dark.

I sat at the desk and perused the drawers for anything useful. In the drawer with pens and rubber bands, I found a key chain with a single car key on it. "Hey guys?"

"What's up?" Griz replied.

"Either of you see a Dodge parked around here somewhere?"

"Yep. A nice Dodge Challenger was parked in back."

I tossed him the key chain. "That must be their loaner car."

Griz smiled. "Nice." And he headed out the door.

A moment later, I heard a car start. My eyes widened. "I'm surprised it started."

Clutch, who had been lying on my couch, sat up and rubbed his stiff shoulder.

Griz hurried back in. "Anyone in the mood to check out the area?"

Clutch pushed himself up with a grunt. "Not a bad idea. Any locals would've heard us fly in. It would be good to know what kinds of risks we might have to deal with tonight."

I pulled my gloves on. "Let me lock the plane."

Once I locked the plane doors, we all stood in front of the airport office, staring at the broken glass door.

"I told you not to break it," Clutch said.

Griz held up a finger. "Hold on."

He disappeared back inside, the sound of pounding and banging ensued, and Griz returned with a wood door with a *Ladies* sign on it.

I sighed. "What am I going to use now for privacy?"

"You can use the guys' bathroom."

I scrunched my face. "You know how disgusting guys' bathrooms are?"

He didn't answer. Instead, he propped the door behind the other and pulled out some paracord. Once he had it tied onto the metal bar in the door, he took a step back and put his hands on his hips. Pride gleaned in his smile. "Problem fixed."

Clutch narrowed his eyes. "I could sneeze and knock that door down."

"I'd like to see you do better," Griz said.

"Well, it's enough that if any animals or zeds tried to

get through, we'd know," I said. "But, it sure wouldn't stop a person with an IQ above forty."

Griz blew us off and headed toward the car. I climbed into the backseat, and enjoyed being chauffeured.

Griz played it safe, carefully plowing through snowdrifts. He stopped after we made a full circle of the airport.

"I could get used to this," I said, enjoying the quiet. We saw only a few animal tracks and no zed tracks. No tire tracks besides ours. Out here, it felt as though we were the only ones left in the world.

"Let's check out how many tracks there are at the edge of town," Clutch said. "It's close enough to the airport that it could be a problem."

Griz agreed. "My thoughts, too."

I enjoyed the view and heated air as Griz weaved down roads toward the town.

"Stop," Clutch commanded.

Griz hit the brakes. "What do you see?"

Clutch pointed to the right. "See those soccer fields over there?"

I slid across the seat to look out. The fields were still a half mile away, but something wasn't right about them. Instead of open fields, tall fences enclosed rows of white trailers lined up like they would be in a RV park. Griz drove toward the soccer fields, and I watched as we approached the fields. Zeds—at least a couple hundred—stood around. Reinforced fences surrounded the fields.

As we approached, no zeds moved, but I sensed their gazes upon us. "There are so many of them."

"They're frozen," Clutch said.

Griz brought the car to a stop not far from the fields. "This must've been a FEMA camp set up during the outbreak. It did a good job at containing them. The fences are still standing."

"Not quite," I said, and pointed to a place in the fence where a tunnel had been dug under. Dirt sat upon snow. Inside the fence, streaks of brown zed sludge stains led to the tunnel. Two large dogs were yanking at a frozen zed in a morbid game of tug o' war. The zed had no face—it had already been torn off by the dogs. When the zed fell, the dogs continued to pull. One fell back with its prize: an arm. The second dog soon followed with the other arm.

They carried their "food" back to the fence and crawled under. When they crossed the road, they paused to look at us. Deeming us no threat, they continued away from town, one of the dogs dragging the leash still connected to its collar.

"Wow," was all I managed to say after the dogs disappeared.

"It's like a deep freezer full of beef for them," Clutch said.

Griz chuckled drily as he turned the car around and started back toward the airport. "Now, that's the definition of irony."

"How so?" I asked.

"Zeds hunted the dogs. Now, the dogs hunt zeds."

Nothing about this felt ironic. It felt sad. Beloved pets had been abandoned and forced to do awful things to survive. They weren't much different from us, I suppose. We'd done some pretty awful things in the name of survival, too.

I noticed Clutch was eying me, and I tried to give him my "I'm okay" look.

But, it was hard to fake it when I knew we were nowhere close to being out of the woods yet.

CHAPTER XXIII

After a cold night, we were anxious to sit in a warm airplane as soon as the sun rose the following morning. The Cessna lifted off the runway easier today, with less weight than when we'd taken off in Nebraska yesterday morning.

Clutch checked the airplane's clock. "We have under three hundred miles left, so we'll be there in roughly two hours, give or take."

"We'll have to be careful when we get close to Moose Jaw," I said. "We know they have an operational air force, and I'm not sure how they are at welcoming other folks flying into their airspace."

"We'll find out soon enough," Griz said.

Clutch dialed in numbers on the radio. "The radio's set to the frequencies listed on the map. If they've changed them, we won't have any way to know unless they're transmitting them."

When we were one hundred miles out, Clutch began to transmit our intention and location on the radio. When we were fifty miles out, someone responded.

"806 Romeo Bravo, this is Wing 15. Squawk 1219."

Clutch read back the instructions and set our transponder to 1219 so they could track us. When we were only ten miles out, the tower fed us landing instructions, which we followed to a T. When I was on final, I could hear Griz praying in the backseat, and I shot him the bird quickly before focusing on my landing.

Fortunately, for my ego and our well-being, this landing was spot on. When I pulled off the runway, the tower directed me where to go next.

"806 Romeo Bravo, take taxiway Alpha to the FBO."

I taxied toward a large hangar bearing an Air Force sign. A man jogged onto the ramp and flagged me to park at a location not far from the hangar.

"806 Romeo Bravo, cut your engines and stay in the plane until you are authorized."

I smirked. "We're the only plane with its engine running. It's not like they need to keep using our N-number."

"Guess they want to stay in practice," Clutch said.

Once we stopped and I cut the engine, I turned to Clutch. "We made it."

He smiled. "Thanks to you."

I couldn't help myself, and I leaned over and kissed

him. "And thanks to my navigator."

"Don't forget me," Griz said. "It was my praying and good luck that got us here safely."

I laughed. "Thank you, Griz, for getting us here."

The flagger approached, and I opened my door to talk with him.

He had a wide smile. "Welcome to Wing 15. We don't see many planes that aren't based here. You can step out and stretch if you need, but please wait by your plane for another minute or two. Our official welcome wagon is on its way."

After a quick glance to each other, we climbed out with our gear, weapons sheathed, and I grabbed the cooler. We stood together. Clutch and Griz stood tall, tense, and still. I fidgeted, waiting to see what came next.

A black SUV came speeding toward us. I found myself shiver, not from cold, but from nerves, as the vehicle came to a stop only ten feet away. The front passenger door and two back doors opened, and three men stepped out, two of them holding machine guns. The third man, a younger one of perhaps twenty or so, walked over to us and smiled. "I'm Peter. Welcome to Moose Jaw, the capital of the Provinces of North America."

CHAPTER XXIV

Peter escorted us into the large hangar where several military jets sat. His armed guards followed ten feet behind us. They had allowed us to keep our weapons, though a machete against a rifle wouldn't exactly be a fair fight.

I knew Clutch and Griz were as on edge as much as I was. We were in a new place, surrounded by unknown people. *Armed* people. And, these people were currently in control.

Despite Clutch and Griz's cool demeanors, I'd bet they were ready to jump into action the instant these people turned hostile. I knew that if they thought anything was off, they'd let me know. They always seemed to know how to handle these situations. I felt much safer that they both came along on this mission.

Peter talked as he led us through the hangar. "Most

newcomers are found by our recon teams and brought here. It's pretty rare to have folks fly in here themselves."

"We're from New Eden, in Nebraska," Clutch said.

Griz added, "New Eden's radios were knocked out. Otherwise, we would've called ahead."

"I'm glad you came," Peter said. "We've been worried that something happened to New Eden. We had planned a trip down there, but mechanical issues have been grounding our drones, and fuel for manned flights has been restricted to training and high-priority missions only."

"We have time-sensitive material to get to an expert ASAP," Clutch said.

Peter held up his hand. "Aline already knows you're here, and I'll get you to her as soon as I can. I'm not trying to be a bottleneck, but we have protocols to follow. Before I can bring you into the capital, you need checked for bites or any signs of infection. Don't worry, we'll get you to the people you need to see."

Behind the jets stood a makeshift room built with plastic and tarps. Peter motioned to a person wearing blue rubber gloves. "Mason has done this a thousand times before. It doesn't take long if you do as he says. I'll take you into the capital after you pass inspection. Now if you'll excuse me, I'll need to get time slated on Aline's schedule so you can meet with her today."

"Who's Aline?" I asked.

Peter smiled. "Oh, Aline Palvery is the President of

P.N.A., the Provinces of North America."

"I've never met a president before." I looked at Clutch and Griz. "It sounds like we're getting the red carpet treatment today."

"She's a good, strong leader. She does everything she can to get this new country up and running," Mason said. "Now, if you'll come with me, there are two rooms, one for the gentlemen and one for the lady. Set your gear and clothes on the table and step into the shower stall for a medical inspection and chem-bath."

I scowled. "Chem-bath?"

"To kill lice, fleas, and anything else immigrants tend to bring in. It doesn't hurt, I assure you. I've been through it myself." He must've caught my expression because he added, "Not that you guys have lice. It's standard operating procedures, that's all."

We entered the small room, and Mason directed us to our stalls. I eyed Clutch. He gave me a tight nod. I took a deep breath and stepped off to the right and undressed.

Thirty minutes later, after a thorough examination, chem-bath, and a detailed inspection of my backpack, weapons, and cooler, I was dressed and reunited with Clutch and Griz. Guards gave us water and flatbread while we waited in one of the hangar's offices.

Peter arrived soon after, smiling. "You all passed inspection with flying colors." He pulled out white stickers and markers. "If you don't mind, put your name on these, so folks know to introduce themselves."

My brows rose, and I looked at Clutch and Griz, who looked just as humored.

We put on our stickers, and Peter hemmed. "Uh, Cash, Griz, and Clutch? Those are your names?"

"They're the ones we go by," Clutch replied.

"Oh. Okay. Well, if that's the case, it's nice to meet you." He shook each of our hands. "I have an appointment set for you to talk with Aline." He glanced at his watch and motioned to the door. "It's in less than an hour, so we'd better be on our way. You can keep your weapons. Everyone carries in the capital, but the laws are strict. Anyone caught fighting or instigating violence is imprisoned until proven innocent."

He escorted us to the black SUV he had arrived in earlier. This time, he had no guards with him, and the tension eased. He drove us up to a fenced gate and waited for it to open.

"So, what do you do around here?" Griz said. "Besides being the welcome wagon?"

"I'm Aline's assistant," he said. "Basically, whatever she needs, I see that it gets done."

We drove down a mile or so before he reached another gate, this one manned by several armed soldiers. The gate was connected to a tall fence with razor wire that went on seemingly forever.

"Does that fence surround the entire city?"

"It surrounds about half of Moose Jaw," Peter said. "We lost the northern parts of the city before we were able to erect the fence through the center of town to save the southern half. We were one of the first cities that focused on defending our town rather than going after the zeds. That made all the difference between why we're alive today and not zeds."

"I heard you guys opened a can of whoop-ass on the zeds that migrated south," Clutch said.

"We did," Peter said. "And, there's a lot more coming. I'm sure Aline will fill you in."

Inside the fence, Peter drove slower because people were everywhere. Dressed in heavy coats, they moved around, working on construction, pushing carts, and carrying bags. It was a blur of activity.

"Holy crap," I said. "How many people live here?"

"Four thousand three hundred and eight. Eleven if you're staying."

"We're not staying," Clutch said quickly.

"We have family in New Eden," I added.

Peter smiled. "I understand." He motioned toward the city. "We're nowhere near the size of some of the bigger provinces, but we have the most resources. We were the best equipped to reach out to everyone, so it only made sense to establish us as the capital of the P.N.A., which is comprised of what used to be Canada, the U.S., and the northern states of Mexico. Moose Jaw is a good, safe place, though I'm not a big fan of their winters."

"Where are you from?"

"New Mexico. Our weather was a lot better, but unfortunately, the state had developed a problem with none-too-friendly 'illegal aliens.'"

He pulled up to a stop outside a brick building that looked as though it had been the city hall at one time. Different flags lined the sidewalk, and I recognized New Eden's about two-thirds of the way down.

Peter motioned to the flags. "As of today, we oversee twenty-four provinces. This winter has been rough, and we had to take down three flags this month. We were worried we'd have to take down another flag until you showed up today. Even though we're keeping a step ahead of the zeds, the cards are still stacked against us. When we're not fighting with each other, there are still plenty of zeds out there, wildlife is taking back the land with a vengeance, and even Mother Nature seems to be against us."

As we walked to the building, Peter pointed to the cooler I carried. "So, what's in there?"

"This," I lifted the cooler, "will prevent another outbreak from ever happening again."

CHAPTER XXV

We waited in the hallway while the president wrapped up whatever meeting she had before ours. Clutch looked at the cooler and then at me. "We're almost done. Then we can get back to New Eden."

The door opened, and Peter appeared and ushered us forward. Inside, a woman stood chatting with two middle-aged men. A large table was set with seven place settings and platters filled with pot roast, mashed potatoes, gravy, green beans, and fruit cocktail. The smell of food—*real* food and not some bland stew of some kind—made my mouth water.

Everyone turned when we entered, and the woman approached us and held out her hand. "I'm Aline, and this is James, the vice president, and Mike, our chief of staff."

Once introductions were made, Aline continued. "It's wonderful to see representatives from New Eden. When we lost radio contact, we were afraid that province was lost to us. I trust your journey wasn't too eventful?"

"It was fine, Madam President," I said.

"Please call me Aline. You'll find we're quite informal around here. Now, please, have a seat. We'll talk over dinner."

I set down the cooler, shrugged off my backpack, and took a seat in between Clutch and Griz.

"You'll have to forgive the lack of fresh fruit and vegetables. Our gardens are just beginning to produce. In the meantime, we're getting by on canned foods."

Griz chuckled. "This looks better than we've had in...hell, let's just say it's been a real long time."

"It's the least we can provide you after your long journey. Peter says you have much to tell me."

I began. "A hematologist came to New Eden. He'd been working on the zonbistis virus since the outbreak, and he had a breakthrough."

Aline's eyes widened. "You've found a cure?"

"Not a cure, but a prevention. A vaccine, to be clear." I reached back and hefted the cooler. "Dr. Gidar was able to isolate the antigen that allows a person to fight off the virus. With the antigen, you can create a vaccine. All of Dr. Gidar's research as well as blood samples are in here. All you have to do is reproduce and distribute the vaccine to everyone."

"That's...amazing." She rang a bell, and a young man

entered. She motioned him toward me. "Take the cooler to Dr. Franzen as quickly as you can, and tell him I'll talk with him tonight."

"Wait," I said. "Don't you want us to talk with this Dr. Franzen, to tell him what we know?"

Aline smiled. "I'll make sure he can talk to you should he have questions."

I reluctantly gave up the cooler to the man, who hustled from the room. I eyed Clutch who sat there with a tight jaw.

Aline watched me. "Thank you for bringing this research to us. I can assure you that Dr. Franzen will look into it right away." She then looked across all our faces. "The promise of a vaccine will improve the morale of every citizen. After Operation Redemption is completed, the vaccine — if it's still needed at that time — will have a role in building the new nation."

I frowned. "Whoa. You're putting the vaccine on a back burner?"

"Tell us about Operation Redemption, and why you don't think we'll need a vaccine," Clutch stated pointedly.

"Yes, of course," Aline said. "Redemption is a multi-phased plan to eliminate the infected. Mike, if you'd please."

"It's a straightforward operation," Mike said. "The first phase was to reestablish government and build a network of survivors. New Eden is a link in that network. We continue to search for new groups of survivors every day. However, we've acquired enough resources to deem Phase One a success. Phase Two is now underway and nearly complete."

"Saturation bombing the south," Griz said.

Mike nodded. "Yes. Bombing was our initial offensive, followed by a cleanup effort. Our losses have been higher than originally forecasted, but we're still making headway."

"What happened down there?" I asked.

"Zeds proved more resilient to radiation than we'd planned. Those that didn't burn didn't die, despite receiving deadly radiation levels. Our fighting force is down over ninety percent since the offensive began."

"Jesus, that's not an operation. That's a slaughter," Clutch said. "How many troops are left?"

"At last report, eight hundred and sixty. But, don't worry. The zeds have suffered great losses as well. We estimate that there are fewer than one million left that pose any kind of threat."

My eyes widened. "Those are impossible odds. Every soldier down there would have to kill over a thousand zeds. Why haven't you pulled them back?"

"We need them to hold the line until we can implement Phase Three, which is our largest offensive yet."

"And, what would that be?" Griz asked, his words dripping with distrust.

"The Orange toxin," Mike replied. "One of the provinces led us to a warehouse supply of a highly improved version of the dioxin TCDD. You see, TCDD was first used in Agent Orange, and it still bears the same color. Orange has killed all the zeds in our tests." He took a breath. "Unfortunately, Orange also kills everything else. Even with carefully mapped drop zones, we expect significant losses when we deploy it. But, it's the only way to eliminate the zed threat."

"You'll kill everything," I said breathlessly, in shock at his words.

"Sounds like you're taking the 'throw the baby out with the bathwater' approach," Griz said.

"We're doing what's necessary to survive," Mike said.

"We didn't even know about the government or provinces until we ran into someone from New Eden," Clutch said. "There must be thousands of others like us. What are you doing about them?"

No one answered.

"Ah," Griz said. "You've already written them off. That's some plan you've got there."

I shook my head. "The Orange won't work. Dr. Gidar said the virus was resilient. He discovered that the virus becomes even more contagious outside the body. That's why the virus spread so quickly during the first hours of the outbreak. If you kill all the zeds, the virus will become even more of a super-virus for some time. You need to vaccinate everyone first. Otherwise, your only other alternative is to kill every living human being on this planet."

Aline gave me a condescending smile, as though she were entertaining a child. "Well, let's hope it doesn't come to that. But, to your point, yes, we will employ the vaccine. However, a vaccine doesn't address the immediate threat of those already infected. You've said it yourself, the vaccine is a prevention, not a cure. We are at constant risk until we eliminate the current zed population. Therefore, spraying Orange must be our highest priority.

"Phase Three has long been approved for delivery," she continued. "The drones can't handle the weight, so we'll spray Orange via fire bombers. We will deliver it over areas outside the vicinity of each province under our protection. Then, each province will be responsible for eliminating any remaining threats outside the kill zones."

"How long will the toxin be viable?" Clutch asked.

"In tests, it has broken down in only seven days," Mike replied.

"As you can see, Phase Three will work," Aline said. "And, the matter isn't up for discussion. We are moving ahead with Operation Redemption."

I was less optimistic. "Orange kills everything. What will be left afterward? What about long-term effects to our food and water supply?"

Mike spoke. "Testing to determine any long-term risk isn't possible. But, we know Orange will work."

I shook my head. "Orange will work. Despite your good intentions, you're going to be responsible for genocide."

"I thought nuking several states was bad enough," Griz said. "That's nothing compared to willingly poisoning your own country."

Aline frowned. "We cannot afford to take moderate measures. People need to feel like we're doing something drastic. The troops in the south are down there to improve morale here as much as to hold back the herds. The idea of them down there, protecting us from the herds, is keeping hope alive here. The Orange is the same. Deploying it is as much for the citizens' hope as it is to kill zeds. The capital is in its infancy. Every step we take now must be to benefit the capital. I hate to be blunt, but no matter what, the capital must survive. If the capital falls, the entire country falls."

My mouth had dropped more and more with each sentence. I thought of Jase and how easily he could be killed by a threat he couldn't see. "You only care about the capital. That's — that's — "

"That's bullshit," Clutch completed for me.

"I was wrong, about what I said earlier," I said. "Your intentions aren't good, they're selfish. Provinces like New Eden and the squadrons in the south are nothing but pawns to you, aren't they?"

"We're not criminals. We value the provinces, and we're not intentionally killing anyone," Aline said. "In fact, we take the provinces into consideration with every plan we discuss. But, the end result must lead to the capital's survival. As long as the capital thrives, we can reform this entire continent. You can't say that for each province."

I came to my feet. "Where's this Dr. Franzen guy?"

Aline frowned. "Why?"

"Because you have no plans to deliver a vaccine to the provinces. And, I plan to make sure a vaccine is available to everyone that's left in this world."

Her lips thinned. "Once Phase Three is complete, if there is still a need for vaccinations, and if it can be safely distributed, we will distribute it outside the capital. I give you my word."

"Those are two suspiciously big sounding 'ifs,'" Griz said.

Clutch shook his head. "Just let us use your radio network. We can find someone else who can produce the vaccine in mass quantities so *everyone* can be vaccinated. That way, you don't need to pull resources, and the vaccine can be made. We'll stay out of the way of your operation here."

Aline sighed. "Believe me, I don't want anyone else to die. I'm not the Grim Reaper. Nothing would make me happier than to see the virus erased from the world. There has been far too much death already. However, the survival of this country is riding on my shoulders, and it's a responsibility I can't take lightly. The preparations for Phase Three are underway. At this time, a vaccine will only confuse people. They'll ask why they need a vaccine if we're destroying all the infected."

"Then tell them about the virus," I said. "Because any person with half a brain knows that killing every zed and every trace of virus on this planet is impossible."

James finally spoke up. "We'll kill every last zed in this country. I guarantee it."

"You sound like a politician," Griz said with a snarl.

After a moment of silence, Aline nodded to Peter who brought over a carafe of red wine from the bar. He poured some in each crystal goblet. She held up her goblet. "I'm disappointed that we aren't seeing eye to eye, but I believe we'll work out our differences. That you've brought us news of New Eden's survival is enough to celebrate. Here's to the future."

We reluctantly held our glasses up, and I took a sip of the sweet wine.

Aline smiled and took another long drink. "This isn't the best vintage, but wine has become such a rarity, I savor it whenever I can."

After I had another drink, I frowned and set the goblet down. A sudden case of vertigo overtook me, and I squeezed my eyes shut. When I opened them, everyone was blurry. I grabbed the table for support. "Clutch."

He kicked back his chair and pulled out his sword, but the weapon fell, and he grabbed onto my chair. I tried to reach out to steady him, but my hands no longer obeyed me. Clutch fell, and I found myself falling.

"Fucking politicians," Griz slurred as everything went black.

CHAPTER XXVI

I woke up with a searing headache in pitch darkness. Even blinking my eyes hurt. I groaned and sat up.

"I apologize for the headache. The tranquilizer is a bit strong, but its effects will wear off soon enough."

I recognized Mike's voice, but could only make out a male silhouette in the darkness. Surprisingly, my hands weren't tied.

"Where are my friends?" I asked.

"We thought it best to talk with each of you separately."

"You drugged us?"

"It minimized the risk of an altercation. You must understand. We preferred not to go this route, but when you and your friends showed animosity, you forced our hand. We need you each to be reasonable. Every survivor has a role in the new country."

I guffawed. "What makes you think I want to be a part of this new country?"

"We're not perfect, but we're trying to make things work. We're trying to save as many as we can."

"Killing survivors is not a good place to start," I said.

"Aline isn't afraid to make the hard choices. She must go certain lengths to ensure the new country succeeds."

"She's not a leader," I said. "She's a bully."

Mike sighed. "The human race is on a precipice of survival. We can't afford provinces to operate separately from us. If we don't work together, we'll all die."

He walked closer and flipped a switch. Light flooded the small room, and I shaded my eyes. The room looked to be a small apartment of some kind.

"We need everyone's help to eliminate the zed threat. We need capable pilots more than anything. Our air force has taken a beating, and we need to replenish. Pilots, no matter how little experience, are needed."

"So I'm being conscripted, is that it?"

"Everyone has a choice."

"And what's mine?"

"You can choose to fly missions, or you can choose to return to New Eden."

"What's the catch?"

"Nothing for you."

I let the words sink in. "And my friends?"

"If you choose to stay and fly missions, they'll stay here, safe. If you choose to return to New Eden, they'll be sent to join the squadrons in the south."

"So you'll send them to their deaths if I refuse."

"They could survive." He paced back and forth.

"Why are you doing this? You can train more pilots. You can find more loyal survivors. Why go to all this effort?"

"Because every survivor is crucial," Mike said before taking a long pause. "And the government is still in its infancy. We can't afford the toxicity of negative opinion to taint it. You would bring toxicity back with you to New Eden, and it would spread, just like the zed virus."

Ah, the truth finally comes out. I nodded as he spoke. "The jobs are to keep us busy. But, you wouldn't let us go home regardless of what my decision is."

"You have a decision," Mike said. "Be a crucial part of our new country."

"This 'new country' has already dropped nukes in the U.S. Now, you're talking about poisoning the rest of the country. What's going to be left for the survivors, if there even are any?"

"Idealism must be a nice trait to have. I haven't had that luxury for some time." He walked to the doorway and dropped a hotel keycard on the table. "You have until morning to make your decision."

He left.

I jumped off the bed, my throbbing head nearly sending me back on my butt. I pushed through it, found my backpack on the floor, and paused at the door. I remembered the plastic keycard, grabbed it, and headed out the door. The hallway was lined with more numbered doors. A hotel of some kind.

I started heading one direction, then changed my mind, did a one-eighty, and headed in the opposite direction.

I opened the door to the stairwell to find a stern-looking Griz and Clutch coming up the stairs with another man. My eyes widened. "You're okay."

Clutch's features lessened in an instant. He hurried forward and lifted me into an embrace. He held me tight. "You're all right."

"I love you," I said under my breath.

Clutch lowered me but didn't let go. He looked me in the eyes. He opened his mouth to speak, but the other man spoke first. "Your friend can show you your room for tonight. I'll stop back in the morning with breakfast. If you need anything before then, dial 0 and ask for Adam." He paused before heading back down the stairs. "Oh, and be sure to walk around town. Take in the scenes. It's really pretty here in the winter."

As soon as the man had gone, we looked at one another. "Where were you going?" Clutch asked.

"To find you," I replied.

We stood in the hallway for a long moment. "What do we do now?" I asked.

"It sounds like they've 'invited' us to stay the night," Clutch said, his voice full of venom. "That's what we'll do."

I pulled the keycard out of my back pocket. "I guess that's what this is for." Mopey, I led them back to the hotel room I'd been in moments earlier. Once inside, they locked the deadbolt on the door and spent the next several minutes looking for cameras or microphones while carrying on a casual conversation about the weather.

Finished, they shrugged at each other, and then Clutch motioned for us all to go into the bathroom. Griz turned on the shower as a sound dampener, and I stood there, watching both.

"I didn't find any bugs," Clutch said.

"Neither did I," Griz said. "But that doesn't mean we're not on someone's very own reality show." He then leaned against the counter. "I've never met a bureaucrat I liked," He rubbed his temples. "Damn, my head hurts."

"What'd they talk to you about?" Clutch asked me.

"They gave me a decision to make. Fly for them or else."

His lips thinned.

"What'd they say to you?" I asked quickly.

"They brought in a 'general' who clearly never served a day of his life. He told us that the military wasn't finished with us yet," Griz said. "The dumbshit droned on and on about the necessity of forming a stable government and how they can't afford to split their troops among the provinces, which was his way of saying we weren't heading home. That we'd find out our orders tomorrow."

"How can they do that?" I asked. "Just because you

were in the military before doesn't mean you have to do what any officer wants for the rest of your lives."

"He said the zeds are terrorists. They've declared war on the zeds," Griz said. "So, yeah, they can basically make any citizen do what they want."

Clutch scowled at me. "And, I'd bet they have some kind of job for you, too."

I swallowed and looked away.

He cupped my cheek. "What did they do?"

I watched an invisible dust bunny on the floor for a while before I spoke. "They need pilots to drop the Orange toxin. If I don't fly for them, they said both of you would be sent to join up with the squadrons to die in the south."

"They can force us down there, but they won't be able to keep an eye on us all the time. We could go AWOL," Griz offered.

"They also hinted that New Eden would be bombed with the Orange toxin."

Clutch shrugged. "We didn't tell them that everyone's living in the silo. They should be safe inside from the Orange."

I shook my head. "They'll be safe as long as they're inside when the area is sprayed. But, if we can't warn them, anyone who went outside during or after the spray could die."

"These guys have got their heads up their asses," Griz added. "They're convinced they can kill off the zeds and then start fresh. It didn't work in Vietnam when we had less ground to cover and more resources. It's sure as hell not going to work now."

"The way I see it, we have three choices," Clutch said. "We can try to escape, but they have a dozen guards posted downstairs. We can tell them to fuck off and get shot or conscripted anyway. Or we can play along with their asinine plan, bide our time, until we find a way out."

"But the antigen will be lost," I said.

Griz smiled. "Not if we find a way to get it back."

I chortled. "That's an awfully big 'if.'"

"The capital has radios here that can reach most of the world. If we can get the word out that we have an antigen for a vaccine, then all we have to do is get the research and samples to the right folks."

"So," I drawled out. "All we have to do is find a way to prevent the entire North American continent from being poisoned, get access to the capital's radio network and broadcast news of the antigen, and not get killed in the process. In a nutshell, we're going to save the world."

Clutch thought for a moment, shrugged, and nodded.

Griz's brows rose. "Save the world? Yeah, that about sums it up."

I smiled. "I'm in."

COURAGE

CHAPTER XXVII

February

The fire bomber's wheels squeaked as they met the concrete, and the heavy plane settled onto the runway. My best landing yet. All fourteen pilots were required to make a test flight once per day until Aline approved the release of the third phase of Operation Redemption.

When we weren't flying, we were in the briefing room working on flight plans. The lead pilot walked to the front of the room and addressed us. "A warm front is coming through. The forecast is thirteen degrees Celsius tomorrow, which means it's finally going to be warm enough to load the Orange onto our birds and start missions. Expect the green light tomorrow afternoon," he said. "Get plenty of sleep tonight. You won't see much of it for the next couple months."

The tension was palpable in the room. Including me, nine of the fourteen pilots had been conscripted into service. At least five pilots were adamantly against spraying the Orange toxin and vocally raised their concerns daily. I was more careful. While I never voiced opposition, I never championed the operation. I tried to blend in so I wasn't noticed, though I suspected Aline kept a close eye on all of us.

She was a relentless wolf wearing the guise of a compassionate leader. Preoccupied with building a centralized government, she refused to see the blood she'd spill to make it happen. She never visited any of the provinces, preferring instead to stay within the safe confines of the capital. She'd convinced herself that as long as the capital survived, there was hope. But, she'd neglected to take one thing into consideration.

Loyalty.

She'd augmented her pilots and troops with people from the provinces. And, we didn't easily forget life outside the capital. The so-called Provinces of North America had forgotten about its provinces, but I hadn't.

The fourteen of us, along with other airport personnel, crammed into a bus and rode back to town.

"It sounds like tomorrow is going to be the big day," Akio, a fellow pilot, said.

"Yeah," I said. "It sounds like it."

He looked off into the distance and got closer to speak quietly. "Well, they can send me out, but they can't force me back."

"Your flight crew may have a different opinion," I said, reminding him that Aline had assigned at least one staunch loyalist on each crew.

He shrugged and leaned back. "They can't fly."

"No, but they can shoot you."

"There are worse things."

"Like what?"

He ignored the question and instead nodded to the sidewalk. "The riders are back in town."

I smiled. As soon as the truck stopped, I hurried to catch up with Griz and Clutch and gave them both hugs.

"How was the supply run?" I asked.

"The usual," Griz said. "A whole lot of nothing."

Clutch and Griz were riders, troops who went out on supply runs and scouted the area. It was the most dangerous of duties, and we weren't surprised when both Clutch and Griz were "randomly" selected to be riders after they were assigned to the capital's military division.

We headed up the steps of the Hotel, where everyone in the capital's forces lived. It actually was a hotel, and the three of us still lived in the same room we stayed in our first night in the city. If we had tried to escape, we wouldn't have made it fifty feet without being trampled by the entire force.

Our room was on the sixth floor, but we climbed all eight flights to the roof. We went up there to watch the sunset on every evening the guys were in town. It was the only place we were confident wasn't bugged.

The three of us stood at the edge, looking across the city. I could see the entire capital from this roof. It looked peaceful enough, but we knew it housed people who didn't care about other survivors, only about building a country in their own fashion.

"My flights start tomorrow," I said.

"Tomorrow," Clutch echoed.

The sun set, leaving only twilight.

Griz clapped his hands. "If tomorrow's the big day, I need a drink."

The following morning

"Good morning."

I scowled at the man standing in our room. "What are you doing here, Peter?"

Clutch and Griz spread out on either side of me so we formed a semicircle around our intruder. After breakfast, Clutch, Griz, and I had returned to our room to find Peter sifting casually through our drawers.

He smiled and held out an envelope. "Phase Three has been given a green light. We begin spraying Orange. I'm stopping by every pilot's room to drop off the flight schedule for today."

I took the envelope. "You could've slid it under the door."

"Yes, but I know how stressful these missions will be for the pilots. I wanted to be available to address any concerns you have."

"Consider knocking next time."

He frowned. "I wish I could change things. After all, we both want the same thing."

My brow rose. "What's that?"

"A world without zeds, of course," he answered.

I shook my head. "I want more than that. I want a world that we can live in after the zeds are gone, too. You've nuked the south. How long before people can live off that land? Now, you want to poison the rest."

"Orange is temporary. The rains will wash it away."

"Orange is a hundred times deadlier than its predecessor used in Vietnam. You said it yourself. It kills everything. How long do you think it will take for nature to recover enough to sustain life?"

Peter clenched his fists. "It will recover."

"Why has Aline set a one-hundred mile radius around the capital with no Orange drops?"

His face reddened. "She's playing it safe."

"For the capital but not for the provinces?"

He didn't reply.

Not caring if our room was still bugged, I continued. "She's not the president of the Provinces of North America, or whatever bullshit name you want to give it. She's president of Moose Jaw, and that's it."

By now, Peter's face had reddened enough that I thought he was about to have a coronary. "Go ahead and think whatever you want. But come this afternoon, you and the other pilots will start delivering Orange. You think you can disobey those orders?" He tossed an obvious glance at Clutch and Griz. "Go ahead and try it."

"I never said I would disobey orders," I said. "I'll be at the airport in an hour, ready to go. I hadn't realized freedom of speech was outlawed along with our freedom of choice."

"Freedom of speech isn't illegal," Peter said. "As long as you aren't talking about treason or hurting the country."

I laughed out loud. "You, Aline, and her henchmen are hurting the country enough on your own."

"Hey, Peter," Griz said.

Peter turned in time for Griz's punch. Peter went instantly down, knocked out cold. Griz rubbed his knuckles. "I've wanted to do that for a long time."

"Now, that was freedom of speech at its finest," Clutch said as he grabbed Peter's lax form. He bound his wrists and ankles with duct tape and slapped a long strip over his mouth. He took Peter's radio, checked the unconscious man's pockets, and pulled out a keychain with at least thirty keys on it.

Griz smiled. "Bingo."

Clutch and Griz dragged Peter into the bathroom and closed the door, leaving Peter inside.

They each checked their gear, and I went through my bag one more time to make sure everything was secure.

My nerves jittered like water droplets on a hot skillet. "I think I'm ready."

Griz hugged me. "Be careful. I'll see you when it's done."

He stepped away and left the room. Clutch pulled me to him, and his lips crashed down on mine. He held me, hard, while we kissed a lifetime of kisses in that moment. His lips softened as he held me, and he struggled to pull himself away. He rubbed a thumb on my cheek and then walked out of the room.

I took a deep breath and followed, though I went in the other direction. It didn't matter if anyone had been listening in on us. The coup had begun.

CHAPTER XXVIII

I took the ten o'clock bus to the airport. The bus was nearly empty, and I suspected that most personnel were still in their rooms. The first flight wasn't scheduled to depart for another three hours. I was one of the later flights, giving me roughly two hours before they would begin to load the orange-colored chemical onto the fire bombers and about four hours before the rest of my flight crew would show up.

The bus stopped outside the main hangar. I stepped off and let the sun warm my face. The air was still cold, but the early winter was already giving way to an early spring. I forced myself to act normal, though everyone had a nervous hustle in their actions this morning. Just like I did every day, I strolled into the pilot briefing room and looked at the weather reports before drafting a flight plan. Though, this flight plan wasn't tied to spraying Orange. This one was for our escape from the capital.

The pilots' missions were posted on a map covering a wall. Phase Three was being rolled out in a circular pattern moving outward from the capital. I'd been assigned to northern Minnesota today. Each load of concentrated pesticide would cover roughly 40,000 acres, which meant a shitload of flight missions. Iowa and Nebraska would be hit in less than four weeks.

Tucking the flight plan into a pocket, I headed out to the fleet of fourteen Convair fire bombers parked on the ramp. The airplanes had been modified from carrying water to carrying the highly corrosive Orange. My plane was third from the end, and I walked around it, doing a pre-flight walk-around. Akio was under the wing of his plane, leaning against a tire. I gave him a casual wave before continuing my inspection.

I did one more walk-around, this time looking under the plane toward nine long, white tanks sitting in rows off the end of the ramp. No one stood around them, not yet, anyway. Thankfully, the airport's security force was small. Aline simply didn't have enough troops to spread across the capital and the airport. Aline had guards posted at every gate, but once inside the airport, everyone went about their business.

I walked toward the tanks filled with Orange. The tanks sat out in the open. There was no way in the daylight to approach them without being seen, so I made no attempt to hide. When I reached the tanks, still no one approached. I casually pulled a gas mask from my backpack and slipped it over my head. At the first tank, I flipped on the power switch, grabbed the handle, and squeezed. Orange sprayed out onto the ground, and I quickly tied a wire around the handle to keep it spraying. I dropped it, continued to the next tank, and did the same.

I continued until I reached the final tank. By then, someone must've seen me or heard the pumps, and a man came running out. "Hey! What are you doing?"

I ignored him and hurriedly tied a wire around the last handle.

I fell to my knees and pulled off my backpack.

When I turned to look at the man, he stopped and his eyes grew wide.

I pulled out the pipe bombs Griz had made. Designed to burn more than explode, I remembered his response when I'd asked him if they would do the job against double-lined steel tanks. He'd smiled and warned me to not stick around after igniting them to find out.

The man's jaw dropped, and he raced back the way he came. Then, he veered to the left and headed toward the emergency power shut-off valve for the tanks. The valve, kept at a small distance from the tanks for safety, was used to cut all power in case of a fire. He was too close before I realized his intentions. *No!*

The man stopped and swung out to hit the big red button, but someone jumped out from around the corner of the building. The pair toppled to the ground. Only one came to his feet, and he held a bloody knife.

Akio.

He watched me, and I pulled my gaze away to light the first pipe bomb. I set it down mere inches from the stream of Orange and ran. As I ran, I clutched the second pipe bomb and my lighter, ready to light it up if the first one failed.

But, whoa boy, the first one most definitely did not fail. I felt the wall of heat before I heard the *whoomp* of ignition. It pressed me forward, and I found more speed. Akio's eyes widened, and he motioned me toward him. He yelled something but all I could hear was the sounds of flames growing behind me.

Like Akio, I wore a Nomex flight suit like all the fire bomber pilots wore. Made of fire resistant material, it served its purpose well today. Exposed skin in between my suit and stocking hat burned against the oven heat at my back, and I hurried as quickly as I could to reach Akio.

He ran around the corner of the building, and I followed, finding a golf cart waiting for us. He climbed behind the wheel, and I more or less fell onto the seat. He floored the pedal, but being an electric vehicle, it didn't go nearly as fast as we needed it to go.

"That was the most ballsy thing I've ever seen," he yelled out with a laugh. "I can't believe you walked right up to 'em and lit 'em up."

"Let's hope it works," I said, cranking my neck to

look behind us while hanging on for dear life. Bright flames shot high, with dark smoke climbing. The air around the first tank morphed a split second before the tank exploded.

I yanked Akio down as I flattened on the seat. The blast hit us, and the golf cart lurched. As soon as I could breathe again, I sat up and Akio kept driving. He slowed as we reached someone who was getting back to his feet. "Climb on."

The man, wearing the orange vest of a flagger, climbed on back, and Akio sped toward the gate. The gate stood open, and the guards were nowhere to be found, likely in search of emergency crews. Akio never even slowed as he drove us through the gate and toward the city.

I glanced back at the man. He looked a bit singed but otherwise all right.

"They have cameras at the airport," Akio said. "Once the fire's under control, it won't take them long to figure things out. They aren't going to be happy."

"They'll have other things to worry about."

"You did that?" the man behind me asked.

I grabbed out my knife handle, ready to unsheathe it, and turned around. "We'll drop you off at the Hotel."

"Take me with you. If there's something I can do to help, I'm in," he said with a heavy southern drawl.

Suspicious, I eyed him. "Why would you help?"

His jaw tightened. "I'm from Louisiana. Listen, I know I made a mistake coming up here when they put out the invitation. I've been looking for payback for some time."

I thought for a second and then held out my hand. "I'm Cash. This is Akio."

"I'm Greg."

Another blast sounded, and I knew the second tank had blown.

"Both of you, act injured," Akio said as he approached the city gate.

I leaned back in my seat, and I heard Greg collapse on the backseat's pleather.

Akio came to a stop at the city gate. "I'm on my way to the hospital," he called out.

I winced through half-closed eyes. Greg moaned.

"Go on." The guard motioned Akio to drive. "Hurry. And tell them to send help."

Akio floored the pedal again, and drove down the main road. "Where to now?" he asked without looking at me.

"Can you get me to the archives?" I asked.

Akio replied, "I can get *us* to the archives."

Greg leaned forward. "My wife works there. If you need a way in, I can get her to let us in the side entrance."

"That'd be easier than what I had planned," I said.

Another explosion, soon followed by two more. The entire airport looked like it was on fire.

"I think our birds are toast," I said.

"Aline's going to be pissed," Akio said.

I watched us approach the city. Fire engines roared past us. "The party's just getting started."

CHAPTER XXIX

"**H**i, honey." Greg kissed his wife on the cheek after we squeezed through the door. "These are my friends."

"Thank God you're all right," she replied, oblivious to our presence. "I saw the smoke. Everyone's talking about a fire at the airport. What happened?"

"There was an accident with the Orange. The tanks ignited," he said. "How about you go home and take a long lunch?"

Her eyes narrowed. "Greg, dear. What's going on?"

He grabbed her hands. "Please, Jenny. No questions; not today. Do what I ask."

It took her a moment to process his request. "Okay, I guess..."

He smiled and kissed her again. "I'll see you at home. Now, go." Greg left her standing confused as he led us down the hallway. "The radio room is in the basement."

I stopped. "How'd you know I was headed to the radio room?"

"Besides books, that's the only thing in the archives."

"Oh. I guess that makes sense."

"The basement is open to the public, but the area that leads to the radio room is off limits. They assigned guards when too many people tried to access the radio room to locate their families." He motioned us down another hallway. "Jenny showed the radio room to me before. The back stairs lead to a hall where all the offices are. There are never guards in that area. That'll get you closer."

We followed him as he weaved through bookshelves and down a flight of stairs. Exactly as Greg said, we found ourselves at a hallway lit with bright fluorescent bulbs and lined with doors.

He slowed as we reached the end of the hallway, where we had to turn either left or right. "It's just right down here." He turned and stopped. "Strange. There's usually a guard standing at the door."

I moved around him and walked forward. "That means they're already inside."

Outside the door that read *Suite 3A*, I found a "V" drawn in white chalk scrawled on the wall. *Victory.*

I smiled and gave the secret knock.

Seconds later, the door clicked and opened, and I found Clutch pulling me inside and into his arms as though I were an oasis in the desert. When he released me, he eyed my compatriots, and I spoke. "They're okay. They helped me. This is Akio and Greg."

Clutch's gaze remained narrowed on the two men with me. He made no qualms about showing his distrust of them, but after a moment, he motioned them inside and locked the door behind us. Griz stood behind a man working at the radio bank. A restrained, gagged guard sat in the corner. Clutch turned his attention back to me. "How did it go?"

"It's done," I said. "All the Orange is burning."

"That's an understatement," Akio said. "The tanks are blowing like it's World War Three out there. The entire airport is going up in flames."

"How'd things go for you?" I asked.

"Easy," Clutch said. "All of Aline's people seem to be so focused on the fires that they didn't even go into lockdown mode. Aline's clearly a politician, not a military strategist."

"We're getting the radio set up for a mass broadcast now," Griz said, standing behind a man sitting in front of the radio. "Thanks to my new friend here." He slapped the man's shoulder who jumped at the contact.

I suspected "friend" wasn't quite the word the radioman would use to describe Griz.

"We should be able to broadcast before anyone gets their head out of their ass," Griz continued.

Someone pounded on the door. "Martin? Are you in there? Martin? Let us in!"

The man spun in his chair. He opened his mouth, but

Griz pressed a knife against his throat, and he clamped his mouth shut again.

"Get those radios ready," Clutch warned.

Griz spun the man's chair back around and whispered something in his ear. The man shook and went back to work.

The handheld radio on Clutch's belt went off.

"Officer team twenty-two reporting in."

"Control station, twenty-two. Report."

"Yusef's not at his post at the radio room. The door's locked, and Martin's not responding."

"Hold your position. We'll send backup."

A brief pause.

"All available teams. Report immediately to the archives. The radio room is believed to have been taken by terrorists."

"Shit," Clutch muttered. "Someone just got their head out of their ass. Come on, Griz."

"It's ready," the man at the radio said softly.

Griz motioned for Clutch. "You're on."

Clutch walked over to the radio and lifted the microphone. He looked back at me once before closing his eyes. He was silent for a moment. When he opened his eyes, he brought the microphone closer to his lips. "This is the New Eden province reporting from the capital. We are hailing all provinces and all survivors. The capital bombed the south, and today we disrupted their plan to drop poison on the entire country. What this means is that if you live in U.S., Mexico, or Canada, you would've been poisoned. Only the capital city in

Saskatchewan was exempt. In their attempt to kill zeds, they would've killed everything outside the capital. We found that plan unacceptable."

He took a long breath. "We destroyed the current supply of poison, but they can create more. If you agree with New Eden, do not send resources to the capital. Do not support their plans, which will cause the death of more innocents. There is a better way. We have found an antigen. A vaccine for the virus is possible. We brought the antigen here, but they have taken it and refuse to create a vaccine for anyone outside the capital. Who among you has the resources to create a vaccine so that we can prevent this virus from winning ever again?"

Something slammed into the door, and the wood cracked.

"The zeds out there can be defeated," Clutch continued. "And, if everyone can be vaccinated, we will be safe from future outbreaks. But we need your help."

The door slammed open, and officers rushed in with rifles. Behind them, two men threw down their battering ram. Shouts erupted as they flocked around us. "Down on the ground! Down on the ground!"

Someone shoved me to my knees, and I found myself on my stomach, my backpack yanked off, my hands pulled behind me. As I fought to breathe, I felt someone go through my pockets.

"This is Helena, Montana," a voice came through the radio's wall speakers. *"We have heard your broadcast. We*

have a fully functional CDC facility that is equipped to create the vaccine. Bring us the antigen, and we can produce enough vaccine for every single person in the world."

"Shut down the broadcast!" someone yelled.

"This is Cheyenne Mountain in Colorado," another voice came through. *"We have air support and can — "*

The radio squealed and then silenced.

I was yanked to my knees and dragged to where Clutch was already kneeling.

When they dragged Griz over, he sported a bloody nose. Akio and Greg were soon added to our lineup.

I knew the odds of our mission succeeding were nil. We'd already accomplished far more than I'd ever anticipated. We'd prevented delivery of the Orange toxin, and we'd told the provinces about the capital's plans and the antigen. They would have to take it from there. The only part of our plan that had failed was for us to get out of the capital alive.

"We have subdued the targets," an officer spoke into his radio. "The room is secure."

A moment later, Aline walked in, with Mike and James on either side. She looked downright pissed, which cheered my mood...somewhat.

She walked in front of us. "Exactly what did you hope to accomplish today with these antics?"

None of us spoke.

She paused in front of Akio. "Why do you even care about what happens? This isn't even your country."

He slowly looked up at her. "Easy. I wouldn't want

this done to my home. I couldn't stand by to watch it done to another's home."

"You're a fool." She looked at each of us. "You're all fools to think you've done any good here today. Four people died in the fire at the airport. They were innocent. Come spring, many more will die from the zeds that will unfreeze and start to walk again. Causing dissension among the provinces is treason. They need a strong capital to look up to, and you took that from them today."

"Lady," Griz said. "You overestimate your value. We got along just fine without a capital before. Hell, we didn't even know you guys existed until a few months ago. You can go ahead and keep on thinking you and your two sheep there are guardian angels, but you got it backwards. You're getting in the way by bullying defenders out in the provinces to do your bidding. From what I've seen, you're leeches, sucking resources and supplies from the folks who need them most."

She wagged a finger at him. "You're wrong. We've helped the provinces. We've distributed supplies to them. You have no idea what it takes to start up a government from ashes and to bring together groups of survivors into a network."

"You should've stopped there. You would've been remembered as a heroine," I said. "But, you didn't know when to stop. You screwed up when you switched from connecting folks to directing their destinies."

An officer hurried into the room. James held him

back from getting too close. "Madame President?"

"What is it?"

"It's the squadrons from the south. They've returned."

Aline frowned. "What do you mean, 'they've returned?'"

"They're here, in the city. And they're demanding your immediate removal."

"That's impossible," Mike said. "What are they doing here?"

"Perhaps," Akio began. "They saw my note in the supplies I dropped last month. A note that may have mentioned the Orange toxin and how they were deemed to be acceptable casualties."

Aline walked over and slapped Akio across the face. "You fool. They'll lead zeds right to our doorstep." She faced the officer standing nearby, and pointed at Akio. "Shoot that man."

The officer's eyebrows rose before he shook his head. "But—"

A herd of heavy boot steps echoed outside the room, yanking everyone's attention toward the door.

The officers nervously held their rifles, the barrels pointing in all sorts of dangerous directions.

"Lower your weapons, and you will not be fired upon," a man yelled into the room. "We've had a lot of target practice, so I recommend you lower your weapons *now*."

The officers looked at one another. None, ironically,

looked to Aline for direction. A moment later, they put their rifles on the floor and held up their hands.

Troops poured into the radio room and herded everyone — except for those of us on our knees — into the corner.

Aline refused to raise her hands, and the man who appeared to be the leader of the new troops walked in and straight for her.

"Hello, Paul," she said to the man with a bronze maple leaf on his collar. "Welcome home."

He smirked. "I bet you weren't expecting to see me around here anytime soon...or, ever."

He removed his helmet to reveal a scarred scalp. "You may remember, I had hair when I left. Radiation is an interesting thing. I've watched thousands of my men die, bleeding out of every orifice and coughing up their own lungs. When you denied my request to retreat, I knew you didn't give a damn what was happening."

"I did care," she said. "You were freeing the world from the infected."

He shook his head. "That's only a half-truth. You also wanted us gone. Us scarred-up soldiers bring back too many memories of what it's like out there. We get in the way of the fantasy world you're trying to create here." He smiled. "Don't worry. You're going to find out what it's like out there firsthand soon enough. I've got a nice spot picked out for you near Texarkana. We call it the devil's dance floor. We lost two thousand men there, and you'll get to meet them for yourself."

"Paul," she pleaded, "it was a hard decision to send you. But, we all have to work at containing the zed threat, in whatever way we can."

He nodded to two of his men, who restrained Aline.

"Paul!" she yelled, but the men took her away.

Paul then looked over each of us.

"You've got some flair for timing, Major," Clutch said. "And, we're mighty thankful to have you come save the day."

The major gave a slight nod. "That your voice on the radio?"

"Yes, sir," Clutch replied.

He smiled. "Your timing was perfect. We were pulling up to the gate when we heard your broadcast. I know Aline, and with a broadcast like that, I knew she wouldn't be anywhere else but here."

"Release them," the major ordered, and we found ourselves free of our restraints.

I grabbed my bag, climbed to my feet, and stayed closed to Clutch and Griz.

"The capital looks like it's fallen on hard times," he said. "Fifty miles out, we saw enough smoke that we assumed the whole capital was burning. While there are a few rats I'd like to smoke out of here, the capital is still a good place for survivors. More important, we could use some real beds to sleep in for a change. But, first, you're going to get me up to speed and show me where the antigen is."

"It's a long story," Clutch said.

"Then, find me a cold beer and a comfortable chair first."

Clutch smiled. "I know just the place."

REDEMPTION

CHAPTER XXX

After Major Paul Mallary and his officers laid claim to the President's home, we briefed him on everything that had happened since we had arrived. Akio was able to fill in the gaps of the time between when the squadrons were sent to the south and our arrival. I learned that Aline had started as a good facilitator with a knack at building relationships. As time passed, the relentless loss of survivors had a profound effect on her, and she'd developed an obsession to sculpt a new country, beginning with the capital.

The major kept his word. He imprisoned Aline, James, Mike, and Peter. Moose Jaw had two airports. The military airport had been destroyed, no thanks to me. But, the city's commercial airport remained functional. With an armed crew, Akio loaded the prisoners into a King Air and flew them south, where they were shoved out of the airplane with nothing but the parachutes on their backs. If the zeds didn't get them, the irradiated environment would. It was brutal, and I winced at the thought of how they met their end.

Akio, a commercial airlines pilot with tens of thousands more flight hours than I had, flew the antigen and research to Helena's CDC facility. I signed on to help deliver the vaccine as each batch was created. The CDC estimated that it would take three years to produce enough vaccine for the world's survivors—and even longer to distribute it—but we'd do it, assuming we could keep the planes running and full of fuel. Akio, I, and three other pilots would be the Pony Express of the twenty-first century. Clutch, of course, had volunteered to be my navigator and co-pilot before I had a chance to ask him.

The major retained control of Moose Jaw, but no longer called it the capital. Before the outbreak, he'd been a history professor in addition to being an Army Reserve officer. He believed the provinces were too spread out with not nearly enough survivors in between to support a centralized government. He called democracy an idealistic notion at this point in the game. Instead, he proposed a cooperative feudalistic system, believing the only way to survive until everyone "got back onto their feet" was to have each province control its own area, with trading and agreements with nearby provinces.

His opinion had its share of dissidents, with people

accusing him of trying to bring us back to the Dark Ages. Personally, I agreed with him. The world was already worse off than what people faced in medieval times. We were homeless and struggling to survive day by day. I figured a feudal system had to be easier to achieve than Aline's idea of a centralized government.

Clutch stepped back from loading our supplies, which included new radios to talk with Moose Jaw and other provinces. He wore a T-shirt, which showcased his full-sleeve tattoos. "Ready to head home?" he asked.

I smiled and nudged into him. "You bet. Let's go home."

Griz had already climbed in the back along with Joe, the only remaining survivor of the New Eden squadrons sent to the south. My Cessna had been destroyed in the fire, and so I opted for a comfortable twin-engine, which could make it back to New Eden without a fuel stop and haul a lot more supplies.

I climbed in, and Clutch took his seat and organized the maps. As I taxied to the runway, Akio smiled and waved broadly from the edge of the ramp. I waved back and smiled, knowing I'd see him in a couple days when he'd come to pick up the zed kids and bring them to the CDC center in Helena.

I'd miss Moose Jaw. It was more than the sense of safety and the electricity and people like Akio. It was the city's potential. Moose Jaw was proof that we could live relatively normal lives, even in all this.

But we weren't ready for that. Not yet.

I throttled forward, and the airplane picked up speed and took to the air as though it couldn't wait to get off the ground. We climbed high, seeing only major landmarks such as rivers, forests, and cities. The sun glistened on a flooded river, and I hoped its floodwaters would wash away the zeds, leaving only pure water behind.

We touched down at the airport outside New Eden by mid-afternoon. Fortunately, there were no signs of wild animals today. The Humvee sat by the hangar, but there was no sign of Zach.

After we tied down the plane and moved the supplies from the plane to the Humvee, we leaned against the Humvee's bumper. Clutch handed me a bottle of water, and I drank greedily. The three of us stared off at the woods, watching the tree line. When nothing emerged, we all climbed into the Humvee and headed back to New Eden.

On our drive, we saw more creatures moving around than when we'd left. Not many animals—only the sick dogs and wolves seemed to venture out during the day. It was the two-legged ones.

Spring was here.

The zeds were thawing out.

CHAPTER XXXI

Later that night

Back in the silo was a bittersweet welcome party for Joe. While everyone had known the risks of sending the squadrons after the zeds, everyone had also hoped more would return home. I didn't stick around when people started grilling Joe about what happened out there. I had no doubt the man had been through a far worse hell than any of us.

Clutch had already disappeared to his tiny office in the lowest floor of the silo to catch up on the daily logs since we'd been gone. I hit the shower and stood under the hot spray for my entire five-minute ration. With my skin still steaming, I headed up to my dorm. I rifled through my backpack and pulled out the special items I had bartered for at the capital and hid from Clutch.

I set the bottle of wine and corkscrew down on the

mattress. I pulled off my T-shirt and pants and slipped on the dress. Before the outbreak, I never would've worn anything like it. It was a slim-fitting, tiny white thing with spaghetti straps and dainty roses printed on the sheer fabric. It was as much a nightgown as a dress, but it fit perfectly. My shoe wardrobe consisted of two pairs of hiking boots, so I decided to go barefoot.

I stood in front of a small mirror. I tried to look past the jagged scar on my forehead and circular scar on my calf where I'd been shot. Hell, I had so many scars now, they crisscrossed my skin like spider webs Then again, Clutch bore far more scars than I did.

I didn't have model looks before the outbreak; I certainly didn't have them now. Curves had toned into lean muscle. My face had lost its softness. Taking a deep breath, I tried to focus instead on the dress and how it fit my body. *Get 'em where I want 'em.* I grinned, thinking of the one rule I had set for myself during the early days of the outbreak. It had meant that whatever happened, I needed to take control to get things to work out so I could survive. I'd never thought it applied to anything except fighting zeds. Until now.

I grabbed the wine and searched around until I found two red plastic cups.

"Holy shit, why are you wearing that?" Jase asked, startling me.

I nearly dropped the bottle. "Jesus. You about gave me a heart attack."

"She can wear what she wants, Silly," Hali scolded,

giving me a knowing smile.

I scowled at Jase and walked past the pair. "Like Hali said, I can wear what I want."

"Have fun," Hali said.

"Where's she going?" I heard Jase ask as I entered the hallway.

I hurried down the steps, not wanting to run into anyone else. If Griz saw me, he'd never let me live it down. Fortunately, most folks were already in bed. My feet flew down the stairs until I reached the right floor.

Clutch's office door was open, and I peeked in to see his nose buried in a stack of paper. I knocked and stepped in the doorway. "Got a minute?"

"Yeah," he grumbled, dropped his pen, and looked up. His features changed from exhaustion to shock in an instant. I had no idea how I didn't laugh at the expression on his face. I'd never seen his mouth drop so quickly. He shuffled his papers to the side in a rush. "Yeah, um, yeah, come in."

He came to his feet rather clumsily, like a schoolboy, and I grinned. He seemed to struggle finding words. "You look nice tonight. I mean, you look better than nice." He finally settled with, "You look really good."

I held up the bottle of wine. "Happy Birthday."

His lips slowly curved upward. "I didn't think anyone knew."

I shrugged. "You told me once, a long time back. We never seem to get the chance to celebrate things like birthdays anymore, so I thought tonight would be as good as any to sneak in a little celebration."

He smiled. "I like that idea."

I shut and locked the door and gave him a mischievous grin. "I don't plan on sharing this wine. I had to trade my machete for it."

He frowned. "Your machete? You shouldn't—"

"I have another one under my bed." I set the bottle, corkscrew, and cups on the table. "Now, do you want a birthday party or not?"

He came to his feet. "Hell yeah. I can't remember the last time I did something on my birthday." He went to work at opening the bottle. He glanced up every couple of seconds while I watched. He filled each cup with the red wine, nearly draining the bottle, and he handed me my cup. "You do look really good."

"Thank you." I took a sip, watching him.

He took a drink, eyed me, and then took a longer drink. After a deep breath, he set his cup down, took mine, and set it down next to his.

He kissed me softly on the lips. "You asked me to say the words once. I couldn't do it. Not then. I was afraid that if I said them, something would happen, and you'd be gone." He swallowed. "But, I can say them now. I love you. With every fiber of my being, I love you." His shoulders relaxed as though a weight had been lifted.

"I know," I said. "But, I like hearing you say it."

He then gave me a kind smile. He deepened the kiss, our tongues meeting for a slow, passionate dance. Our bodies pressed tighter together, moving in a rhythm only we could feel.

He broke the kiss, and his smile widened then, enough to show the wrinkles at his eyes. He lowered himself, kissing first my neck, then moving a strap aside to kiss my collarbone. His kisses were innocent, yet they sent tingles across my skin. Already, my breaths were coming faster. His hands ran down my shoulders, my hips, my thighs, and then back up under my dress. He chuckled when he realized I wasn't wearing underwear.

I held on to him; his heart pounded under my palm. He pressed tighter against me, and I wrapped a leg around him. I felt a shudder surge through him, rippling down his body into mine. He stared at me, the wildness on his face making my heart pound harder. Unable to stand it anymore, I tugged off his shirt as he unbuttoned his pants and shoved them down. He lifted me off the floor and took me right then and there. In perfect rhythm, he kissed me, devouring, violently satisfying kisses as he drove into me.

We made love, and it was sublime.

For the next hour, he went about showing me exactly how he felt about me, until someone pounded on the door.

"Hey, I know you guys are in there," Griz's voice yelled out. "These walls are thin, you know."

Clutch threw a stapler at the door. "Go away," he yelled back before grinning down at me.

"Come on," Griz yelled. "Wrap things up in there. Deb's water broke. She's having the baby!"

CHAPTER XXXII

The following morning

Groggily, I woke when the chest under my head moved. "Hm?"

Clutch stroked my black hair, which I'd let grow out during the cold winter. "Vicki has an update."

I pulled myself up and rubbed my eyes. Everyone from Fox had been here all night. Benji lay sleeping on Diesel at Frost's feet. Other residents had come and gone, checking in to see how New Eden's first birth was coming along. The excitement was palpable. Nerves were on edge as everyone waited.

Vicki, one of the two people assisting the doctor with Deb's birth this morning, stood in her scrubs, smiling. "Dr. Edmund says she's fully dilated. It should be any time now." With that, she turned and hustled back into the room.

I stood and stretched. Jase and Hali stopped their card game to stand and watch the door. Clutch and Griz also came to their feet. Only Frost remained sitting, but his gaze never left the door.

Five minutes passed. We waited. I paced the floor. Jase and Hali joined me. Ten minutes passed. I wanted to be in there, with Deb, but the doctor had been adamant about keeping the room as germ-free as possible.

Deb cried out, and I froze.

"It's time," Frost said. "She's having the baby."

I could hear Dr. Edmund's muffled voice and Deb's cries through the door. The doctor was giving orders, and I heard a flurry of movement behind the door.

"She's seizing!" the doctor yelled. "Hold her down."

I moved toward the door, but Clutch held me back. With my back to his chest, I clasped onto his forearms that wrapped around me. My heart pounded as we waited.

As quickly as the ruckus began, everything silenced. Then, the sound started softly but grew in volume. A baby's cry.

I let out the breath I'd been holding, and turned in Clutch's arms. We smiled and kissed. "It's going to be okay," I whispered.

I tapped my foot, waiting for them to bring out the baby.

"I wonder if it's a boy or girl," Hali said.

Then, a second cry broke free, adding to the first. My

eyes widened. I squealed and covered my mouth. "Twins!"

"Two?" Griz asked. "Wow, Tack had some strong swimmers."

A moment later, Vicki and Izzie emerged, each carrying a baby, and neither looking up from her precious cargo. We rushed the two women to see the babies. They were wrinkled and purple and adorable.

"Are they healthy?" Frost asked first.

"Yes, they are a perfectly healthy boy and girl," Vicki said softly.

"Can we see Deb now?" I asked, excited to congratulate the new mother.

Izzie sniffled and started to cry.

I swallowed and looked at Vicki. "Deb?"

Her lips trembled, and then she slowly shook her head.

"Oh, no," Hali gasped. "Not Deb."

"She hemorrhaged," Vicki said after a long silence. "She lost too much blood, and we couldn't stop it. We tried."

No one spoke. I found I could only stare at the babies, the weight on my chest making it hard to feel anything.

"I promised her I would look after his babies," Vicki said quietly.

I swallowed, then placed a hand on her shoulder. "You don't have to do it alone. We'll all take care of them. Together. Because that's what families do."

CHAPTER XXXIII

Easter Sunday, one year after the outbreak

"How about Jack and Jill?" I asked.

Clutch guffawed. "That's as bad as Griz's idea for Dick and Jane."

I shrugged. "Jase wanted Fluffy and Wuffy."

His eyes widened, and I held up a hand. "Don't worry, I shot those down."

"Their names are Ted and Debra Nugent," Vicki said, settling the debate.

Her words silenced the Humvee.

It took me a moment to place the male name before I remembered. Tack's real name was Ted. Theodore Nugent, to be precise. Vicki had named the twins after their parents.

My smile was bittersweet. "Those are good names."

The other Humvee pulled around us to take lead.

Griz waved from the driver's seat. It was the vehicle we'd hidden in the shed before going to New Eden. It was still packed with all the gear and supplies we'd crammed into it. We'd told Justin about it and offered to share the supplies, but he'd been adamant that we needed everything we had if we were going out on our own.

I turned to make sure Jase and Hali were following us, flanking our tiny convoy. The old Chevy truck was dirty, but Jase didn't seem to mind—if his wide smile was any sign. Of course, that could've also been because Hali was sidled up next to him.

Boxes piled high to Hali's right nearly hid her. All three of our vehicles were weighted down with food and supplies we'd bartered for in New Eden. Even our Humvee, with only room for the three of us, was chock full of supplies, including a radio so we could stay in touch with the other provinces and for me to plan flights with Akio.

Clutch drove. I sat in the front seat with one of the twins and a rifle propped against my hip while Vicki sat in the backseat with the other twin.

Frost had decided to remain at New Eden with Benji, which had come as no surprise. He'd made it clear he preferred to return to Fox Park, but he decided Benji fit in with the kids at New Eden and needed stability. We promised we'd stop by for a visit every chance we got.

When it came to Vicki and the twins, we left the decision up to her. We made it clear that we would stay in New Eden if she chose to stay. Not that she'd need help raising the twins, because she'd have an entire village to help with them, but because we'd given our word. Those babies were part of our Fox family. We'd do everything in our power to ensure their safety.

Vicki hadn't given her decision for a full month after the twins were born. During that time, Justin had tried his damnedest to convince Vicki into staying with the twins. But, on the thirty-first day, she stood before us and stated that Tack and Deb would've wanted their children raised in Fox Park and not a silo.

I was relieved Vicki chose Fox Park. The truth was, Vicki and the rest of us weren't cut out for city living. We'd all been on the run for so long that being confined in New Eden's silo suffocated us. We needed freedom and fresh air.

As Clutch drove, I stared out at the fields of massive white turbines, all still. I enjoyed the scenery as it became more and more familiar.

"We should be there in about an hour," Clutch said as he avoided a zed lying on the road.

With spring, the zeds reemerged, but they'd changed. Most had freezer burn. Bugs ate at their flesh, and they seemed to be putrefying in the warm air. Most could barely walk. They would rot away, and we'd burn the corpses.

When I saw the first zeds walking after the flight back to New Eden, I was terrified of having to face the herds again. It hadn't taken long to realize that the zeds were decaying. These were only the remnants of the vicious monsters that had erupted from the depths of hell a year ago.

But, we'd never be free from the virus until every last zed was gone, every sick animal died, and every survivor was vaccinated. We were lucky. We had a head start on a new life. Our small group was one of the first to receive vaccines because I was part of the delivery crews. We were free from the virus, but we still had zeds and "zabid" animals to deal with. Only when both those predators were gone, would we have a fighting chance.

Baby Ted Nugent kicked out his legs before settling back into his nap. The twins slept much of every day; evidently, newborns did a lot of that. The baby girl—who I'd already nicknamed Little Debbie—must've woken, because Vicki cooed, "Happy Easter, sweet Debra."

"We're almost there," Clutch said, and I looked outside.

Trees had replaced fields, and we passed a sign that read *Fox National Park, 3 miles.*

I leaned back against the headrest and took in a deep breath. Fox Park seemed a dream, and warmth suffused me at the idea of being back there. Out of everywhere we'd been in the last year, Fox Park was the place that held the most potential for being somewhere we could start a new life. We followed Griz's Humvee as it turned into the park.

New grass was fighting to sprout up through trodden ground. Regularly, a zed would be found lying on the ground, trampled by the herds and now freezer burned into a crusty-looking shape of something that had once been human.

"They sure got close to the park," I mused at the telltale signs of the herds.

"Yeah," Clutch said. "We were lucky to get out when we did."

I thought for a moment, back to the days of the outbreak, to Doyle's militia, to living on the river, and to living below ground in a silo. "You're right. We have been lucky."

"It's getting late," he said and picked up the handheld radio. "We'll stay at the old town hall for tonight if it's still secure. Tomorrow, we'll go through the park and assess if we can rebuild."

"Copy that," Griz's voice chimed in.

"Roger," Jase's voice came through.

"We'll be able to rebuild," I said confidently. "It's not like we need more than a cabin to start with. And, I can't imagine the herds managed to trample all of our gardens."

As we pulled up next to Griz's Humvee at the old Fox town hall, which had been the state park rangers' office before the outbreak, I looked for signs of danger but found none. "It doesn't look like the herds came into the park. They must've just stayed on the roads."

"My guess is that they were getting too clumsy for all

these hills and trees," Clutch said. "I noticed their paths stayed on flat lands and only veered off when there was something that drew their attention."

"We weren't here to entice them," I said before stepping out of the Humvee and inhaling the woodsy air.

Jase joined me, with Buddy at his heels. Sometime while Clutch, Griz, and I had been at the capital, Jase and the self-sufficient dog had decided they'd make a good pair.

"It's good to be home," he said with a smile before his eyes widened. "Whoa. Check it out."

I followed his finger. My mouth dropped.

He twisted around. "Hali, get over here. You gotta see this."

Hali ran over and covered her mouth. "Oh my God."

Clutch stopped in front of the Humvee. "Is that...a deer?"

Sure enough, crossing the road was a young buck. It paused to look at us before continuing its journey into the trees.

"Yeah," I said breathlessly. "I assumed they'd all been killed."

"A deer," Hali said breathlessly. She turned and kissed Jase, giggled, and skipped toward the large cabin.

Jase watched her leave. After a pause, he made eye contact with Clutch and then me. "She's my girlfriend. I thought you guys should know."

Clutch belted out a laugh. "Everyone knew that."

"It was that obvious?" Jase asked.

"Yes," I said, biting back a laugh. "But, it feels good to say it, doesn't it."

The corners of his lips curled up. "Yeah. It does."

It took Clutch and Griz only a few minutes to make sure the large cabin was clear of any danger. Fortunately, it showed no signs of trespassers—human or zed. We had our sleeping bags out and dinner ready by the time Jase and Hali fed the twins with the formula Marco had found in the big store back in Omaha.

While everyone sat around after we'd cleaned up, Clutch stood, took my hand, and led me upstairs. "Remember this room?"

I smiled and nodded. "It was the first time we had sex," I said bluntly. I'd almost said that it was the first time we'd made love, but it hadn't been like that at all. It had been only a couple months after the outbreak. We'd been stressed out, afraid, and in need of human contact. In some ways, things hadn't changed much. In other ways, things were completely different now.

He smiled. "Yeah."

We sat down on the floor, with me in Clutch's arms, and looked out the window. We didn't talk. We simply sat there and enjoyed the peaceful silence together.

It had taken one year for the zeds to destroy our world and the world to come back and destroy them. We still had work to do. Fortifying the park, flying missions, and avoiding sick animals—it wouldn't be easy. Not by a long run. I didn't even know if the few survivors who remained had what it took to survive as a species. But, we'd try.

Who knew what tomorrow would bring. Until then, I was content. We were safe in this building. We had seeds to plant and enough food and supplies to get us through the next couple of months. I kissed Clutch, and together, we watched the stars.

ALSO BY RACHEL AUKES

The Deadland Saga
100 Days in Deadland
Deadland's Harvest
Deadland Rising

Short Stories in the Deadland World
Fat Zombie
At Hell's Gates

Colliding Worlds Trilogy
Collision
Implosion
Explosion

Guardians of the Seven Seals
Knightfall
Hellbound

Other Fiction
Never Fear
Stealing Fate
Tales from the SFR Brigade, Vol. 1
Stories on the Go

AFTERWORD

Thank you for reading **Deadland Rising**, the final novel in the three-part **Deadland Saga**. Inspired by Dante Alighieri's **Divine Comedy**, the **Deadland Saga** takes the reader through a journey that echoes the one Dante took in the three poems that comprise the **Divine Comedy**.

In **Deadland Rising**, reminiscent of "Paradiso," Dante (represented by Cash) and Beatrice (represented by Clutch) discover redemption and salvation in the final part of their journey. Zeds play a smaller role as the survivors switch from running from sin (monsters) to rediscovering their humanity.

Like "Paradiso," this story covers virtues and how love can heal the worst of wounds. The thirty-three chapters reflect the thirty-three cantos of the poem, and Easter eggs can be found throughout **Deadland Rising**. Here are just a few items you'll find similar between the two stories:

- In Uncertainty, Cash and Clutch come across a nun (Piccarda Donati) and other historical people.
- In Ambition, they learn from Justinian, a Roman emperor and talented orator.
- In Prudence, they are surrounded by light (both sunlight and candlelight).

- Fires are an underlying theme of Fortitude.
- In Courage, they look from high (on the roof) over the wolves (of the capital).
- As with all three poems, all three novels end with "stars."

For the full list of over one hundred Easter eggs, visit my website at www.rachelaukes.com.

ACKNOWLEDGMENTS

With many thanks to Stephanie Riva, Glenda Moleski, Michael Koogler, and Amber Schmidt for taking a decent story and making it infinitely better. Thanks to my husband for hanging in there through all the crazy times. And, thank you, my reader, for your messages, cheers, and enthusiasm. Live with endless hope and watch out for zombies!

BONUS STORY

"PERFECT"
A short story from the Deadland Saga

(This is Benji Hennessey's story during the outbreak.)

Mom calls me Perfect, but all my friends call me Benji. She said I got more chrome-zomes than everyone else and so I'm special. When she'd first told me I had Down Syndrome, I was worried that kids wouldn't like me. But, other than a few jerks, no one picks on me because my eyes look funny or because I talk a different. Sometimes, I wish I was just like everyone else. But, most of the time I'm happy with who I am. I have lots of friends, and one day, I'm going to be an actor on TV. Maybe even in the movies.

Some of my classes are in a smaller room with kids who have a tough time learning like me. We were in there the day everyone went crazy. Mrs. D left the room to talk to someone, and when she came back, she was scared. She called our parents to come get us, and we all waited while she paced the room, talking about zombies. When we asked what zombies were, she said they were monsters. That made sense why she was afraid of them then. I was scared of monsters, too.

Mom was the first to arrive. She rushed through the

door, grabbed my wrist and yanked me away.

I reached back for my bag. "But my homework —"

She didn't even slow down. "No time."

Mom worried me because she didn't stop to talk with Mrs. D. She *always* stopped to talk with Mr. D.

"Bye! See you Monday!" I called out over my shoulder as my mom pulled me through the doorway.

I wasn't the only kid leaving early. A few other parents were there, too, some with their kids, others heading into classrooms. Mom hurried us down the hallway lined with lockers. My mouth fell open, and I pointed to a woman leaning against a first-grader's locker. "Mom, she's hurt!"

Mom stopped, looked at the woman and then yanked me away. "She's sick."

I had to jog to keep up with Mom's longer steps. When we burst through the glass doors, outside was even crazier. Horns were honking and people were shouting. At the Home Depot next to my school, two men were locking people into the outdoor section behind big black gates. My heart pounded in my chest. It was so crazy that it didn't even seem real, so I sucked in a deep breath to make sure I wasn't dreaming.

It sure felt real. And it wasn't fun.

Mom led me to where she parked the car on the front lawn by the flagpole.

"Get in, Benji," she said in a rush. "We have to hurry."

I swallowed. This wasn't like Mom at all. She was

always happy and chatty. I pushed up my glasses and climbed in. She'd locked the doors and gunned the engine before I even had my seatbelt fastened. I shivered even though I wasn't cold. "What's wrong, Mom?"

She glanced at me and gave me a half-smile, but it fell into a frown all too quickly. "I—I don't know yet. People are...they're...well, people are getting sick."

"Like the stomach flu? *Blegh.*" I hated the stomach flu almost as much as I hated the chicken pox.

"Something like th—"

Tires screeched, and I saw the blur of a car outside my window. Mom swerved onto the median and back onto the street. I held onto the dashboard. I snapped around to watch the other car drive away. "Did you see that? He's driving the wrong way."

Mom didn't say anything. Her eyes were wide and she was taking really deep breaths. She clenched the wheel so hard I could her white bones through her skin. I turned on the radio so she could listen to the country music like she always did when she drove. Voices came on instead. They must've been in between songs.

Mom turned off the radio. "Not today, sweetie."

She was acting weird, and it scared me. I squeezed my eyes shut and clenched my teeth and rode out the rest of the drive home in a nervous silence.

As we reached our driveway, the Jacobsens ran over to meet us. Mom hit the garage door opener button. "C'mon, c'mon, c'mon," she said, pounding her palm against the steering wheel with every word.

Mr. Jacobsen ran straight into the back of the car, and I jumped. "Whoa." When Mr. Jacobsen punched at our back window, I frowned. "Why is he so mad?"

"He's sick, sweetie."

Mrs. Jacobsen leaned against the hood on Mom's side of the car. Blood oozed from her neck, and she clawed at the windshield. I shrunk into my seat, trying to get away from both of them. "Mrs. Jacobsen looks sick, too."

"Yes. They're both very sick. And we have to stay away from them, or else we could get sick, too."

Mom gunned the engine, and the car lurched forward. As soon as we were in the garage, she hit the button. We both turned around and watched as the door descended—so slowly—as our neighbors approached. Mr. Jacobsen was the first through the door. The door stopped moving and the garage light flashed.

"Shit!" Mom hit the button again, but this time the door climbed, and she mumbled something as it opened all the way and she hit the button to descend again.

This time, Mrs. Jacobsen set off the sensor, and the door stopped.

"No," Mom whimpered and she repeated the process, but more neighbors were filtering into the garage, and some folks I didn't know. There were five, no six in the garage now.

"Look, there's Jackson," I said, pointing to the fourteen-year-old who lived four doors down. He walked right up to Mom's door and punched at the window. I jumped in my seat. Jackson wasn't smiling like he usually did. And his lips and teeth were covered with red.

"He's sick, so he's not your friend anymore, Benji."

"You mean he won't get better?" I asked. "They've got something like Gramma had?"

Mom shook her head. "It's not cancer. But it's bad like it." She lowered her head and didn't say anything else. The only sounds were all the people growling and banging on the car. I didn't like getting sick, but they must really hate this bug for how angry they were.

Mom's long hair covered her face, so I brushed the strands to the side to find her crying.

I wiped a tear away, but more kept coming. I hadn't seen her sad like that since Gramma died, and it made me sad. "Don't cry, Mom. It's okay. We won't get sick."

She took my hand and kissed it. She let go, grabbed her purse, and rummaged through it.

She pulled out a gun, and I my eyes grew wide. "Where'd you get *that*?"

"I need you to do something for me, and it's important you do exactly as I say. Can you do that?"

I pushed up my glasses and nodded.

"When I yell, 'run', I need you to hurry inside the house and lock the door behind you. Then I need you play your best game of hide-and-seek ever. I need you to find the very best hiding place in the world and don't make a sound. You can do that for me?"

I swallowed and nodded. "But you're coming, too. Right?"

"Of course." She gave me a small smile. "I've got a key. I'll come in as soon as I make sure no sick people try to get in the house."

"I'm scared. I don't want to be alone."

She pulled me into a long hug. "I'm always with you, Perfect."

She clicked something on the gun and held it on her lap. "Are you ready?"

I nodded again, and then clutched her to me. I tried to ignore all the sick people, but they were so loud. I finally pulled away, sniffled, and pushed up my glasses.

"You'll always be my Perfect." Still crying, she scowled at the people banging on our car. "Hold onto the door handle. When I yell, 'run', you run. Got it?"

My lips quivered. "O-okay."

"Roll down your window. Cover your ears. It's going to be loud, but you won't get hurt."

My fingers trembled but I did what she told me. Mom raised the gun and then a huge boom hurt my ears. My hands snapped over my ears. Mr. Jacobsen fell back, and Mom grabbed at me. I couldn't really hear her because there was some kind of loud siren going off in my ears, but I could see she was yelling.

"Run!"

I tensed, nodded, grabbed at the handle, shoved open the car door, and tripped over Mr. Jacobsen who reached out to me. I stumbled around him and toward the door to the house. Jackson ran at me, but Mom shot him, too. She stood outside the car now, and started shooting everyone near me, just like she was the Lone Ranger. I was watching her instead of where I was running, and I tripped going up the two steps, but caught the door handle and threw myself inside. I fell against the door, shoving it closed, and twisted the lock.

Panting, I raced around the house like a blind mouse, checking out my usual hiding spots like the closet and under my bed. Finally, I decided to hide in the basement and tucked in behind the furnace. That area had always been off-limits to me, so it had to be the best hiding place in the world. As I sat in the dark, brushing away cobwebs, I waited for Mom to come find me, just like she'd always done when we played hide-and-seek. I was careful to keep quiet. Mom would be so proud. This was my best hide-and-seek yet.

I heard more gunshots and a woman's screams, and then it got quiet. After a few minutes, I heard the garage door close, and I tensed. Mom would come inside soon and try to find me!

I was glad I wouldn't have to hide for much longer because I didn't like the basement. It was dark and damp and there were funny sounds in the basement. The furnace would growl and hum. Something else would kick on that sounded a little like the furnace, too. The phone rang upstairs but otherwise it was completely quiet upstairs. It was getting pretty scary, but I stayed hidden and waited for Mom, just like she'd told me.

When I'd gotten dressed for school this morning, Mom had said it was too cold for shorts, but she'd let me leave the house in my favorite pair, anyway. I should've listened to her. It was really cold on the concrete. It made my teeth chatter.

Mom still didn't come to find me.

I cried myself to sleep sometime after the sun went down and everything went black.

When I woke the next morning, I had to pee so bad. I crawled out from my hiding spot, with shivers running all the way into my deepest bones, and hustled up the steps, grabbing my crotch to keep from wetting myself. At the top of the stairs, I looked both ways before running for the bathroom. My eyes watered as I stood at the toilet and relieved myself.

Finished, I tiptoed down the hallway and into Mom's bedroom to find her bed still made. With a frown, I headed to the kitchen, but Mom didn't have breakfast ready. The TV wasn't even on yet. But I was too hungry to wait for Mom. I grabbed a box of cereal and ate straight out of the box, just like I'd seen Grampa do when I stayed with him.

The phone rang, and I jumped, dropping the box. Cereal flew everywhere, and I scrambled to sweep it into a pile. As I swept, I realized that it could be Mom on the phone and I rushed over and grabbed it.

"Hello?" I asked.

"Benji? Oh, thank God you're all right!"

My heart felt like it was going to burst with happiness. "Grampa! You'd never believe what happened. First, Mrs. D let us go home early. Then, Mom—"

"We'll talk about that later," Grampa cut in. "Let me speak with your mother, kiddo."

My bottom lip trembled, but I swore to myself that I wouldn't cry again. "Mom said she'd be right behind me, but she hasn't come home yet. She took out a gun and shot the neighbors in our garage because they were sick. She told me to run and hide."

"God, no, Anna. My girl..." Grampa drifted off, and it sounded like he was crying.

"I hid just like she told me," I said. "And I was really quiet."

"That's good, Benji. You did really good," Grampa said, but his voice cracked. "I just miss Anna, I mean, your mother."

"I miss Mom, too," I said softly. I wanted to go into the garage and check on Mom. But if she got sick, she wouldn't want me to get sick, too. And so I had to wait until she came inside.

Grampa wasn't talking so I munched on the cereal in my hand while I waited. It wasn't until after I wiped my hand on my shorts that he finally spoke. "I'm coming to pick you up, Benji. I need you to hide until I get there."

"Okay," I said, but I worried about how long I'd have to hide. Hide-and-seek wasn't fun anymore. Grampa lived far away. The car ride to his house took three hours each way. I took a deep breath. "Please hurry."

"Hang tight, Benji. This mess will be over in no time. I'll be there later today."

"Okay. Love you, Grampa."

"I love you, too, Benji," he said, his voice rough, and hung up.

I held the phone in my hand until the dial tone switched to beeping, then to nothing. I hung it up and picked it right back up again. I hit 1 on the speed dial. The phone rang, echoed by a ring that sounded like it was just on the other side of the door. Just because I couldn't Mom if she was sick, there was no reason I couldn't at least talk to her.

"Come on, Mom. Pick up," I said, cradling the phone against my ear. She might be upset that I didn't stay quiet and hidden like she told me, but she'd understand. I hid *all* night.

A thump. The sound was raw and crude, not gentle like Mom. But, if it was Mom, why didn't she use her key to get in before she got sick?

The ringing finally stopped and I got her voicemail. I held my breath. Why didn't she answer?

She was too sick to even talk to me.

When the truth hit me, I looked at the phone in my shaky hand and hit 2 on speed dial.

Grampa answered on the first ring. "Hello?"

I was too scared to talk.

"Benji, is that you, kiddo? I'm just about to start driving your way."

I nodded.

"Is everything okay?" he asked.

"I think Mom's sick," I whispered, my words echoed by a pounding on the door. I gulped. "She sounds mad, and she wants inside."

Grampa cussed. "Can you hide?"

The thumping was so loud, but I could still hear the fear in Grampa's voice.

"I can, but," I sucked in a breath. "But, Mom always finds me."

"I need you to be strong, Benji. Hide where she can't get to you. I'm coming for you."

"Okay," I replied in a quiet voice and hung up the phone.

I shivered as I walked away from the pounding at the door and toward the cold, dark basement. At the top of the stairs, I stopped and my jaw slowly dropped. I turned around and hurried for the pantry instead. It wasn't a large pantry, nothing bigger than a tiny closet. But, I'd always been small for my age. I crawled onto a shelf, shoving canned goods against the wall, and tugged the door shut as quietly as possible.

I'd hidden in pantry once during a game of hide-and-seek. It was the only time Mom hadn't found me, and I'd won the game. But, I couldn't open the door from the inside and had gotten scared (I was just a kid back then). When Mom had finally found me, she scolded me for not calling out for her, and then she held me because I cried. After a week of night terrors, she put a door handle on the inside of the pantry. But I'd never hidden inside since.

Mom would never find me here.

After many minutes, there was a loud bang, like the door was slammed open. Someone was definitely inside, because I could hear clumsy stomping, things crashing to the floor, and angry grunting and moans. The voice sounded somewhat like Mom's but...different.

When something brushed against the pantry door, I hugged myself, clenched my eyes shut, and held my breath. *Please don't find me. Please don't find me.*

The next sound came from a bit farther away, like she was walking away from me. I tried to breathe quietly and slowly but it was hard. My heart was beating too fast. A ruckus erupted, the sound of pans banging together, and I bit my tongue to keep from giggling when I imagined Mom banging her head onto the pan rack hanging from the ceiling like she'd done so many times before. But this time, she didn't cuss and then apologize and chuckle like every time before. She didn't say anything at all except grunt.

She's sick.

My lower lip trembled as the shuffling sounds moved away from the kitchen. I bit my lip to keep from crying.

Over the next few hours she moved through the house, and I never made a sound. I was so hungry that I'd almost reached for a snack cake on the shelf above me, but I was afraid she'd hear and find me. My muscles felt weird from not moving, and I wanted to stretch out. After what felt like forever, the sounds neared my hiding place again and I heard her tumble down the two steps into the garage.

I let out a big breath.

I waited until I hadn't heard a thing for a really long time.

I slowly reached out for the door knob. A can rolled off the shelf and landed the floor with a thud, and I froze. I strained my ears, but I couldn't hear Mom.

I inched my hand to the door knob and turned it as slowly as I could. When light peeked through, I waited, then pushed it open. I jumped off the shelf and fell to the floor. Both my legs were fuzzy feeling, but I managed to get to my feet.

I ran over to the door and tried to close it, but it wouldn't stay closed. The wood was all splintered on the frame where it was supposed to lock. I grabbed a chair from the kitchen table and dragged it across the floor. The metal legs vibrated against the floor, so I pulled it faster and pushed it against the door, and I could hear movement in the garage.

I jogged over to the phone and punched 2 on speed dial. The phone rang and rang until it went to voicemail.

"I'm okay, Grampa," I said into the phone. "Mom is in the garage again. And I put a chair against the door."

Something banged against the door.

My eyes widened. "She's back! Got to go!" I hung up

the phone just as the chair slammed into the wall, allowing the door to open partway.

Mom struggled to squeeze through the doorway, and she looked so sick I barely recognized her. Her skin looked look someone had colored her with a yellow magic marker. But much of her neck and face was covered with dried dark brown mud or something. Even her eyes were yellow as they zeroed in on me.

The chair between the door and wall kept the door closed just enough she couldn't get through. She reached out to me. Bites, gouges, and scratches covered her arm. It was like she was gesturing me to come to her, and I found my feet taking me closer. Only this time, as I drew closer, she growled and tried to claw at me.

I jumped back and bit back a sob. "Oh, Mom. I can't. You're sick," I muttered. Then I turned and ran.

I ran from the kitchen and down the hallway to the patio door. I heard a ruckus in the kitchen and footsteps behind me. I was too afraid to look back.

I slid the glass patio door open and jumped outside, slamming the door closed behind me just as Mom slammed into the glass. Some of the dark brown mud on her face smeared against the glass and she lunged again. I pumped my arms as ran across the patio and to the small storage shed in the backyard. I pulled up the wide door and looked inside.

In the corner sat my dusty bicycle. I was the only kid my age who still had training wheels. I'd quit riding last summer because I'd been too embarrassed to ride with the extra wheels.

I was still embarrassed, but I could pedal really fast, faster than I could run. I spun the bike around and climbed on. I nearly spun out on the concrete as I pedaled as fast as I could out of there.

Mom was slamming herself into the glass door, trying to get outside. Other people I didn't know (but couldn't be certain because they looked *really* sick) all started chasing me. They could run nearly as fast as I could ride, so I had to pedal faster than I'd ever pedaled before. A mean-looking man covered in brown stains reached out and tore off some streamers on my bike handlebar.

A bigger kid grabbed at my arm, and I nearly flew off the bike. It took me awhile to get my feet back on the pedals, and I kept pumping. One of my training wheels was wobbly after that and squeaked every time I leaned too far over.

After three blocks, I was finally putting distance between all the people in my neighborhood but new ones kept showing up from behind houses and cars. I had to swerve around sick people and crashed cars. The wobbly training wheel fell off, and I had to lean on the other wheel to keep from falling over.

My legs burned, but I kept pedaling. My chest hurt and I couldn't get enough air, but I kept pedaling. Sweat burned my eyes and kept making my glasses slide down my nose, but I never slowed down. I rode away from all the sick people until the houses started to spread out and fewer cars sat on the road. But, I didn't feel any safer until I passed the Wal-Mart on the edge of town. I finally slowed my pedaling when I passed the sign *Thank you for visiting Fox Hills, Midwest's Hidden Gem.*

This was the way to Grampa's house. I slowed down, but I didn't stop. I rode until the sun climbed all the way up into the sky. My other training wheel was getting wobbly. I kept hoping to see Grampa's truck, but I never saw anyone else on the road.

I gritted against the hurt inside and kept pedaling. I'd ride all the way to his house if I had to.

I was so thirsty. Hungry, too, but my stomach didn't hurt as much as my chest and legs. Both felt like I'd walked through fire, they burned so much. But I was afraid if I stopped, I'd never be able to get going again. And I'd never get to Grampa's house if I stopped.

I saw two sick people in a parked car not far from town. After that, I didn't see anyone, sick or otherwise.

My bike slid on loose gravel, and my other training wheel flew off. The bike tipped over. I was too tired to jump out of the way, and I cried out when my knee hit the hard pavement. Hissing through my teeth, I pulled myself out from under the bike and sat on my butt. I took off my glasses, wiped the sweat — and maybe a tear or two — from my eyes, and pushed my glasses back on. Sniffling, I picked out pebbles from my bleeding knee. It really, really hurt.

Mom would definitely put a band-aid on this. I hope I don't bleed to death.

After several minutes of watching my knee bleed and looking for sick people, I pushed myself to my feet. It was really hard because my knee throbbed, and my legs felt like they didn't have bones in them anymore. But I managed to get to my feet, and I started limping down the road. It was three hours to Grampa's house. I rode way longer than that already, so I should be there soon.

Walking was easier than riding, but it was slow. I don't know how many hours I walked, but the sun had gotten to get low in the sky, and my wet clothes were making me shiver. My mouth was dry and my head was starting to really hurt. I watched my feet drag over the pavement with every step. *Fifty-two, fifty-three.* Every time I hit one hundred, I started over because it was hard to think straight.

A loud engine sound made me lose count and I looked up. A long ways down the road were bright headlights heading right toward me.

As it drew closer, I saw it was a big green truck, with a man standing behind a big *something* on the back of the truck. I smiled and waved my hand. Maybe he'd seen Grampa!

"Zed! Ten o'clock!" the man shouted from the back of the truck.

"Hold your fire!" another man yelled as he ran around the front of the truck and toward me.

He was holding a gun, too, and it was a lot bigger

than Mom's. He slowed as he approached as he looked me up and down. He was wearing green, just like the color of the truck.

"Hi," I said and rubbed my sore throat.

The turned back to his friends. "He's okay. He's not infected."

The man came down on a knee and held out an opened bottle of water. I grabbed it with more speed than I thought I could muster and chugged the water, though I spilled some by accident.

The man gave me a nice smile and handed me a candy bar. I liked him already.

"You're safe now," he said. "I'm Captain Tyler Masden with the National Guard at Camp Fox. You can call me Tyler."

He held out his hand, and I gave him my empty bottle.

"My name is Benji Hennessey, and I live at One-Fourteen Maple Street," I said as I tore into the candy bar, and then added, "But my mom got sick, so I had to leave."

Tyler gave a sad nod. "Sorry to hear that. There are a lot of people getting…sick lately." After a moment, he frowned. "How'd you get to be all the way out here?"

"I rode my bike, but then it broke, so then I walked."

Tyler whistled. "That's impressive. I bet you could use a ride."

"Yeah," I said with an eager nod and quickly added, "I have to find Grampa."

"And where's he?" Tyler asked.

"That way." I pointed. "Grampa lives three hours from my house."

"Three hours? That's an awfully long ways. It's getting late. How about I take you to Camp Fox for the night? There are no sick people there. How's that sound, Benji?"

"That sounds nice, but I can't," I replied. "I have to find Grampa. He's looking for me."

Tyler's lips tightened but he didn't seem angry. "Well, we'd better see if we can find him. Do you know your grandfather's phone number?"

"Two."

"Is that all?"

I frowned and then smacked my head. "Oh, no. You have to hit the tic-tac-toe button first."

Tyler smirked. "Well, maybe we'll try to find him another way."

"Hey, Maz, You're not going to believe this," the man said from the back of the truck. "The Camp reported that Lee's squad brought in a guy with the same last name a few hours ago. He said he was on his way to pick up his grandson named Benji, but he'd had a car accident on the way."

Tyler reached out his hand. "How about we get you to your grandfather, Benji?"

I put my hand into his and smiled. "I'd like that very much. It's been a bad day."

ABOUT THE AUTHOR

Rachel Aukes is the bestselling author of 100 Days in Deadland, which was named one of the best books of 2013 by Suspense Magazine. Rachel lives in Iowa with her husband and an incredibly spoiled sixty-pound lap dog. When not writing, she can be found flying old airplanes and trying to prepare for the zombie apocalypse.

Connect with Rachel at
www.RachelAukes.com.

Made in the USA
Charleston, SC
26 February 2016